Recruited

Recruited

A Novel

Lauren E. Anderson

Stormbird Press

Stormbird Press

Stormbird Press is an imprint of
Wild Migration Limited.
PO Box 73, Parndana, South Australia.
www.stormbirdpress.com

Cover Júlia Palazzo.
Typeset by Alice Teasdale, Big Quince Print,
with fonts Antique Olive and Kazimir.

National Library of Australia and State Library of South Australia
Legal Deposit
Anderson, Lauren E. – Author
Recruited
ISBN – 978-1-925856-31-6 (hbk)
ISBN – 978-1-925856-32-3 (pbk)
ISBN – 978-1-925856-33-0 (ebk)

The publishing industry pulps millions of books every year when new titles fail to meet inflated sales projections—ploys designed to saturate the market, crowding out other books.

This unacceptable practice creates tragic levels of waste. Paper degrading in landfill releases methane—a greenhouse gas emission 23 times more potent than carbon dioxide.

Stormbird Press prints our books 'on demand', and from sustainable forestry sources, to conserve Earth's precious, finite resources.

We believe every printed book should find a home.

Dedicated to my husband, Brian, and our children, Dylan and Lia.

There aren't words to express how much I love you, how grateful I am for everything you've given me, and how much I hope I can make you proud.

Contents

Rodrigues

This cement block with a tin roof had been my home for the last seven months, and I wasn't ready to leave it now. Not like this. It had been a rock-solid plan, spending a year in paradise on a university-sponsored, all-expenses-paid trip. I was studying some of the rarest plants on the planet.

Just an hour earlier, I had climbed one of these treasures—the *aureum*. The tall, skinny tree looked like something out of a Dr. Seuss book. A thirty-foot stick with a tuft of fronds at its crown, ironically nicknamed the hurricane palm. It grew nowhere else on Earth and had been eaten to the verge of extinction. Rats loved its seeds, and people loved palm hearts in their salads. There were nine left on Rodrigues, a rocky island so small and remote, it had taken me as much time to fly there from New York as it had to walk its circumference—about three days.

The tree grew on a bluff overlooking the vast

Indian Ocean. Its seeds hung in wiry batches at the top. The team chose me to retrieve them because I was the lightest. With the winds picking up, I was the least likely to snap it in half. I reminded myself of this, as the bole to which I clung narrowed and swayed in the circular gusts. Under different circumstances, we would have never taken this risk. We would have just waited for the seeds to ripen and fall and collected them from the ground. But Emma, a Category 5 cyclone, barreled towards the coast, promising a direct hit. If she came as predicted, her record-breaking winds would level the island, blowing millions of years of evolution into the sea.

In my haste, I had climbed without a backpack or even a water bottle. I yanked the marble-sized, black seeds from their husks and shoved them into my cargo pockets, my bra, and my socks. I worked fast, but even in that situation, the view at the top was worth taking in. Rodrigues looked like the place where God perfected the Earth's palette of blues. Every imaginable shade from the queerest of teals to the darkest of navies sparkled on the expanse of ocean around the island. I scanned the horizon for what I knew was coming, but saw only boundless tranquility.

Looking out over the sea, it was easy to wonder why I was 3,000 miles away from my home dangling from a palm tree. This trip had been the ultimate pivot, a diversion even. "Mom, Dad, I'm not going to medical school. I don't want to be a doctor." They hardly had time to gasp, to ask, what then? What do you do with a biology degree to pay off student loans? I wasn't going to speculate. I followed up one factual statement with another—that I'd gotten a scholarship to study abroad, and I was leaving in two weeks.

I didn't just leave, I ran. I flew. I traversed the Earth away from the rank competitiveness of pre-med classes, hot dissection rooms reeking of formaldehyde, and vials of mating *Drosophila melanogaster* soon to be anesthetized. With no notice, I left my internship shadowing doctors through the antiseptic halls of hospitals. Corridors of empty gurneys under buzzing fluorescent lights. Sallow faces waiting for me to dress the bed in sheets crisped with bleach. I went instead to put my hands in the dirt, to feel the sun on my face, and to see the natural world all around, far beyond the confines of prescriptive medicine, of my college nestled in rural New Hampshire. Under midnight stars, I watched ancient sea turtles crest in the Caribbean. I held mildew sodden sloths, and I chased hotrod yellow frogs and electric blue butterflies through walls of rainforest. Now, with my arms wrapped around the aureum, I knew there was a path—however off-script— for me. Maybe I didn't have a plan for what was next, but, somehow, I'd figure it out. I'd make them proud.

Back at basecamp, I labeled and stowed my hard-earned treasure in the seed room. I placed the airtight container among dozens of others each bearing the name of a plant our team intended to resurrect. When the World War II-era sirens started blaring, I ran to my room and threw some clothes, a Walkman, and a couple of notebooks into a duffle bag. There wasn't much else to take. I had traveled light and the care packages my parents sent either never arrived or arrived half eaten by rats. I took one last look around, and then I evacuated back into my senior year at Dartmouth University.

Emma eviscerated the island, the images on the news brimming with heartbreak. When I finally got through on the phone, friends told me of the devastation. They spoke with the resolve and the anguish of people who had nothing, save their breath, left to lose. Their homes flattened; their livelihoods destroyed. The storm stripped the land clean, everything from the touristy bougainvillea-flowered retreats to the thorny acacia fences holding livestock to the last of the *aureums*—all felled and swept away.

"And the seeds?" I asked, hoping for a lifeline to what had been, something—however small—around which they could plant hope.

"*Tout ine aller.*"

Translated from Creole, "All gone."

Black Pants

"Olivia!"

I sat up and started clicking my keyboard. The computer took up most of my desk. A square plastic castle, it loomed over a serfdom of balled up paper, old coffee cups, and nubby pencils.

"I'm working," I yelled at my reflection in the grease-smeared monitor.

Heels commanded their way down the hall. I slouched when the door clicked open.

"It stinks in here," Sky observed, opening the door wider.

"Must be the flowers." Dry bits of dead birthday lilies and baby's breath littered the desk. Sky had given them to me for my twenty-third birthday. "Or the laundry." My bed cried for air from beneath the pile.

She considered the situation, cocking her head, and wrinkling her nose. "Your computer is off. Smells more like procrastination."

"I know." I dropped my head into my hands, which was easier than looking at her.

It had been months, but I still hadn't adjusted to life back on campus. I had evacuated from one swirling storm into another, my senior year of college. Not only did I have to finish my coursework and write a thesis based on the soggy data I had collected abroad, but I had to find a job. One that sounded more important than medical school and paid bank.

My peers were already announcing spectacular post-graduation plans. Sky had won a Fulbright to study for a year in Rome, while our hallmate had accepted an offer with an investment bank in Chicago. Others raised the banners of the law and business schools they would attend. Dartmouth had always felt like a pressure cooker, but now it was way worse. I was muddling through, no exit plan in sight. I breathed in the stale air of my room and exhaled into the rotting bouquet.

"Why don't you go tonight?" Sky's suggestion was gentler than her entry.

"I don't want a beer," I mumbled into my palms. I rubbed my eyes, as though that would bring clarity.

"It's free beer. And just an information session. An info session, you know, for networking?"

"Sky, it's a software company."

"It's supposed to be cool. What else are you doing tonight?"

It didn't matter that she already had plans for next year. Sky wanted something tonight, her agenda cloaked in concern for my unemployment. I knew better than to argue with her, but I did anyway. "I don't know anything about computer science."

"What are you going to do? Buy an $8,000 plane ticket to go back to Gilligan's Island? To get paid in coconuts? There's more out there. You have to look." I winced. "There is nothing to go back to. It all got destroyed. And maybe my parents were right. I should have applied——"

"This company is up and coming. Everyone's talking about it. The CEO is a young billionaire." Oh, that's what you want to go and see. "Here. Wear my shirt." Before I could object, I was cupping a puddle of violet silk. The exquisite material smelled of lavender. The tag said Marc Jacobs. "Just. Get. Dressed." She clacked her way back down the hall.

I held up the gossamer shirt, careful not to let it touch my desk. She wasn't wrong. Even if I could go back to Rodrigues, I couldn't pay back student loans on the pittance a conservation job would offer. It was the same for every opportunity I researched, even plain humanitarian work. Build wells in poor villages so people could have fresh water—get paid in mosquito bites; Type numbers into an excel spreadsheet for a seedy investment bank in the city—earn $70,000 a year. Of course I applied, but they weren't calling me back. The salary paying consultancies and banks weren't looking for a pre-med drop out turned crunchy eco-warrior. They wanted polished economics and business majors, the kind of guys with slicked back hair and tortoise shell glasses, or brawny boys who could swing a golf club, throw their weight around, literally, on the stock exchange floor. I dropped resumes anyway, but my phone stayed eerily silent. I was falling through the cracks.

"What's the name of the company again?"

From another room in our dorm, "Kava Technologies. It's a start-up. Rich techies in t-shirts. But, wear black pants. Jeans are so last year."

I fumbled through the clothes hanging out of my makeshift closet. It was 1998, and while I was away, everyone started wearing black pants when they went out. Baggy ripped jeans and Pearl Jam flannel shirts were over. I could no longer disguise my student poverty as fashion.

"Found them." Victorious, I pulled a pair from the bottom of the pile.

Sky materialized in my doorway again. How did she move so fast in those shoes? "They're giving away a laptop as a door prize, just for dropping off a resume." She looked at my wrinkled pants. "You should bring a resume."

We made our way up campus. It was a cool spring night, and what the trees lacked in leaves, the lamp posts made up for in neon flyers, each advertising a different company hiring graduating seniors. The birds were just coming back to campus, but we were getting ready to fly the coop.

Sky pulled a hot pink advert as we walked past. "Deloitte is tomorrow night. Free BBQ."

"Consulting with greasy fingers?"

"Sounds awkward," she agreed.

"So why is this Kava place supposed to be the *it* company? Besides the CEO?" I asked.

"I heard they party. And are very unconventional. No peep toe shoes and panty hose. You might like it." She gave me a friendly shrug.

I smiled at her. We had been friends despite her being one of those campus girls who traded their academy skirts and blazers for Seven-brand jeans and North Face parkas, the lift tickets from Vail left dangling from the zipper. Tall, blonde, and understatedly beautiful, Sky was like a J. Crew model with finishing school manners and a private education. Classic Ivy League. Freshman year they gave us facebooks—hardcopy books with the headshots and names of everyone in our class—to help us find familiar ground. Upper class guys used it to invite hot girls to parties. Sky was a facebook celebrity. I was her sidekick with the wild hair.

But, over the years, I learned a lot. I knew how to handle a scene. I could hold a keg stand as well as I could navigate a snotty club dinner where guests got the kelly green napkins, members bright white. Even after you got in, Dartmouth was all about getting in.

"I'm on the list."

"I'm a member of the club."

"I'm with him."

"It's the right color wristband."

"I'm on the varsity team."

"The bouncer knows me."

"The stamp's still on my hand."

"Do you know who my dad is?"

To get access, you needed status. It's what got you served everything—from food to beer to a place to dance on a Saturday night. Privilege. If you didn't come with it, you had to figure out how to get it. Or how to get around it. You had to learn to network in, and once there, to look like you belonged. That was the real-world education that came from within the ivory tower.

That night, I went with Sky to a different kind of party, but I knew the rules would be the same. They always were. Meet people. Make an impression. Look like you've been there before. I smoothed a wrinkle out of my black pants.

The Info Session

Kava Tech held its information session at Victory, the new place just off campus on Main Street. We stepped into the warmth of the pub, its two floors of bars framed by enormous pewter tanks of micro-brewed beer. The shiny cisterns funneled into an elaborate schematic of chrome piping tacked to faux brick walls. The pipes appeared to empty into the taps below. The bar smelled like an ambitious Saturday night—liquid yeast and fermented cologne. It was upscale, but our feet stuck to the floor.

"This place ... Sky, it's like your ripped designer jeans."

"How's that?" she said over her shoulder, disappearing into the crowd.

"Soulless. Just yearning for authenticity."

"Doesn't stop you from borrowing them." I laughed because it was true. I followed her as she picked her way through a group of guys in suits. Some still had their conference name tags pinned to wrinkled jackets. Beer made them predators, ready to pounce, spring-loaded from hours of sitting. I watched them watch her. Talking heads turned and Adam's apples swallowed. We walked to the safety of the area roped off for Kava Tech's session.

"Your CEO isn't the only one here recruiting," I said.

"Gross. Stay here. I'll get beers."

While Sky went for drinks, I grabbed a sandwich off a tray. It came with a company pamphlet. I skimmed the empty industry catch phrases like "paradigm shift" and "business solutions," until I got to the story of Levi Tyleck, Kava Tech's wealthy CEO. After earning degrees in math and philosophy at the University of Chicago (computer science was a hobby), he'd spent years making a fortune on Wall Street. Then it sounded like something snapped or maybe he just burned out. As quickly as he rose to the top, he dropped off the map. He reappeared years later in the Pacific Islands, where he developed a taste for flip-flops, cargo shorts, and a traditional drink called Kava. One night in Kiribati, after way too much of the powerful beverage, Levi saw the future—a world, he believed, that would be powered by software. He had since leveraged all of his personal wealth to turn his hallucination into Kava Technologies.

The company was Levi's manifesto on business and life, and he was Kava's cult of personality, having woven his most intense and defining experiences into the company fabric. He eschewed the artifice of Wall

Street—its suits and ties and its hierarchical rules, as well as the veteran businessmen that came with it. Instead, he grew his company out of the unbridled ambition and messy creativity of newly minted college graduates. He loved competition, relished risk-taking, and nurtured new ideas, all while ditching the confines of traditional corporate culture. His start-up was thriving, at least according to company literature.

I recognized Levi now from his picture in the pamphlet. His feathery hair, tastefully graying at the temples, was just long enough to qualify as unkempt, maybe even a little middle-aged sexy. While his sharp blue eyes moved like a new Intel Pentium, his face looked worn, perhaps from gambling his entire fortune on this company after partying for years in the equatorial sun. He leaned casually, one foot against the wall, away from the growing crowd around him.

While Levi was a lesson in contrasts, the students filing in were nearly uniform. Most had no doubt just crawled out of a computer science lab. Young men in cloth sneakers and logoed t-shirts, hair unwashed and pimples unpopped. Skinny shoulders slumped under backpacks. I recognized one from a molecular bio class I had taken. He chewed his nails to nubs waiting for the electrophoresis gels to run. He never talked to me in precept, just turned pink when we exchanged lab and problem set notes. But he was chatting now, they all were, amongst themselves, not daring to approach Levi, a God among them. Levi had made it. Done what they aspired to do. Started a tech company, poised to go public, for a big chunk of change.

She altered the dynamic when she walked in. A beautiful girl in a pair of tight jeans and a company t-shirt, the Kava Tech logo perfectly distorted by her ample breasts. Levi reached for her hand, shook it, and then pulled her close. She leaned down and whispered something in his ear that made him chuckle. Her hand on his shoulder, a flirtatious grin. The spoils of a billionaire? The boys stilled. Their heads cocked, could they have that too?

Sky handed me a beer.

"Check it out." I pointed to the woman. "She's stealing your man's show."

"Oh."

"What?"

"He's older than I thought he'd be," Sky said.

I handed her the brochure. "Something money can't fix?"

She leafed through the booklet. I drank beer. It was the expensive kind they serve with a slice of orange on the rim. "And he isn't a billionaire. Not even close. It's just company valuation." She flipped the brochure open to a graph I didn't bother to look at. "But, check this out. Kava Tech is in Austin."

"Texas? Who the hell wants to live in Texas?"

"You do."

"I do not."

"My parents had a house on a lake down there. It's fun. I'd call it the liberal oasis of Texas."

I rolled my eyes. "Where haven't your parents had a house? New York would be better." I drank more beer, wondering what made it taste better, the orange or that it was free. Or maybe it was the fancy glass. I was used to chugging warm light beer out of opaque plastic cups. A microbrew in a nice stein was a different experience altogether.

She shook her head. "You don't want to be some spreadsheet jockey riding the Big Apple." She handed me her untouched drink, "Hold this," and reached for her coat.

"These are strong. Maybe that's why they taste so good. Wait. Are you leav——" I stood, holding a mug in each hand. She stuffed something in her purse.

"Yeah, this isn't for me. You should stay." Her coat was on. She was hugging me. "Let's meet later at Quad."

I stood there weighing that she was ditching me with the fact that I had two really nice, free drinks in hand. I took another sip and watched her leave. I should have gone with her. What was I doing here anyway? Sky walked by a guy who didn't belong to the wrinkled conference crowd or the ill-fashioned engineers. White dress shirt unbuttoned to the collarbone, sleeves rolled to just below the elbow. His clothes fit the way *GQ* said they should, and I couldn't tell if it was because they were expensive or because he had the body designers dream of when they cut cloth. He crossed his arms, impatiently. He was looking for something. Then he was looking at me. The t-shirted beauty turned on the mic and told us to find a seat. I dropped out of view into a folding chair.

"Thank you all for coming to learn about Kava Technologies," she began. The crowd settled. Some jostled to sit up front on the floor, closer to Levi. Others lined the walls. "I'm Laurie Davis, a recruiter for Kava Tech, and I'd like to start this session by reflecting on this year ...".

I looked between heads, but GQ had moved. Now it was me scanning the room, searching for the opposite of *Where's Waldo*. I giggled at the idea of an Armani-clad Waldo with a smoking hot body hidden amongst thousands of geeks, and I was smiling when I met his eyes a second time. I jerked my head back to the recruiter's speech.

"... 1998 is a unique and lucky time to be graduating college. New technologies like email and the internet are driving an unprecedented economic boom. I know the 90s will be remembered for this tech-driven growth, which may even rival Monica Lewinsky and *Seinfeld* for a place in history." The crowd laughed and I peeked at him. He had the kind of smile that brought you in, dimples softening the hard angles of his cheekbones and chin. I stared until he caught me, again. Embarrassed, I knotted my shoulders, put my hands on my lap, and forced myself to look straight ahead.

"... we start-ups are the heart of this growth. We're spawning innovation and disrupting age-old business models in every industry. We're the innovators. And we at Kava Tech want to shape how business happens in the future. But to do so, we have to hire the right people, the best and the brightest. This is why Levi makes talent acquisition and retention a core company priority. He knows his business is only as good as its people, will only grow as his people grow; so he dedicates serious resources to building Kava Tech's human capacity. And I can tell you, while competition for hiring is fierce in this electric job market, I'm confident you will want to work for us." She called on a presumptuous hand in the front row.

"Why? What's so different about Kava Tech?" he asked.

"Great question. Thank you for that. Kava Tech is revolutionary not only in what it creates, but how it creates it. We're changing the way business uses new talent. We're resetting the expectations of graduates everywhere on how an office should look, feel, and function. The average age of our employees is 25. We don't care what you wear to work. We encourage flip-flops. Air out your feet like you air out your ideas. We don't care when you take your vacations or for how long. We give you the freedom to think, to create, and to innovate."

Laurie wrote the word "YOUth" on the flipchart.

"Levi believes in youth. Right out of college you're used to exploring new ideas and you aren't afraid to take risks. We reward that at Kava, and it's working. Our products are cutting edge and our people are happy. This is why the best of the best college grads want to work for Kava, and why the big consultancies, the investment banks, and the established software giants are bleeding talent to us." Laurie sipped her beer. She took her time placing it back on the stool next to her.

"We offer unparalleled opportunity in an insanely fun, high-energy culture. If you're one of the smartest here and you'd like to learn more about Kava Tech, please drop a resume. To say thank you, later tonight, I'll pick somebody to win the latest IBM ThinkPad. It's got 32 MB of RAM."

The audience broke out in hardy applause and clapped harder when Laurie introduced Levi. I waited for him to talk about his travels in the Pacific, but instead of paradise, he told us about software-as-a-service, the core of his business. Under "YOUth," Laurie wrote "Software-as-a-Service = SaaS."

So that's what Kava Tech made? Software-as-a-service? I skimmed the brochure again. Its vague language and generic photos of people staring meaningfully at computer screens offered very little explanation. Levi glossed over it too, assuming, I guessed, that anyone who wanted to work for Kava would already know why SaaS was visionary.

"Web-based software means companies will purchase less system hardware," Levi explained, and then his lecture took off like a college course. I watched the people around me nod in agreement and fascination as he leapt through semesters worth of computer science and economic theory. My old lab partner gnawed his finger. I finished my beer and wondered where GQ went. I watched the pretty recruiter fold t-shirts that looked like the one she was wearing. I scribbled on the Kava brochure.

It wasn't until the end of his speech that Levi caught my imagination. "We're growing fast and there is sound potential for a very lucrative initial public offering," he said and drew a graph on the next page of the flip chart. "Kava is already valued, by some, at close to a billion dollars."

While I didn't have a clue about software or business, I knew that getting in on an IPO could mean serious cash. I needed money. And a career. Plus, I reasoned, the possibility of controlling my corporate destiny dressed in jean shorts and flip-flops sounded pretty good. When the formal speeches were over, I nudged my way to the front of the room. Meet people.

I was sure he would be impressed. I shook Levi's hand. "I lived on an island too, once."

Levi's ice blue eyes scanned for data. "That's great," he said and waited for me to make the connection.

"It was beautiful."

"Yes, they usually are." The lights of his eyes dimmed and refocused on something behind me.

"I worked with endangered plants, but I've never had Kava," I stuttered.

"I see. That's very interesting."

"I just meant to ask——" An impatient guy behind me stuck out his hand and blurted something about algorithm configuration. The question immediately turned into a conversation in which I couldn't participate. Basking in the intensity of Levi's baby blues, the guy edged me aside. I was cut off and boxed out. I stood there, a lurch, my arms suddenly too long for my body. I didn't have a drink to pretend to sip.

"Hi. I'm Laurie." The recruiter shook my hand with both of hers. "Can we chat?" Grateful, I let her lead me a short distance away from Levi and the crowd of students. When she moved, the boys gave her space.

She was taller than all of us.

"Would you like to submit a resume? I'd love to see it."

She was gorgeous, but approachable. A hard balance to strike. Her demeanor said she wanted to help, and I let her. "Thank you." I reached into my bag and handed her a copy.

She took the paper and started rooting through a box of t-shirts. "These are the best advertising ever. Small? You want one, right?"

"Of course. That's the real reason I came."

She laughed. "You'd be surprised. Some people do." She alternated between reading t-shirt tags and my resume. "Wow, you've traveled a few places. And a bio major. This is great stuff."

"It is?" I glanced over my shoulder. The algorithms guy and Levi were still at it. Make an impression. "Yes. Yes, it is. I have a 3.8 GPA and I studied in Latin America and in the Mascarene Islands. Kava Tech sounds like a very interesting company. You gave an excellent presentation; much more dynamic than the others I've attended." I hadn't been to any others.

Laurie handed me a shirt. "I'm glad you liked it." She had a cheery southern drawl I hadn't noticed earlier. "Why don't you grab another beer on us at the bar? Maybe we can talk for a minute when I'm done with the drawing? But for now, for me, it's more t-shirts." She pulled a tangle from the box.

An Invitation

A short while later, Laurie picked the laptop winner. She worked the crowd. Two hands down, she drew a resume, then dropped it back in the box, demurely. In the end, the winner also got a congratulatory hug. Judging by his expression, this was a way better prize than a piece of hardware. When the show was over, the students dwindled. I studied the pamphlet, thinking of what smart thing I'd say about software-as-a-service—whatever that was.

"You're interested in Kava Tech?"

I looked up and GQ was there. Next to me. Leaning on the bar. Black eyes brilliant. The material of his shirt starched stiff but soft enough to cling to his chest. "You're with the company?"

"I'm affiliated. I'm Marion. A lot of people call me Mars." My hand in his. The warm expanse of his fingers around mine.

"Olivia ... Olivia Gesso. You're a recruiter?"

He chuckled, and I knew it was the wrong assumption. "I'm on the board." Of course you are. "Can I get you another beer?"

I'd had three. "Thank you."

"Well?" He drew out the one-word question.

"Well, what?" Was he flirting? Or was I just hopeful? You didn't get to meet men like this on campus. Men. Not sweaty boys peeing in the bushes outside your dorm at three in the morning.

"What do you think of Kava?"

"Oh." The company. Right, that's why I'm here. "It sounds wonderful ... for a software company."

"Is that like, it's riveting ... for a C++ textbook?"

I laughed. "Not exactly, it's just that, well, the culture sounds great, but——"

"You're not a techie. You don't code."

"No. Nothing binary here. How could you tell?" I knew the answer, but I wanted him to look. He didn't. It made me want to try harder.

"There's more to building a company than ones and zeros," he said. "There's a compendium of needs to meet. People with different backgrounds fill different gaps. You should consider——"

Laurie blew in, a sweet southern breeze, and dropped her computer bag on the bar between us, left-over XL t-shirts suddenly piled on the stool. "Mars, are you doing my job for me, again?" She hugged his shoulder. The only man here taller than her. The only man here. Period.

"I'm not pretty enough," he said. He grinned. I stared.

"The hell you aren't," she said. Coming from her, I felt vindicated. "You think the bartender wants one?" She threw another shirt on the pile. Mars shrugged. "Laurie, this is Olivia." He made the unnecessary introduction. "She's unsure about fitting in at a software company. Wants to know why we'd consider a non-techie." I did? Marion gave me a reassuring glance. I held on to it.

Laurie plopped her purse on top of the t-shirts. "Olivia, Kava Tech believes that if you're smart, you'll contribute. But we're also hiring culture fits. It's as important as being brilliant."

"What's a culture fit?" I asked, conscious he was watching me. I crossed my legs and leaned in.

"Success hinges on being bright and working hard 20-hour days for as long as it takes to launch a successful product. But just as important is being the kind of person somebody wants to work with for 20 hours a day. We're looking for brainiacs—and it doesn't matter what major—who will have a blast while building this company. We're looking for the right combination of humility and hubris, of pensive and impulsive, of people willing to take big risks for even bigger rewards."

"That sounds intense, I mean, exciting," I corrected.

"It is. Your resume tells me you're a risk-taker. Smart and dynamic. The kind of person we invite to interview at Kava. Why don't you come out for a first-round interview?" I was beyond flattered. When people looked at my resume they usually thought "crazy," but Laurie saw something else, something important: "risk-taker." I inflated, instantly. "Think of it as a chance for us to find out more about one another," she encouraged.

"I'd like that," I said and glanced at Marion. Earlier he'd been scanning the room for something or someone. Now he looked at me as though he'd found it. When I met his gaze, the tiny electrical currents that made my heart beat fired a new rhythm. I could hear it, I could feel it, but I could not control it.

Laurie didn't waste a second. She opened her laptop on the bar and started typing. It gave me a reason to look elsewhere, telling her what day and time were best for the interview. "Next week?" She typed the answers into a spreadsheet and explained the logistics. I yanked a planner from my bag and jotted down the important stuff. Marion waved down the bartender and pulled out a credit card to settle the tab. I watched his hands. They were decisive. He slid the bill under a glass. The tendons came through the lean muscle of his forearms. I knew it wasn't the cut of the shirt, but what was underneath. When he looked up, I blushed.

"Good luck in the interview. Let us know if you have any questions," he said.

Of course I had questions. Why me? What am I interviewing for, exactly? Why does the world need software? What happened to the algorithms guy? But I played it cool, like hot tech company reps gave me job opportunities every day. "I will."

Marion reached to shake my hand and put his other hand on my shoulder. "Take care, Olivia," but his eyes said, I'll see you later.

Make an impression. Say something witty. I mumbled thank you.

Laurie gave me a solid corporate handshake. And they were out the door. I stopped thinking about him when I remembered that I had just signed up to interview with a software start-up. Ridiculous. I laughed and swallowed the warm dregs of orange rind and lager. I'd interview because I was a risk-taker, wasn't I? I lifted my chin. Yes, I was. And maybe, if I had to be honest with myself, I'd see Marion again. I looked at his signature, the sharp angles now a blurry mess in a puddle on the bar. The receipt was for just over $5,000.

What I could do with the money this company just spent on beer and burgers.

Chanel

Sky came in unannounced. "What are you gonna do about that laundry?" She skirted the pile.

I looked up from the textbook I was reading. "Wait until I graduate and then throw it out. Why? What's up?"

"Well, what are you wearing to your interview next week?"

"Good question. I guess I should get a suit from Ann Taylor. Isn't that what they sell?"

"They do. But their clothes are predictable."

"You mean affordable."

"That too," she conceded. "But, just think, if you get this job, you can get a wardrobe."

"Why are you in here?" I loved my roommate, despite our differences. She was a window to a world I didn't inhabit. A world my parents wanted me to inhabit. She reveled in my curiosity, and I in her generosity. I thanked her by being her entertainment, her personal fixer-upper project. Sometimes it stung, but it never hurt more than it helped.

"I'm bored. Tired of studying."

"You weren't studying." She never studied. She was one of those annoying people who did well anyway. A skill cultivated in prep school.

"Aren't you excited about the interview?"

I gave up and put the book down. "It's the only one I have."

"Is that desperation or enthusiasm?" Sky leaned on the door.

"Both," I admitted. Interviewing at a tech start-up felt like when I borrowed her jeans. It was exciting to be somebody else for a night, but anything longer, like a career, and I wasn't sure I could pull it off. "We'll see how it goes."

"You'll be fine. And Kava sounds awesome."

"Still hunting for a rich techie?"

"Nah, not for me. But maybe you'll find one."

I threw a pencil at her. "Did you book your tickets for Rome?"

"About that. My closet won't fit in the suitcases I have."

"That's why you're in here? Closet philanthropy?"

"Come on, help me downsize. It'll be a lot more fun than ... what are you reading?" She picked up the textbook on my bed. "*Mating Habits of African Ungulates*? No wonder you can't find a job."

I laughed. "Fine. Let's go." There was no sense in being proud. Since my stint abroad, my threads were a ratty mess, and I needed interview clothes.

Sky's immaculate closet was organized by color,

possibly by theme. All the shiny gowns and sequined shirts hung in the back. Neat cubes of folded t-shirts, jeans, and sweaters lined the perimeter. On the bed were a dozen or so shirts, skirts, and dresses, the tops of the hangers all facing the same direction. "Impressively OCD."

"Check out what's on the bed. Take what you want. Just try to hang it up," Sky said.

"You sure?" I picked up a caramel-colored dress. It was a delicate piece with capped sleeves and lace at the hem. "Could I use this for the interview?" I held it to my body and looked in the mirror.

"If you want this job, any job, you need to make an impression. That dress is Chanel."

I looked at the label. "Woah. Yes, it is."

The silk lining felt cool against my skin. I zippered the side and the material went taught. Last year I quit Dartmouth's track team, but my ass and thighs were still bulked to win a 100-yard dash, and without all the calorie-devouring workouts, my breasts had filled out to a C-cup. Janet Jackson had nothing on my silhouette, and the dress loved all of it.

Sky's eyes lit up with delight. "It's gorgeous. *You* are gorgeous. Everyone will show up in navy polyester with gold buttons. But you'll be the Audrey Hepburn of the interviewees."

"She wasn't this curvy."

"Her loss, that waif."

"You sure you don't want to keep this?"

"Take it. All of it." She waved at the bed. "I'll shop in Italy."

I looked again at my reflection. It wasn't that I didn't love my body, I just had no time or money to dress. And it didn't make sense. Chemistry and bio labs weren't for frills, unless I wanted to ignite myself over a Bunsen burner. But when I saw what was in the mirror, I wondered why I didn't try just a little harder. Even though I couldn't run a race or a titration in it, the dress made me feel powerful. Why? When did the curve of my ass become so important?

The Interview

On the morning of the interview, I slipped into Sky's dress and a pair of heels. It was novel walking through campus without a backpack hanging on my shoulder and without my jean cuffs dragging on the ground. Transcendence. I'd never felt it here. There was always something lurking, undone—an impossible problem set, an exam, a 30-page paper—and somebody doing it better and faster than you. Dartmouth was full of perfect people and that's what stripped away everyone's perfection. So we all worked harder. I held onto the coattails of the grading curve, and if I was honest, I went abroad to escape the stress. The tower of library books sitting on my chest. The ivy strangling the grey stone buildings. The cold sores on my lip. The crows.

But that morning, I felt light. I saw robins on the green, where there would soon be white folding chairs for our graduation. The spring of my future. I wasn't sure what was next, but this was a start. A pretty dress. Something new to try. A career, maybe. I walked around the main gate, paying tribute to the university's seal and the statues that guarded it. At the Main Street Inn, a man held the door. Laurie greeted me in the lobby, every bit as exquisite and hospitable as the first time I met her.

"You look ready," she said approvingly.

"Thank you. I feel ready."

"Any questions before I take you up to meet Garrett Sanders, your interviewer?"

"No. But, thank you, again."

We took an elevator to the third floor of the Inn and walked to a room with the door propped open by the deadbolt. Garrett stood to greet us. He wore a man's business casual uniform: blue button-down shirt, simple khaki pants, and brown loafers. He was slight, his face as nondescript as his clothes and wire rimmed glasses. His laptop sat ready on the table of the suite.

I extended a hand. Garrett reached to shake it and blushed the moment he touched me. His eyes flashed from my face, to my chest, to the floor, where they stayed when he asked me to join him at the table with the computer. Laurie whispered "Good luck" and ushered herself out of the room. I pulled my own chair and sat across from him.

Breaking the silence felt like the right thing to do. "Laurie told me to bring an extra copy." I slid my resume across the table.

"Thank you." He took the paper and studied it. He cleared his throat. "Why did you major in biology?"

"It's the study of life. Of interconnectivity. But it's also the study of change, slow and incremental. Evolution over hundreds of thousands of years. But sometimes brutally quick, one event, altering the course of everything. I found it fascinating."

"Can you give me an example?"

"The dodo is a classic case of adaptivity over many millennia to its environment. But the flightless bird went extinct with the introduction of man. Men are pretty good at destroying things." He focused on the keyboard, recording my answers.

"How do you apply it?"

"Biology?"

"Yes, your degree. What's a practical application?"

"I apply it every weekend."

"You do?"

"Sure. Take animal behavior, for instance. I've got to avoid male displays of dominance just about every Saturday night at the bar." He cracked a smile. It was brief, but it gave me courage. "I also wanted to go to medical school. Biology was the best major for that."

"Why aren't you going?"

"Medicine isn't the career for me. I don't want to spend the next ten years studying. I want to get out in the world and work." It was the answer I'd rehearsed.

"Why do you want to work for a software company?"

Another practiced response. "Because I think it will be challenging. I went to another country to learn tropical ecology first-hand. I want to go to a software company to learn about business and technology."

Garrett nodded. I relaxed. "Tell me about a time you failed, besides not going to medical school."

"That wasn't a failure."

"No? What was it then?"

"A change of direction. There's a difference."

"Okay, so when did you fail?"

"I quit the track team last year." Nobody just got into the Ivy League. Okay, maybe some people did, but not me. I was one of the ones who owed their admission to something, like the legacies or the kids whose parents donated a building. I was a recruited athlete. And it was hard. I was always a week behind in class, having to study on a Greyhound bus driving six hours away to the next meet. And there was the stigma too, that athletes like me were admitted against lower academic standards, as entertainment, a profit center for boosters. The varsity letter on my jacket said I was as academically deficient as I was physically gifted. Maybe it was all in my head, but after years of working harder than everyone else and being branded for it, I got tired of running. I quit. I bit the hand that fed, or rather admitted, and I'd never shaken the guilt.

"Why?"

"I wanted to spend more time studying, and sports took too much time."

"Why was that a failure and not a change of direction?"

"Because, maybe, I could have worked harder to balance sports and school. In a way, I gave up, and I think that's a failure."

Garrett accepted my logic, which I think was the

only thing he was looking for. Everything else was just noise. He couldn't care less that I quit track.

"What are you most proud of?"

"My senior thesis. It's almost finished."

"Tell me about it."

"It's about sex and gambling."

"Excuse me?" He looked up from his laptop and I knew I needed to change course.

"Reproductive Stochasticity in *Dermochelys coriacea* ... uhm ... sea turtle reproduction, and not putting all your eggs in one basket." He typed something and shook his head. I kept talking. "They're a pelagic species, so nesting——"

"Why are you interested in Kava Tech?" His tone was flat. He wanted to know why I was sitting in front of him, possibly wasting his time. I expected this question, but I had lost my footing.

I forgot my script. "Well, I don't know very much about software or computer-related technologies, but I like the company's culture, at least the way Laurie described it." I had just told my interviewer that substantively I had nothing to offer, but I did like to wear flip-flops. I wanted to ask for a mulligan. Please don't write that answer down. But, he did. And then he asked me a non sequitur.

"How many tennis balls can fit in an airplane?"

"Excuse me?" I put both hands on my knees and fidgeted with the hem of my dress.

Garrett repeated the question, though this time he handed me a dry-erase marker and motioned to the whiteboard behind him. I had heard about these interview questions, the kind meant to evaluate how you think and if you could think critically. They were the business world's version of brain teasers. I stood up with the marker and accidently brushed his knee with mine on the way to the board.

"Sorry," I murmured, but his blush went purple.

My hand shook. I put the marker to the board. Tennis balls in an airplane? I drew the oblong center of a jet and two compartments for luggage at its base. I stepped back to observe my sketch. It looked like an erect penis. Shit. I added wings. Then it looked like an open maxi-pad. I quickly erased it with my palm, which I wiped off with the felt eraser I should have used on the board. Then I accidently dropped the eraser on the floor, but there was no way I was bending over in this dress to pick it up. I nudged it to the side with my toe.

"Okay," I breathed. "I'm going to start again," I whispered to the smeared board, thankful Garrett couldn't see my face. I redrew the diagram and wrote equations to estimate the size of the balls and the available space within the plane, assuming it was filled with passengers. I put balls in the bathroom, the beverage carts and the spaces under the seats. I added in suitcases and carry-on luggage, figuring their capacity. Pockets. People have pockets. How many pockets per person? I kept calculating. I added a service dog, one tennis ball for him too. Was the luggage compartment pressurized? I'd have to account for that, because balls could burst as the plane ascended, couldn't they? And then there would be room for more. Ten minutes later, my hand was sticky with sweat and black marker residue. I circled my final answer on the board. I returned to my seat at the table, careful to go the other way around.

Garrett noted something on his computer, forced a smile, and moved on to the next question. He pushed an empty water glass across the table to me. "Can you sell this to me?"

Sales and marketing. Sky told me how to answer these. Bullshit and bravado. "This glass is top of the line crystal, but it's unbreakable and microwave safe. This is because it's made from a special kind of New Jersey sand from the Pine Barrens." I dropped the glass on the rug. It landed with a thump and rolled under Garret's chair. He looked at me like I'd lost my mind. Then he narrowed his eyes, pushed back from the table, and scooped the glass up off the floor. He placed it again on the table in front of me.

"This is a different glass. Tell me why it's better than the first one. Why do I want to purchase this glass?" He tapped the top with his thin finger, looking smug.

I leaned forward. "This glass will surpass your every expectation. It has all the features of the first glass, but it also releases ions into your water, which improve focus, energy, and mental acuity."

A look of appreciation appeared and then vanished from his face. He crossed his arms. "Tell me the parts of a computer and their main functions."

It was a simple question, wasn't it? "There's a keyboard, a power cord, and a screen, and those have obvious functions. Internally, there is a motherboard, and it controls ... it is used for ... uhm ... it talks to a processor that has memory ..." I fished in the well of my head and found an endless blank space. A minute passed, or maybe it was an hour. Garrett observed me in silence. It was my turn to flush. "I'm sorry, I don't know much about hardware." I looked down at the table.

"What about software?" he asked while typing. "Do you have any experience coding in any language? If not classes, perhaps as a hobby?"

A hobby? Who codes for a hobby? "I don't code." Hardware, no. Software, no. He moved on to the close.

"Well, thank you for coming today. Laurie will be in touch with any next steps. Before you go, do you have any questions for me?"

I made the obligatory inquiries about what it was like to work at the company. Garrett's replies were rehearsed responses to my rehearsed questions. Towards the end, he mentioned that Kava Tech was getting ready to expand.

"How many people are you hiring?"

"I can't discuss it in too much detail, but if I know Levi, it's going to be bold." He said it like he was letting me in on an important company secret.

After a few more short, compulsory exchanges, Garret escorted me out of the room. He held his laptop in one hand and the door in the other. We managed a concluding smile and eye contact. No need for a handshake.

On my way out, I thanked Laurie. There was no gentleman to hold the door, which I expected to hit me in my curvy ass. I stood on the sidewalk in front of the Inn, my adrenaline fading. The interview questions and my answers ran through my mind. I cringed at my deranged academic humor, at my lack of preparation. Of course they were going to ask about hardware and software.

"Damn it." I imagined the rejection letter. Two paragraphs or one? Probably one. I exhaled. Why did I care? I didn't, I assured myself. I picked my way through downtown. I told myself I'd find something else besides a software start-up. I pulled the door to the nearest café.

As if the smell of freshly roasted beans wasn't enough to jolt me, there, on his way out, was Marion. He had a small paper shopping bag in one hand, a coffee in the other, and a newspaper tucked under his arm. He greeted me with warm familiarity and the confidence I'd be happy to see him too.

"Olivia. How'd your interview go? You had it this morning, right?" He glanced at his watch.

I overcame momentary paralysis to answer. "Good. Okay? Really, I'm not sure," I admitted, with an honest sigh.

"Talk about it over a coffee?" he asked and gestured to an empty table.

"That'd be great," I said and followed him into the cafe. He was definitely older than me, maybe in his mid-to-late twenties. Tall and wiry, he had the kind of strength that was all tendon, no bulk. His eyes, expressive and warm, crinkled around the edges when he smiled. In 30 years, he'd be just as beautiful.

He pulled a chair for me to sit and leaned in to

nudge it forward. "How do you take it?"

His cologne smelled like spiced citrus. I breathed it in, sweet, mulled. From you? Any way that I can. "Dark please. Splash of cream. No sugar. Thank you."

"My pleasure."

A minute later he sat across from me. His red golf shirt was loose everywhere, except where his biceps strained the elastic. He watched me stare and when I met his eyes, he flashed a raffish grin. The floor dropped down and the heat rushed up. I reached for the steaming coffee.

"Did Garrett give your interview?"

"Yes. Do you know him?" I asked.

"I know everybody at Kava Tech. I'm not sure why Laurie had a techie interview you."

"What do you mean?"

"Garrett's a brilliant developer. He writes code. It's probably best he interviews other techies."

"You mean men."

Marion laughed. "Yes, I guess so." He sipped his coffee but did not take his eyes off me. "He's not the most socially adept guy. Sorry. What did he ask you?"

"A brain teaser, some marketing questions." I recapped our discussion but left out what happened with the tech questions.

"Marketing. I'm sure you'd be fantastic, but I envisioned a different role for you at Kava Tech."

"Like what?" I focused on the fact that he envisioned me at all. Had he thought about me too, after the bar?

"I have a couple of ideas of how somebody with

your attributes could contribute."

The way he was looking at me, I knew it. I had seen it in other countries, where men stared at women like hungry wolves. There it made me furious. Here, with this stranger, I was flattered, exasperated. I wanted him to stare. And I wanted him to like what he saw.

He leaned back. "There are a lot of ideas for expansion being thrown around right now at Kava."

"Garrett mentioned something about that."

"What did he tell you?"

"Not much. Just that Kava planned to grow. Are you involved ... in all of that? I mean, as a board member?"

"I'm also invested. My venture capital firm gave Kava seed funding. And I'm friendly with Levi. So, I lend my influence where I can. Where I think it will make a difference."

"Is that why you're here?" I meant with me. "Uhm, recruiting?"

"Even if it means helping to find the right people to do the right things. With sound planning now, things could get even more exciting."

"I see." I didn't see at all, but I couldn't look away. I logged the details. The angle of his jaw. His skin scrubbed to a soft glow. The edge of his collarbone peeking out of his shirt. Manicured hands. The sleek masculinity of a metrosexual.

Something below the table beeped and vibrated. Marion silenced the unwelcome commotion, looking somewhere between disappointed and annoyed. Then he reconnected the beeper to his belt.

"You'll have to excuse me. I have to take care of

something, but I'll see you again." I didn't have time to ask what he meant. He rose abruptly, and I stood too, unsure of how to end these precious minutes. He left no room for error. He leaned down and kissed my cheek. The gesture was intimate, but distantly professional. I breathed him in, coffee and cologne.

"Goodbye Olivia." I opened my eyes.

"Bye." By the time I said it, he was already out the door.

An Audition

In the weeks I waited to hear from Kava Tech, I thought about the company, my interview, and Marion often. Just when I got excited about the idea of working at Kava, I'd remember that I flubbed the tech portion of the show. I still didn't understand why the company bothered to interview me. Then little rays of hope would stab their way into my heart (and other areas) when I remembered how Marion said he'd see me again.

It was unlike me to be so quickly smitten, but it was also easy to explain. The last boyfriend I'd had, Kevin, broke up with me before I left to travel the world. He was on the track team too, and we dated for almost a year. While I was miffed he had cut it off so easily when I told him I'd be away, I couldn't say that I was all that hurt. It had been one of those dysfunctional college relationships that happened because we had the same track practice schedule and because we both had fabulous runners' bodies. We had little else in common other than excellent stamina.

When I lamented to Sky that he had ended it, she shrugged. "Was he good in bed?"

"It was like dorm food." I was busy, but I needed to eat.

"Well, then." And that was the end of that conversation and my relationship with Kevin.

When I left the country, I vowed wholeheartedly to keep my panties on, no matter what. There was an AIDS epidemic raging around the world, and there was no way I'd risk contracting something in a country that lacked basic medical supplies, like antibiotics. My self-imposed sexual exile got a whole lot harder in Rodrigues where the men had green eyes, light brown skin, muscular builds, and high cheekbones. This collection of genetic treasures, courtesy of Indian, European, Australian, Chinese, and African ancestry, made for the most beautiful people I'd ever seen. Nevertheless, I persisted.

Now that it had been too long since I'd had contact with the opposite sex, it was easy to get preoccupied with someone who looked like Marion and, as Sky pointed out, could probably afford to buy me more than a burrito for dinner. I fantasized about him with ease, which, along with my financial situation and lack of employment options, kept the company on my mind.

One sunny afternoon after class, I checked my voicemail from a campus blue phone. Along with several messages from my mother and a drunk dial, there was a message from Laurie Davis. Her cheery southern drawl congratulated me on passing the first round of interviews. She invited me down to Austin, Texas, and said I'd receive a FedEx with all the information. I sprinted home for the package.

I pulled the envelope apart, wondering how I'd graduated to the next step. I read the letter inviting me to Kava Tech's office to "interview on-site for the position of recruiter." Recruiter? Maybe recruiters didn't need to know that much about hardware or software. I thought about Laurie. She was in the business of finding and selling people, not tech ware. I'd done well on the other interview questions, hadn't I? Maybe that's why Garrett mentioned the expansion at the end, and this is where Marion thought I could contribute? Marion. "I'll see you again." In Austin? Is that what he meant?

The letter said I'd spend an entire weekend in Texas, the agenda packed with networking sessions, dinners, and hours and hours of interviews. How many tennis ball brain teasers could Kava Tech possibly ask over the course of two days? Would the interviews be the same now that I was pegged for recruiter? Would the company be as fun and exciting as they said? I had a lot of questions, and the only way to answer them was to go.

A week later, my flight to Austin routed through Dallas. Though I flew economy, Kava Tech spared no other expense. I arrived in my room at the downtown Four Seasons and flopped on the squishy king-sized bed, a heavenly upgrade from my prison-style dorm mattress. I curled up in the crisp white sheets until it was time to catch a bus to a 'Recruit Meet and Greet.'

The shuttle was full of nervous people like

me. I sat towards the front and watched out the window, eavesdropping on the uneasy introductory conversations behind me. I had expected to see desert tumbleweed, but the scenery surprised me. The sun hung low in the distance, lighting up white rock hills that lined newly paved highways wider than any four northeastern streets put together. Fluffy clouds floated in a sky devoid of dampness and darkness. It felt open and warm in a way that made me want to lift my face upward, unlike back in Hanover where I was always huddled in a coat.

From my seat I heard the names of universities, "Stanford, Harvard, Rice, Georgia Tech ...." The list of brand-name schools tossed around was absurd. When I finally introduced myself to the girl sitting behind me, Dartmouth seemed ordinary.

"What are you interviewing for?" asked a guy in the seat across the aisle.

"Recruiter."

He smirked, head up, eyes down. A full once over. Was there something on my shirt? I checked.

"You?" I asked.

"Developer." He looked the type. Male. Asian. Hair vigorously styled to stand straight up off his head. "I'm Course 6. MIT."

"Course 6? Is that like Area 51?"

He laughed. "No, no aliens. It's what MIT calls computer science. William. I'm William Chang."

"Olivia Gesso. Biology. Dartmouth." I shook his outstretched hand.

"What kind of bio?"

"Extraterrestrial," I joked.

Deadpan, "Any evidence here?" He looked around.

"That guy over there. Totally suspect." Eyes closed, rocking it out to whatever was playing on his headphones. His orange and white striped shirt two sizes too big, messy hair everywhere. "There's something going on there."

William laughed. "Nah. Not an alien. He's just a developer. For real, what kind of bio?"

"Evolution. Species dynamics. Reproductive behavior. That kind."

"That'll be useful."

"For what?"

"Recruiting."

"Yeah?"

"Recruiters and developers are different species. You'll have to bridge the gap." William looked at the guy in the headphones. "You'll be a natural. You look right. Even if you're not a comm or psych major."

"I look right?"

"You look the part. You know, of recruiter."

"What's a recruiter look like?"

"You." I looked at my shirt again. "You'll figure it out, Dartmouth."

"Thanks, Course 6. I usually do."

The shuttle banged across a metal, semi-circular bridge, a wide waterway coursing underneath. It looked like Christo and Jeanne-Claude went rustic with a singular structure, and then everything modernized. A separate drive led to a glass-plated building reflecting the sun off its every angle.

"The building," William said, "they call it the campus. Don't say office."

"Why not?" I asked.

"Offices stifle people."

"So do stereotypes." It gave him pause. "You'll figure it out, MIT." He grinned.

The bus lurched to a stop. William stood and held out his hand, "Recruiters first." He leaned forward and I waited for a geeky bow, but crazy-hair headphones guy pushed by us both.

"At the campus, it's aliens first," I pointed out.

"You're stereotyping." William smirked.

"I'm classifying," I corrected. "It's what biologists do."

He laughed. "What's the difference?"

I shrugged and hopped off the bus.

We were led through enormous glass doors and a large lobby with 20-foot ceilings, and then out to a courtyard overlooking the Austin landscape. We descended the steps into a stone amphitheater-style patio with a view of the river, the bridge, and the tops of the city buildings to the south. I understood immediately why they called it Texas hill country. Out to the horizon, the land ran in beautiful waves of cedar forest and crumbled stone. The sun dropped lower, promising a cotton candy sky.

People gathered around blue plastic tubs filled with ice and beer, the kind with funny names like 'Shiner' and 'Fat Tire.' Were it not for the name tags, you couldn't tell the prospects from the personnel. We were all the same age. I spotted Laurie and waved. There were other recruiters like her here. They dotted the party landscape, serving drinks and patting name tags onto people's hearts. Circles of conversation, always a recruiter at the center. They braided people together, making introductions and finishing sentences. They weaved recruits with employees and doused reticence with beer.

The polite, predictable conversations were redundant but easy.

"What do you do?" Sip, smile.

"Do you like your job?" Sip, smile.

"Where did you go to school?" Sip, smile.

"What was your major?" Sip, smile.

"Do you like Austin?" Sip, smile.

"Recruiter, can I get another?"

Over the next two hours, the light made its quiet descent behind the hills, as the volume of the happy hour steadily rose. Stevie Ray Vaughn serenaded over the sound system and I saw William stumble up one of the steps. He had turned a bright shade of pink, his cheeks a different kind of sunset. Later, when the recruiters ushered us from the happy hour, I sat next to him on the shuttle.

"Okay, William?"

"I'm fine. I'll hang in there for tonight. It's gonna be awesome," he said.

"Another two hours of small talk is awesome?" I asked. "You really are a developer."

"What, is this your first on-site?"

"It's my first interview weekend," I admitted.

"Geez. Well, expect more drinks at dinner. Lots

more. Then bar hopping and dancing. I did this at Pegasus last weekend, and at Sun Microsystems the weekend before that, and——"

"... and we're supposed to interview tomorrow?" I asked, wide-eyed.

"Well that's it. The whole culture fit thing. See if you can party, but then get it together to answer the hardest questions they can think of. It's too bad for you if you're too hungover to think."

"What do they ask recruiters?"

"What are you talking about? This is your interview. Look at what they're doing. Your whole job would be this—take out recruits, wine and dine them. And believe me, getting some of these computer science geeks to socialize is a total job." I giggled at his self-deprecation.

"You must be ... something ... if you've interviewed at all those places?"

William perked up but lowered his voice. "Yeah, it's been a pretty fun couple of months, getting flown all over to party. I've got a couple offers. I just have to decide. I keep telling them to give me more stock and bigger signing bonuses, and they do."

"I'll be lucky to land a job that pays me at all."

He scoffed. "You'll get an offer. It doesn't take a whole lot of mental oomph to take people drinking and dancing for a living. You just gotta look good."

"I used calculus on the fly in my first-round interview." I meant to say I'm smart.

"So what? Doesn't matter, now. Not for you." I crossed my arms. I knew this feeling. Recruited athlete at an Ivy. Recruiter at tech company? Out of the frying pan and into the fire. "This matters." He waved at the shuttle of recruits laughing and chatting in their seats. "Same scene everywhere I've interviewed."

"Tell me about it." And he did, until our bus pulled up to Ruth's Chris Steak House. The shuttle had stopped, but my head felt like it was still moving.

We were escorted into several private dining rooms in the restaurant. There were no formal speeches or presentations at dinner, just lots of Kava Techies mulling around to make conversation, answer questions, and sell the company. They talked up Austin. I was told about pristine lakes, famous music festivals, green spaces for hiking, bike trails, and a food scene full of ribs, Tex-Mex, and steaks. Austin is sunny 300 days of the year, they said.

I leaned over to William, "If the streets were gold, I'd swear Austin was Oz."

He mimicked the sales pitch. "This isn't Texas, it's Austin. This isn't a job, it's Kava Tech."

"Maybe you should interview for recruiter," I laughed.

"I lack the assets."

Dinner ended. In a beer–martini haze and a steak coma, I envisioned late-night TV and down pillows at the Four Seasons. Laurie dashed my plans when she asked if I'd join some people going over to the Elephant Room.

"It has live jazz, a tiny little place with great atmosphere," she offered, "We're catching a cab now."

I remembered what William said about this being my real interview. As much as that bed was calling, I knew going along was expected and the right decision if I wanted a shot at the job. I followed Laurie and a few others out the door.

The bar was a local favorite. We walked down a flight of steps into what felt like a house basement, the damp air heavy with smoke. At the center of a small stage, a scantily clad vocalist perched upon a stool, one of her ankles wrapped around its base. Her hair swung along the length of her tiny waist as she rocked to the music played by the accompanying bass and sax. Her soulful voice filled the room in a way that was rhythmic, captivating, and just plain sexy—the exact opposite of the nerdy, drunk, and awkward assortment of recruits descending on the scene. Led by Laurie, we made our way to a couple of reserved tables off to the side of the stage.

I ended up sitting with four guys I didn't know, two recruits and two employees. Somebody bought a round of shots. We toasted Kava. And then another. We toasted Austin. And then I was holding a cold pint, both my palms around it for stability. Talking over the jazz felt criminal. I closed my eyes and breathed in the slow whine of the sax.

The guy next to me yelled, too close to my ear. "You like jazz?" It felt like when you're buried in the best part of a book and a stranger wants to know what you're reading. But I was supposed to be networking.

"It's excellent."

"You're a recruiter?"

"No. I'm a recruit."

"For recruiter."

"Yes."

"Do you dance?"

"What?"

"Do you like to dance?"

"Sure."

"All recruiters dance."

"They do?"

"Yeah."

"Like, they have to audition?"

"No." 'Alex Clark, Technical Sales'—still stuck to his chest—looked at me like I was stupid. "They dance. You know. Like this." He stumbled up from his chair and pulled me into the small space between the tables. He reached for my waist, steadied himself on my hip and rested his forehead on my shoulder. Was he too drunk to stand or was this dancing? I looked around. It was too crowded for this eighth-grade nonsense. I held my beer between his stomach and my chest and watched the liquid slide from one side of the glass to the other like a warm urine sample. The song ended, and he picked up his head. "See? You do dance."

"Uhm ... yeah. Hey, you need more beer. I'll get you one. Can you hold mine?" I took his hand off my hip and put the pint in his palm. "Finish that, and I'll get us more."

"Thanks, sweets." He slunk into his chair.

I backed out of the space and saw Laurie watching from a few tables over. She gave me a thumbs-up. This was my audition.

The On-site

The Texas sun poured through the shades I had forgotten to close the night before. It seared holes in my head, which, after a while, I realized were my eyes. To save them, I crawled to the bathroom away from the light and rested on the cool tile floor. Three hundred days of sun a year might not actually be a selling point for this company. I choked down water and ibuprofen and waited before moving again. I let the shower take care of the rest, boiling and steaming the hangover out of my body.

It took time, but I got ready for the day. Apply makeup. Control unruly hair. Find Underwear. Zipper Chanel dress. Locate shoes and purse with room key. One last check in the mirror revealed a puffy, but presentable face. I made my way to the lobby for the 8:30 a.m. pick-up.

William sat there in an oversized, King James-style armchair. In a black suit with a leather briefcase, he looked like a boy playing dress-up in his dad's clothes. Next to him sat a girl in a dark purple pantsuit. Her jet-black hair was pulled tightly back, except for short straight bangs that framed her forehead and brushed against the tops of her large green eyes. Though her face was a cute mess of freckles, she looked serious. She sat bolt upright, her thin legs crossed at the ankles.

I plopped across from them. "Hi," was all I could offer in the way of an introduction.

William was effervescent. "Olivia, this is my friend Viola. We interned together the last two summers and keep running into one another at these recruitment extravaganzas. She's from Cal Tech."

"Great to meet you." I extended a hand. "Were you there last night? I don't remember seeing you."

She shook her head. "I flew in late last night and missed all the fun. I already interviewed with Kava Tech, so this is my sell weekend."

"What's a sell weekend?" I asked.

William butted in. "This is Olivia's first time interviewing anywhere."

I shot him a look.

"I was offered a job with Kava Tech in technical sales about three weeks ago, but I haven't decided between them and another start-up. They've flown me down to convince me." Viola's delivery was factual, but not boastful. I liked her.

"Congratulations. What will you do today if you're not locked in a room with a whiteboard full of brain teasers?" I asked.

"You know, with this company, could be anything.

I'm having brunch with Levi and some of his inner circle people, but beyond that, who knows? The recruiters told me to pack a swimsuit, so we'll see what that means."

"What are you interviewing for?" Viola asked.

"Recruiter," and feeling the need to fill the void, I joked, "I can't imagine what my day will look like either. Brain teasers about dinner, drinks, and dancing?"

"I don't know Olivia, I'm pretty sure they drill the recruiters too—just not with questions." William covered his faux-shocked open mouth with his fingertips.

"Wow." I wasn't one to overreact to social ineptitude, having had plenty of practice hanging out in the chemistry and genetics labs at school. I let an awkward silence descend.

"That was supposed to be funny," he said, and then turned to Viola. "Olivia's a bio major from Dartmouth. Not typical for a recruiter."

Viola was quick. "Well, you're typical for a developer. A socially backward male with an intelligence complex. Congrats again on alienating yet another of the opposite sex, *Willy*. It gets funnier to watch every time it happens." Viola puckered her lips and blew him a kiss. "You should have seen him last summer."

"Willy?" I snickered. "Isn't that a cute nickname for such a serious coder."

"It makes me less academically intimidating." William's nose was in the air, in the space where indignant meets wounded. "And that's not fair, what happens over summer doesn't count. It's summer."

I rested my forehead in my hand. "I'm going to

find coffee before the shuttle comes. Good luck today, *Willy*. Viola, I'd love to meet up for a drink later."

"Good luck, Olivia. You'll need some thick skin to be a recruiter. Social skills are an art. The recruiters are the most organized, efficient, and best judges of character I've ever met. And they have incredible patience." She glanced at William.

"What?" he said.

Viola ignored him. "Really, good luck. Hopefully, I'll see you tonight."

The shuttle ride to campus was quiet. People were either reviewing notes, reading last-minute printouts about the company, or simply trying not to throw up last night's exploits. I was in the latter group. I doodled on my legal pad.

At the Kava campus, we sat through a brochure-based company presentation followed by a basic question-and-answer session. At least a hundred candidates, buttoned up in dark suits, jotted notes in faux leather binders. It felt like a dress rehearsal for adulthood. The prospects asked questions I knew they knew the answers to because we had all prepped with the same materials. Anything to raise a hand, get noticed, and stand out.

We were led from this room into a holding tank with floor to ceiling windows and a view of the city's forested hills. It was nauseatingly full of coffee, tea, and snacks, and the cushy chairs were all taken. I stood and watched out the window. Blackbirds, shining purple in the sun, darted synchronously between the trees. The flock, organized chaos in the sky, disappeared into the canopy. The birds were safer moving in this tightly orchestrated mob. Outliers were easy for a predator to grab.

"Olivia Gesso?"

"Here." I raised my hand and followed my interviewer to a small windowless room.

"Please." He motioned to a chair. "Did you have fun last night?"

"Too much. The music was great."

"Good, I'm glad. We like to show our recruits a nice time."

"You succeeded." I rubbed my forehead, the headache finally fading.

He snapped open his laptop in a way that said, okay, enough with the small talk. I opened my legal pad.

"Last week I was in New York City and I got stung by a bee. A honeybee. Can you believe that? Walking down the city street."

"That stinks." I put my pencil down.

"Yeah, but it got me thinking. How many bees do you think there are in Manhattan?" I waited for him to continue his story. "Well?"

"Is that a question? You want me to answer?"

"Yes."

"You want to know how many honeybees there are in New York City?"

"Just Manhattan, the main borough. Can you make an educated guess?"

Tennis balls in an airplane. Honeybees in Manhattan. Another way to ask, show me how you think. Last year I took an animal behavior class. The professor loved honeybees; their orderly, high-functioning society run by women for women. Female drones feed, clean, and protect. They ensure the order, loyalty, and longevity of the hive, all in the service of their queen mother. The males? They do nothing. Absolutely nothing, except wait around to mate with the queen. They die afterward, their abdomens ripped off by explosive coitus. What an existence. I set to work on the legal pad.

Manhattan is what, about 30 million acres? Who knows? Two colonies per acre? Why not? That's 60 million colonies. One colony has about 100,000 bees. That's six trillion bees. I circled the fast math. "Wait. That's not right. There are apiaries." How many buildings, 500,000? How many have apiaries? Who keeps bees in the city? I pictured a commune of people in Birkenstocks getting together to taste each other's honey. In Manhattan, I guessed five million more bees. "In the borough, there are 6,005,000,000 honeybees." I looked at my interviewer. "Wait, cut that in half. No, a quarter."

"Why?"

"The calculation assumes regular grassland. But it isn't. It's dense city. Pavement."

"So?"

"So, it's way less. About 1,500,000,000 to do quick math."

"Done?"

"Done." I showed him the math. He moved on. "You're at an important client presentation giving a demo on a Kava product that will sell for $50 million if you can close the deal. Everyone is seated around the table and you begin your pitch." I looked around the room, trying to imagine myself selling software. "Then you spill your water on the keyboard."

"I do?"

"Yes. And the computer shorts. You and your clients are staring at a blank screen."

"That sounds bad."

"It is. What do you do?"

"I pull out the back-up hardcopy of the presentation I have in my bag. Request copies and continue on. I'll email the demo later."

"Do you prefer working in teams or alone?"

"Depends on the team."

"Why?"

"Because some people do better on their own."

"How do you handle competition?"

"I destroy it."

"What about pressure?"

"I make sure it doesn't destroy me."

"Tell me something amazing you've seen."

"A hundred-year-old, thousand-pound turtle disappearing into the ocean."

"What's your favorite color."

"Yellow."

"A colleague makes an inappropriate comment about your clothing. What do you do?"

"Tell him to knock it off."

"Do you go to HR?"

"For a comment? No." I thought about William's joke this morning. He'd made a mistake, and it was over.

"What if he inappropriately touched you?"

"The colleague? I don't know. What's the company's policy on harassment?"

"We're small and hire great people, so I'm not sure. It's never been a problem."

"Then why ask that question?"

"It's standard."

"Are all these questions standard or are they specific to me?"

"Standard. We don't have much time. Can we continue?"

"Of course."

"What does this picture look like?"

"A butterfly. Wait, a dog. Both. I see both."

"What food do you hate?"

"Liver sausage. Tastes like rotting organs."

"What scares you?"

"Guns. But they also make me feel safe. Maybe it's the need for a gun that scares me. I don't know."

"How would you make a shy colleague more comfortable?"

"Invite them to a private space to talk. Establish a connection."

"What would you do if a recruit got too drunk at an event you were hosting?"

"See if he needed medical help. Get him home. Call him in the morning."

"Do you consider yourself adventurous?"

"Yes, very."

"Have you ever committed a crime?"

"Like, do I have a police record?"

"It's what you consider a crime."

"I shoplifted a necklace when I was 12. Got caught. Been straight ever since."

"Are you a risk-taker?"

"Absolutely."

"Tell me why you think so."

"I shoplifted once." He looked up, the first time he broke form. "I'm kidding. I once climbed one of the world's rarest trees in near hurricane-force winds."

And on and on it went. Forty-five minutes of rapid fire questions to construct a vague psychological profile defined by my likes, dislikes, tendencies, and preferences. He never asked for an explanation, beyond my initial answers, no matter how weird. Just wrote them down. I returned to the holding tank for a short break and was farmed out again 15 minutes later. The other interviews were more standard, full of brain teasers and behavioral scenarios. We had sandwiches for lunch in the campus cafeteria and by 5 p.m., after almost eight hours of grilling, I felt wilted. My eyes burned. I didn't have it in me to look at one more business case or explain again what I hoped to gain by working for Kava Tech.

The end of the day was celebrated with another happy hour on the veranda. The formal questions were over, but for recruiters, if William was right, the interview was just beginning. I made my best effort to ask important questions about the company, to smile, and to casually impress. After an hour, I walked over to a cooler to help myself to a beer. I unfurled with the first sip and let myself stare into the quiet of another spectacular sunset.

"Gorgeous." A voice behind me. I turned. Marion. He meant the view, but he was looking at me. His dark eyes endless. They swallowed the paling light. They swallowed me. What had slack in me, tightened. I braced for impact but kept falling.

"It is."

"Can I get you another?"

I shook my head. "I have everything I need now." I meant it.

"Do you know what you're looking at?"

"I'd like to think I do." I searched his face.

"Let me show you." He leaned closer. I sucked in the air, like I'd been holding my breath for the last eight hours. "That's the 360 Bridge, over the Colorado River." I reluctantly looked away from him to take in the scenery. "Over there is hill country. And there is downtown. It's small, but entertaining." The tops of the buildings reflected the fading light.

"Can you swim? There?" I pointed to the bridge.

"Would you like to?"

"With you." I meant for it to be a question, but it came out as a definitive.

"Hey, Mars." An interruption without introduction. A clap on the back. A Kava Techie. All the most important people in the company had beepers in a black case attached to their belts. Some also had cellular phones.

This guy had both. He talked business, putting me suddenly out of place.

"I'm sorry, would you excuse us?" The interrupter acknowledged me.

"I'll see you tomorrow," Marion said, his expression rakish.

"Yes, of course," I replied, like I had any idea what he was talking about. I didn't get the chance to ask him. I watched him leave, talking intently with the Kava Techie until they disappeared into the building.

I dissolved back into the happy hour, went back to networking, and let the drinks and the small talk wash over me. When it ended, William wasn't the only pink-faced recruit boarding the bus to dinner. He sought me out. "You know I was only kidding this morning."

"Is that an apology?" I asked.

"How 'bout I buy you a beer?" He grinned and held out half a cup from the happy hour.

"The least you could do is get me a cold one." And he did. He ran back to the patio and then all the way to the bus with his peace offering, sloshing half of it on his shirt when he sat next to me.

At dinner, we exchanged war stories with the other recruits, arguing the answers to the brain teasers and business cases. We dripped jalapeno-laced queso on the red-checked plastic table covers and slurped frozen margaritas. This was Tex-Mex. This was comradery. And when I stopped thinking about Marion, I started thinking that I really liked the people at Kava Tech. I felt like I was fitting in, finding common ground in the business riddles and white papers. Maybe I could do this software thing after all, if these were the kinds of problems I'd have to work through, and if we did it together over liquid cheese. I sat back from the table and listened to Willy argue why artificial intelligence was the future of everything. Could I call this my career? Mom, Dad, I'm revolutionizing business. I'm building human capacity at a company that only hires geniuses. And if the money was what everyone said it would be? "Definitely," I said, smiling into my margarita.

After dinner, they took us dancing at Polyesters. We piled into the seventies-themed night club, exhausted but ready to party. The recruiters passed out more drinks and baited every uncoordinated one of us onto the packed dance floor. Things got hazy. I forgot to behave. William and I climbed on a pillar and dethroned one of the professional dancers. A disco ball-illuminated, maladroit sweaty mess, we electrified the crowd with our moves. Hours later, a recruiter found me and ended my reign as dance floor royalty. She stuffed me in a cab.

Lake Travis

The phone rang inches from my ear. "Hello?" I mumbled.

"This is your 7 a.m. wake-up call," a recorded voice informed.

I cursed and dropped the phone between the nightstand and the bed.

Then there was the door, the knocking too loud to ignore.

"Coming." My aching feet, the victims of last night's heels, hit the floor. I held my forehead, because my neck needed help.

"Yes?" I peeked through the chained space.

"Ms. Gesso? A package for you."

I fumbled the lock, still hiding behind the door. A man in a dark hotel uniform handed me a white box.

"Thank you."

"You are wel——"

I slammed the door, dropped the box, and lunged for the toilet. When my stomach had nothing left, I rested my head on the porcelain pillow and looked under my arm. The glossy white box was there, out of reach. I kicked the bathroom door shut with my foot, regretting the noise instantly. Without lifting my head, I turned on the shower. I crawled out of my clothes and over the ledge of the bath like a salted slug. I laid my back against the cool tub and let my mouth hang open to catch the warm spray.

I stayed that way until I could sit, and then that way until I could stand. And with time, I emerged from the steam to find another irritatingly bright Austin day behind the blackout curtains. When I could bend with confidence, I picked up the mysterious box and sat on the bed to open it.

Under tissue paper, a small card rested on top of canary yellow material.

It read, "Hope this fits. Meet in the lobby at 10 a.m. Enjoy, Mars."

The yellow material was a one-piece Body Glove swimsuit. The neoprene-like material zippered lengthwise up the front, the cut neither ample nor skimpy. I'll see you tomorrow; is this what Marion meant?

"How am I going to interview in a swimsuit, Marion?" I asked like he was in the room. I leaned back on the pillows and closed my throbbing eyes, the pain dulling the thrill of the gift, proof that I was on his mind too. The other present in the box was time. I fished the phone out from under the bed and ordered room service. The caffeine brought clarity, if not concern. Would Laurie know where I was? Had Marion made arrangements with her? Was this, whatever it was, part of the interview process? I reminded myself that I came to Austin to see about a job, not a boy. I nibbled my way through a bagel and decided to roll the dice. Instead of calling human resources and asking questions, I went to the lobby wearing the bathing suit, jean shorts, and a t-shirt, the only informal clothes in my suitcase.

I looked for Marion. Instead, I found Viola.

She looked surprised to see me. She was wearing a loose, woven cover-up over shorts, and sandals. A bathing suit halter hugged her neck, and she held a large black sun hat. "I thought you'd be in day two of agony. What happened?" she asked, concerned.

"I'm not sure. I got an invitation to come swimming. Or, at least, I got a bathing suit."

Viola looked happy, relieved even. "That's great. I thought I was going to be the only girl. You're probably coming on the boat."

"What boat?"

"Kava Tech keeps speed boats on Lake Travis. Employees can use them whenever they want. I guess to sell recruits too. You must've done pretty well yesterday to graduate to the sell group already."

I shrugged. "This just sort of happened, uhm, last minute."

Viola waved her hand. "It'll beat inhaling marker fumes all day. Willy will be so jealous."

"We had fun last night."

"Willy is a good time. We hung out a lot last summer."

Other recruits walked over and introduced

themselves. We stood there, college kids in bathing suits, sipping coffee and chatting in a five-star hotel lobby. Then we climbed into a black Yukon waiting out front.

The drive was peaceful, quiet even, with everyone nursing hangovers. I draped my arm out of the window and watched the white cliffs fly by under the bright blue sky.

Viola leaned over. "They say it's sunny 300 days a year."

"I've heard. Coming from New Hampshire, I might spontaneously combust."

Speaking to herself as much as to me, she said, "I could do this, I think."

"It's nice to know you already have the option," I said and worried, again, that I was supposed to be somewhere else.

Thirty minutes later we turned onto a dirt road that ended at a mooring dock. The slips were full, the boats bobbing despite the stillness of the lake. We walked down to the sparkling water, to a ski boat with the Kava logo painted on the side. A guy, prepping its interior, bounced over the side and greeted us. He had paired a red Hawaiian shirt with a lime green bathing suit, Teva sandals, and a severe sock tan.

"I'm Thomas." He bounded between us making introductions, his Canadian accent thick. Then he hopped back in the boat, talking as he moved things here and there. He checked the engine. He threw us life jackets. He held up a wakeboard. "Anyone ever tried it?" Nobody answered. "You will today." The Canadian jumping bean was electric, prattling instructions, safety directives, and activities. He asked questions and then answered them.

I looked around for Marion.

"Everyone in." Thomas helped recruits off the dock, pointing to seats, explaining something about counterbalance in boats. He turned the key and the engine rumbled the fiberglass. I had misjudged. I should have gone to my interviews.

"Mars! Let's go!" Thomas yelled to nobody and everybody.

A creaky spring-hinged door, the kind on every rural grandma's house, swung open from the lean-to we had walked past on the way to the boat. Marion, statuesque in white linen pants, reflective pilot's glasses, and carrying a clipboard of papers, strode to the dock.

Viola's whisper was involuntary. "Whoa."

Marion quickly shook everyone's hand and with the engine on, wasted no time taking the wheel and maneuvering the boat off the dock. Thomas took a backseat, fiddling with more gear. The engine hummed and we picked up speed, cutting through the morning air. Marion's attention was on the water. Mine was on him, the broadness of his shoulders, the wind whipping his t-shirt against his chest. I felt the grip of his hands on the leather of the steering wheel. He was one person, but he took up the whole boat, the lake, and the view. I saw only him.

I don't know how long we sped over the water, but it wasn't long enough. We reached a place, somewhere in the lake's middle, and it was time to pretend I wasn't preoccupied.

"Any of you ever wakeboarded?" Thomas asked again. We shook our heads, and he set out explaining.

"It looks like a skateboard," one of the recruits, Shawn, commented.

"Similar." Thomas handed him the board. "Give it a go?" Shawn inspected it. "Getting out of the water is the hardest part. Then it's just balance. But catch an edge, and you're on your ass. Let me go first."

Thomas jumped over the side, strapped the board to his feet, and swam to the tow rope. He gave a thumbs-up and Marion revved the engine. Hundreds of horsepower pulling a gnat. Thomas skidded, turned, jumped, and hopped with flare. Never tiring, like a kite dancing behind the boat. A good while later, he tried to flip and finally crashed into the water. He swam to the boat ladder and celebrated his ride.

"I can totally do this." Shawn ripped off his t-shirt with confidence. He was the palest human I'd ever seen. In the water, his long dangly arms were bioluminescent like one of those squids. Eventually, he anchored his feet to the board. The rope in hand, he gave Marion the sign to go. The boat took off, but Shawn slumped to the side. Determined, he held on, and it looked like we were towing a lump of albino seaweed. This went on repeatedly, and after each flop, Marion circled the boat, bringing him the rope to try again. It was exhausting to watch, but eventually, out of sheer willpower, Shawn stood. He held on, hunched, and fought to keep his shoulders from dislocating. Then everything gave way at once. He went down face first.

From somewhere under her hat, Viola said, "Ouch."

I giggled. We sat side by side, our feet propped on the seat cushions and watched the others try. Their results were comedically similar. Viola stifled a cackle that got Thomas' attention.

"Try it?" He asked, earnestly.

Viola lifted her oversized brim. "I'm good."

Thomas looked to me. "Somebody needs to represent my half of humanity," I said. Viola tipped her hat.

"Let's see it then." It was the first time he had addressed me directly. Marion sat in the captain's chair, a model in a magazine shoot. Not a drop of water on his light blue V-neck. He crossed his arms.

And it wasn't just him waiting for a response. The dripping, defeated recruits, Viola, Thomas, all watching. The heckler had the mic. I tugged my t-shirt over my head and dropped it next to Viola. They stared in silence. I wiggled out of my jean shorts. Wake rocked the boat, and I planted my feet wide for balance. The sun on my thighs, my ass hanging out of the angular swimsuit. I walked to the stern and dove into the cool water. A seconds-long respite. A blackout curtain around me, until I bobbed for air, and he was there, leaning over the side.

Marion handed me a life vest and slid his glasses onto his head. It felt like a private moment between us, the engine drowning out the others. "Relax. Lean away from what's pulling you," he said.

"What if I can't? Don't want to. Lean away."

"Then you'll fall. Hard."

I unraveled. I drifted with the rope. The current silent, faint, but dragging me, nonetheless. Lengths away, I heard the engine before I felt it, a force I couldn't fight. It lifted me up, out, and over the glassy lake. So fast, I choked on the wind. I was flying then, and it felt right somehow, hurtling towards something I could never catch. Every time I got an inch too close, proximity dissolved the tension. The choice clear: keep my distance or sink. So, I held tight to the thrill and he pulled me harder, faster. The spray stung my face, and my muscles screamed for it to be over, but I dug in, wanting more. The tether somehow freeing, my adrenaline coursing. It wasn't enough to glide, the scenery blurring past. I jammed the board against the wake, expecting air. Instead I caught the crest. It ate the board and the water swallowed me up, cool and soundless.

"Again!" I hollered when I surfaced. Every time I said more, he said yes, until I was almost too tired to swim back to the boat. I climbed the deck ladder into claps and compliments.

Viola handed me a towel. "You killed it."

I was slow to wrap it around my quivering arms. The sun felt good, and I knew Marion was looking. I didn't care if it helped get me a job—or him. They felt like the same thing.

Later, we lunched at a restaurant on the water. Thomas entertained. Marion took work calls on his phone and then toured us around the lake's nicest real estate. He was cordial and accommodating, but impersonal. I was just another recruit, and I got to worrying again that I should have been in an interview room instead of on a boat. By late afternoon, we were back at the dock. Thomas showed us the changing rooms. When I came out, bathing suit balled up in my hands, Marion was waiting for me. The tow rope between us was tight.

"You left these in the boat." He handed me a pair of sunglasses.

"Viola's. I'll give them to her. Thanks for today." I wanted to ask him what it meant, for me. For him. For a job. Keep your distance or sink. "They're waiting for me." I motioned towards the full truck, engine running.

"Olivia. You need a ride to the airport." He didn't ask. He told me.

"Tonight?"

"Were you planning on staying longer?" His dimples teased.

"I mean, if I need to make up an interview day. Do ... do I need to?"

He shook his head. "I'll meet you in the lobby. Just us. Give you a chance to ask any last-minute questions about Kava." I felt the rush, like I was flying over the water. The driver honked. "You'd better go."

I jogged up the path to an open door. We rode back to the hotel, windows down and the warm wind howling through the truck. A beautiful day, and for me, and the best part was yet to come.

La Salsa

After a long hot shower in the sparkling hotel bathroom, I flopped on the bed and exhaled a sea of tension out in one breath. The weekend was over, but the banter, people's faces, their names flashed through my head. A cacophony of interview questions, music from the nights out, and the carefully orchestrated conversations at happy hours. I needed to get dressed.

My only casual outfit, jean shorts and a t-shirt, was damp with lake water. Instead of comfortable airplane clothes, I buttoned myself into the suit I had brought for my second day of interviews. I pinned a rose broach to the lapel. I had picked it up at an antique junk store for a dollar. The suit needed it. Something else besides the lace camisole to break up the black. It was the nicest I'd ever looked for a flight, but it felt right for Marion. I was a contender for him, and for this job, wasn't I? I wanted them both.

I thought about it on a bench downstairs, my

suitcase propped against my leg. The lobby felt empty
without the recruits' nervous chatter, their speculation
about what would happen next. I liked joking with Willy
and Viola, and the others I'd met. We were different,
but all dialed into the same intense frequency. It
wasn't what Kava made, it was how they were making
it. Risk and reward, we were told. Kava drew a certain
kind of person who liked to test the limits. I imagined
that working there would be like an adventurous trip.
Some things would be difficult, but in the end it would
be worth it. I'd have a career; I'd earn good money; I'd
make smart, new friends who liked problem-solving
over beer and queso; and I'd get to see about Marion.
Marion? Marion! I looked at my watch. He was late.

The airport shuttle had long since departed, and
another 15 minutes ticked by. If I missed the plane, I'd
have to call Human Resources, but on a Sunday, who
would be there? I had no place to sleep and couldn't
afford a last-minute reservation at the Four Seasons.
I started for the concierge. Marion strode coolly
through the revolving door, sunglasses on his head,
face radiant. A handshake turned into a kiss on the
cheek, and I forgot about my flight.

He scooped up my bag. "Sorry I'm late, but I've
made amends."

I assumed he meant the Porsche 911 that was
waiting out front, engine purring. He opened my door.
I breathed new leather. Then he was next to me, hand
on the shift. Everything under control.

"You look great." The compliment was matter of
fact, like the once over that came with it.

"So do you. Always. Like you're in a magazine. How do you do that?" His watch looked expensive. His hair was not so much styled as expertly cut; left just long enough.

He shrugged. "Business is about appearances."

"You must be very good at business."

"I am." He looked at me, everywhere, but my face. "And you will be." He nudged the gear shift, and my heart and the engine said, Yes. Go faster.

"Is that why I spent today soaking up the sun, instead of interviewing?"

His eyes on the road, we darted through traffic. "Levi asked if I'd sell some recruits on the boat. Figured you'd want to see what recruiters do. At least the soft sell. Didn't mean for you to embarrass everyone with your professional wakeboarding skills."

"It felt like flying."

"Kava often does. One way or another. If you're willing to take risks."

"I am." I uncrossed my legs and let the air conditioning lift the edge of my skirt.

"The company needs people who think like that, to get where we want to go."

"You mean an IPO?"

"Yes, but you didn't hear that from me." He flashed a dimple.

We were streaking down the highway, and an airplane icon blurred by on an exit sign. "Marion—the exit." I pointed back at the sign.

"You can call me Mars."

"*Mars*, you missed the exit." I looked from my

watch to him and back to the highway sign. "Or is there another——"

"Have dinner with me, Olivia."

"Wait. What?" I was still looking over my shoulder for the sign, when I processed that he was asking me out. Was it a date? Part of the recruitment process?

"Dinner. With me. Tonight. You can fly out later. There's a red-eye."

"You changed my flight?"

He put a reassuring hand on my forearm. "It's okay, I can still get you to the airport if you want."

"Yes."

"Yes?"

"I mean no." I looked down, to see if my arm could blush. "No to the airport. Yes to dinner."

"Great, because you were going to miss that first flight anyway." He gave me a beautiful, guilty look. "You did skip your second day of interviews. Thought I could give you some extra time to ask any questions you might have."

"Is this a company dinner, part of my interview weekend?"

"Does it matter?" he tutted.

"I just want to know who to thank."

"You can worry about that later." His voice silken, his smile wicked.

I wanted this attention, but when I got it, I didn't know what to do with it. I looked for a place to put my hands that didn't feel awkward. I tucked them under my legs and pinched my knees together.

He glided the car into a spot on Second Street, and

we walked a short way to a tapas bar called Dama. It was crowded, but cozy; upscale, but not formal. He had reserved a table in the back corner.

"Chef is a friend," Marion said, after we were seated.

I hadn't managed to control anything from my interview schedule to my travel plans and saw no reason to worry about what I ate. A waiter brought two cactus pear margaritas, and Chef came out of the kitchen to greet us. Marion introduced us and Chef greeted me in halted English, excusing the switch to Spanish, which Marion spoke perfectly. Of course he did. I wanted to tell them, with three semesters and a study abroad stint in Costa Rica, that I could understand it too, at least a little, but they were already talking quickly and quietly.

I sipped the margarita, the rim of salt marrying the tart and the sweet, and observed their conversation. Where Marion was tight, his friend jiggled. Occupational hazard, I mused. Chef had superbly chubby cheeks, childlike in their plumpness, and I could see him licking the batter off the beaters. His accent was soft and loose too, a European lisp smearing his syllables together, buttering their chatter. Chef thanked Marion for coming, told him that Kava had been giving him a lot of business. Marion congratulated him on a five-star review by the city paper. Then Chef wanted to know who I was. I pretended to fish something out of my purse.

"The others, they were pretty, but this one, there's something else."

Or maybe Chef said, "She's something else." I
didn't care. I wanted to know who were "the others?"
Other dates? Other business people? Other recruiters?
Who was Chef comparing me to? Had I misunderstood?

Then I thought Marion said, "She might take some
time."

"I hope she works out," Chef said. What works out?
Me as a hire? As a date? "I'd like to see her again. Enjoy
her. Let Arturo," he pointed to the waiter, "know if you
need anything at all." Chef clapped Marion's back and
gave me a polite nod.

Mars picked up his drink, "To your recruitment."

"Apparently." I took a long swig. "Where'd you
learn your Spanish?"

"University. Europe. Life." He shrugged off the
question. "Careful. Those are stronger than they taste."

"I'm okay. How do you know Chef? His accent is
hard to place."

"I think he prefers Catalan to Spanish. He's one of
many business contacts I keep up with. When my firm
was just a start-up, before we had good offices, we used
this restaurant for a lot of meetings. In the beginning,
Chef gave us quite the line of credit and space. Now I
pay back the favor, in a lot of different ways."

"Business is about relationship building." I said it
with authority I didn't have.

Marion glanced towards the kitchen door. "Chef
has places in San Fran and New York, and, for whatever
reason, has sway with the business communities there.
Something in his drinks, I don't know. He's the right
guy to have on your side."

I took another swallow, and before I put my glass down, Arturo brought another round.

"Place has serious service."

"I warned you."

"*The others*—did you warn them?"

Marion looked amused, but his expression gave nothing else away. He shifted the candle on the table between us. "I warn all my business partners."

"Is that what I am?"

"Not yet."

"Why do you warn them?" It came out as a whisper.

He leaned closer, his voice soft, his black eyes somehow darker. "Because they need to know I'm going to get what I want."

I waved my hand over the candle, making it flicker. "And what do you want?"

He traced the top of my hand with his fingertip, then tapped my knuckle into the heat. "Careful. Don't get burned."

I didn't flinch, my eyes locked on his. "You didn't answer my question. What is it you want, Marion?"

"I think you know."

And I did, because I wanted it too. And I didn't care if it burned.

A succession of tapas came to the table, each culinary treasure arranged on a tiny plate. Foie gras shaped into flowers, wild mushrooms hidden under clovers, cuttlefish tentacles hugging caramelized onions. Sometimes the wine glasses changed, so did the color of the wine. There were explanations. Pairings. I lost track. I drank to calm the fire I felt inside. I ate whatever Marion fed me, dabs of sauce from his fork, slick oysters off the shell, stories about European travel, college, and Kava.

"*Bunuelos de viento.* Dessert," he told me.

I pinched the doughy ball between my fingers. "What's inside?"

"A surprise. Eat it whole. Like this." His hand around my wrist, he took the tips of my fingers and the dessert into his mouth. I closed my eyes when I felt the tip of his tongue.

"Okay?" he asked, brushing my hair away from my cheek and tucking an errant curl behind my ear. I blinked against the lightness of his touch, the warmth of his palm as it skimmed my jaw. His expression was mischievous. "Let's get out of here."

He waved for the check, wrote something on the back and helped me out of my chair. It was one blurry motion. Outside, crickets serenaded the street lights, cars parked beneath. We walked past the Porsche, my arm in his. My fingers curled around his bicep, I held on because I needed to. Because I wanted to. At the end of the block, we stopped in front of a square cement building, teal paint peeling off the walls. A glowing sign read Azucar.

I thought he'd hail a cab or call a car service. Instead, he took my hand and led me into the blaring music of a live Cuban salsa band. I knew when we walked through that door, the night would go from professional to personal, not like it already hadn't. I knew, and I didn't care about getting woven into Kava, or tangled in his arms. I followed him through the crowd to the edge of the wooden dance floor, its planks shaking beneath a crush of couples.

I unbuttoned my jacket and wrapped my arms around his neck. His hands were already on my waist, and we pushed into crowd.

Salsa-merengue lives in your hips. Not the tasteless grinding of cheap night clubs, but a perfect melding of two people to a palpable beat. It ties you together, no part of your body left untouched. Marion's leg between my thighs, his hips rocking mine, and my hands under his shirt, pulling him ever closer. The songs flowed through one another, an endless and evolving rhythm that left our hearts racing and our shirts soaked through. I pressed my cheek to his chest and breathed the sweet commingling of his cologne and sweat. He slowed then, letting the music go on without us, and brushed my neck with his lips. When I looked up, he cupped my face in his hands.

"Baby, you've got a flight."

"No." I put my finger to his mouth to shush reality. He nibbled the tip.

I leaned to kiss him, but he brought his lips to my cheek. His breath in my ear, "Not yet. You've got to come because you want to."

"I want to." He meant Kava. I meant the other thing.

Seeds of the Future

My remaining time in college flew. I was busy presenting my senior thesis, taking exams, and trying to graduate. I waited to hear from Kava Tech, and I got another job offer from the New York City Department of Parks and Recreation. It was a position with their Forestry Division. It paid $30,000 a year.

"In New York City?" Sky shook her head. "You'll have eight roommates and live in a closet in Brooklyn. Haven't you heard from Kava?"

"Not yet."

I hadn't heard from Marion either, and I tried not to give my bizarre recruitment weekend too much thought—or at least it only kept me up most nights a week. Usually, when I was falling asleep, I'd think about dancing with him, replaying what he felt like in my arms, how he smelled. The memories hit my nervous system like a shot of heroin.

I ran home between classes to check voicemail so often that I felt like I was training for track again. This time, I found the phone sitting on top of a FedEx envelope. Breathless, I shook the package. It was light, maybe one sheet of paper. That's what college rejections felt like. I sat down on the couch and pulled the cardboard open. Below the Kava company letterhead, I saw the words "Congratulations" and then, "the position of recruiter." I squeezed the offer letter to my chest.

"Can I see it?" Sky asked. I didn't realize she was standing there.

"They want me, Sky," I said. "They want me." She smiled back at me. I handed her the letter.

"Nice salary, $40,000 and they're going to pay for you to move. This is great."

The phone rang and I scurried to my room to answer it. Laurie's sweet twang greeted me. "Hi, Olivia. I called to make sure you received an envelope today."

"Thank you!" I sang. "Thank you, I did."

"Well, congratulations. You did fantastic in your interview weekend, and we're looking forward to having you join the recruiting team. Are you thrilled?" she asked.

Was this supposed to be when I accepted the offer? I wasn't sure. "It's exciting. Thank you again." The pit in my stomach hardened. Was this it? Was it time to commit to a future in software-as-a-service? I felt the nervous nausea that accompanies sudden indecision.

What was wrong with me? This was a great job. I needed to say something and when I didn't, Laurie got right to the point.

"Do you have any other offers you're considering?" she asked.

"With the New York Department of Parks and Recreation." What was I waiting for? I needed a job, and this was the best offer I had. Who the hell cares about trees?

"I understand. It's a big choice. How 'bout this? Why don't you join us for dinner tomorrow night? I'll be there, as well as a couple of other employees and recruits with outstanding offers. It'll be an opportunity to ask any last-minute questions and see what happens at a sell dinner. Maybe it will help you make up your mind."

"That sounds great."

"Meet at 7 p.m. at Le Savoy. Food's delicious. I look forward to seeing you and hopefully calling you my colleague."

When I hung up the phone, I looked around my disgrace of a room for something to wear to the dinner. It was easier than trying to understand why I hadn't just said yes or how by stalling I had gotten a dinner invitation. I pushed the dirty laundry on the floor into piles. Of course, I'd accept the offer, right? When I had cleared the floor, I moved to the suitcases I had taken to Austin. I unfolded the camisole I wore when I had danced with Marion. That night felt like a distant dream. I held the lace to my nose to see if I could smell his cologne, but there was nothing. Just the stale smell of suitcase. I threw the shirt in the dry-clean pile, along with the rest of the suit I'd worn that night. I imagined myself buttoned into the blazer, shaking hands at a business meeting or talking software with recruits. Was that me?

I pulled an even mustier duffle bag out from under my bed. It had been there since I returned from Rodrigues, but I didn't remember emptying it. I tugged the drawstring open. A few pieces of clothing clung to the bottom. I pulled out a crusty t-shirt. Inside it was an equally stiff and foul-smelling sports bra. When I shook the bra, seeds scattered from the mesh cups onto the rug.

In my haste to evacuate, I'd left them in my underwear. The last of the Rodriguan Hurricane Palms, the seeds of the *aureum*. In disbelief, I collected them from the floor. I remembered climbing the palm, the breathtaking view, stuffing them everywhere, and then running to leave. I had fled to safety, watching from afar as the storm stripped the island down to its foundational rock. I went back to complaining about Friday morning classes and grades, while my host family and my teammates sifted through the wreckage of their lives.

Could I be sure they were *aureum* seeds? From my bookshelf, I pulled down one of the notebooks I had saved from Rodrigues. I leafed through it looking for a sketch and a description of the palm. Many of the drawings were signed by Rani, an 11-year-old girl who had followed me everywhere when she wasn't in school or working on her parents' vegetable plot. When I realized she could draw, I offered her a couple dollars a week to draft pictures of the specimens I collected. Her parents came to thank me in person. They brought me cucumbers. I wondered if their farm survived the storm.

The seeds matched the description and Rani's rendering perfectly. Like I had been taught on the island, I pulled down the desk lamp and inspected each for damage. The shirt and the bra were moldy, but the seeds looked healthy. I marveled at their defiance. Little miracles in perfect condition. I took a plain piece of paper, wrote the full species name in pencil, *Dictyosperma album, var. aureum,* and made a protective envelope. I took the envelope and stuffed it into an old Styrofoam cup and secured the lid, leaving the sip flap open for air. The seeds could stay like this for a long time, dry and dark, before needing to germinate.

I looked again at Rani's rendition of the majestic palm. She had added in a setting sun and birds and colored them meticulously. It looked like the art you'd see on a hospital wall where there always hung a gold framed picture of some natural wonder—a sea of flowers, a peaceful brook, or the soft green moss under cool shade trees. The sick and the dying stared at those pictures or asked to be wheeled to the hospital garden, where the leaves sung to the breeze and the delicate splendor of the stargazer lilies assured there was something magnificent, beyond us, that could orchestrate such beauty.

Nature gives us hope.

Now I had kernels of it to give back to Rodrigues, whose people had been so welcoming, generous, and supportive of me—an awkward, gawking foreigner pretending to be on a serious academic mission, but who was really just a girl hiding from life decisions she didn't know how to make. I tucked the cup away in the bottom drawer of my desk and carefully placed the notebook back on the shelf.

The next day I considered calling some of the world's famous botanical gardens. They'd know what to do. Instead, I phoned Rodrigues. To my surprise, I reached my former team lead and Rodriguan national, Henri. Most of the conservation efforts on the tiny island went through him.

When I asked if I should bring the seeds to a garden or a zoo, he yelled over the shaky connection. "No, Olivia! You must not do this."

"Why not?"

"Because. These people. They will keep the seeds for themselves, and if they germinate, they will use them to make money, all in the name of conservation. But the trees will never make it back to Rodrigues."

"Oh my." I had never given much thought to the competition between countries and conservation organizations.

"Can I mail them to you? Maybe like a certified service?"

"No. Even worse, they will be eaten by rats. Or

they will be lost. Nothing works here. Nothing. No mail services or any services. We've only just begun to rebuild. We could never track the package." He paused, and over the static, he hollered, "You bring them."

"But how? I'd have to declare them at customs."

"No. They would never allow that. Hide them ... *voilà*, in a girl product."

I laughed. "You mean a tampon box?"

"Oui. In your purse."

I thought about this. The Rodriguan culture was proper and respectful. Customs would never mess with a feminine hygiene product, and it wasn't like somebody would be looking for a handful of palm seeds. It could work.

"How long do I have? Before they need to germinate?"

"I cannot be sure. One year? Maybe a little longer. Keep them dry." The static on the call picked up, and Henri sounded even further away. "Bring them back," was the last thing he said before the connection cut.

The Sell Dinner

On the way to Kava's sell dinner, I thought about how I was going to buy a round-trip plane ticket to Rodrigues to hand deliver palm seeds, while paying off loans. Henri thought I had about a year to do it. Anything longer, and the seeds might never grow. I needed money, and as much of it as fast as possible. A slow-moving job that paid nothing in the most expensive city in the country wasn't going to get me there. I had to take the job with Kava Tech and save everything I could.

The narrow entryway to Le Savoy was a hectic, crowded mess of parties trying to get their names on a waitlist. I pressed my way through the tight space into the dark varnish of what looked like a nineteenth-century living room. I squinted in the dim lighting, looking for Kava Tech's reserved space.

"We're downstairs. The private dining room." Marion's voice washed over me.

"You're here."

"I am. I heard you needed convincing."

The night we danced came back in flashes, and I fought the urge to touch him, to ask him why he hadn't called, to ask him if he'd thought about me. This wasn't the time or place. "Marion, something's changed, and I need to talk to Laurie."

"Talk to her." He motioned towards the steps. "You should meet the other candidates too. I'll introduce you." I knew this tone. Cordial business Marion. Polite, accommodating, and professionally distant, like on the boat with the other recruits. Still, I knew what he felt like in my arms.

He walked me down a spiral staircase into a room walled in by wine bottles. The narrow, rectangular space held an equally narrow, rectangular table. With ten people, the room felt filled to capacity, with barely enough space for the waiter to swish by offering glasses of red. He poured them from the bottles on the walls.

"They only rent this room to a select few," Marion said.

"I can see why."

"Even we don't ask to open the bottles at the top of the walls. But for you, maybe ...". He flashed a naughty grin and then left me with a circle of recruits. I sipped my expensive wall wine and watched him from across the room. He whispered in Laurie's ear as she walked around the table placing name placards.

When we were asked to the table, I sat between Marion and a "star tech recruit," the Star Tech Recruit told me. Marion talked intently with a girl on his other side. She batted her stumpy eyelashes at everything he said and bantered endlessly. As the salads were served, Star Tech Recruit started to pick his nose. He wasn't discreetly trying to remove a cliffhanger. He was full on digging in and rolling the boogers between his fingers before flicking them. He did it absentmindedly, chatting with a Kava rep next to him. I inched my chair closer to Marion.

Because of the shape of the table, my only entertainment was an enthusiastic small-talker across the linen. I listened. I agreed. I didn't hear a word he said. I was dodging boogers and watching Marion thrill Stumpy Eyelashes. The night wore on, like this, with us paired off into fixed conversations over a fixed menu. Breaks came when the waiter topped the wine, which he did often. I had no idea how much I'd had because my glass was always full. By the time dessert came, the airless room felt soupy.

The wined walls were closing in and I had long lost eye contact with the guy across the table, though on he talked. I swirled my fork through the meringue on my pie. Under the table, Marion nudged my leg. Then he rested his hand on my knee. I straightened at the unsolicited advance, the first attention he'd paid me all evening, except for when I asked for the salt. Without looking at him I wrapped my ankles around the legs of my chair. He skimmed his fingers along my knee, and then he made slow circles, brushing upwards a millimeter at a time.

My inner and outer selves became disparate beings. My body shell was present, it smiled and even spoke, but everything within processed only, and with laser focus, what was happening to the two inches of my leg he touched. My inner monologue purred like a cat and marveled that this was happening. She wondered where it could possibly go in this tight little space.

But her moment was stolen, literally shattered by a hail of glass and splattered wine. Like a Malbec Molotov cocktail had exploded on the table. And Star Tech Recruit had thrown it. Gesticulating over a story or perhaps shaking a big one off his finger, he elbowed a large crystal carafe across the table, splintering it and several recently topped-off glasses.

Chairs toppled when people jumped away from the sparkling red mess. Star Tech Recruit didn't have the sense to be embarrassed. He wiggled his nose, which was at least free of his finger, and shrugged an "I'm sorry." Everyone talked and moved at once. Mars helped me and Stumpy Eyelashes away from the table. We scuttled to the bathroom to blot the chickenpox stains from our clothes.

The spilled wine and scattered glass shards brought dinner to an early close. Between the thick burgundy wines, the heavy food, the tortured conversation, and whatever was going to happen under the table, I was relieved to be out of the basement and out on Main Street again.

"Olivia, what a crazy night. I meant to spend more time with you," Laurie apologized.

"It's okay, I meant to talk to you as well, you see――"

"Mars told me about your other offer." He did? But I hadn't told him anything about it. "We can up your starting salary by 5k. But, that's if you accept tonight."

She sounded drunk, her southern drawl the heaviest I'd heard it.

I didn't hesitate. I had come with a purpose they had made that much easier. "Yes."

"Yes?" She hugged me. A big, sloppy embrace. Then holding on to my shoulders, "You're gonna be a fabulous recruiter."

Marion took my hand and held it between his. "Congratulations, Olivia. I can't wait to have you."

Laurie didn't notice what he said or the way he said it.

Roller Derby

College ended almost the same way it began—a frenzy of teary-eyed parents moving boxes and mini fridges and saying goodbyes to children eager to make their way in the world. I was sad it was all over, but it was hard to be nostalgic with my parents hovering. My father busied himself lifting heavy objects and strapping them to the roof of the car. He knew how to stay out of the way, asking only what he should move next. I thanked him for his reserve by leaving a six-pack of Corona in the fridge. He leaned against my kitchen counter, took a sip, and winked at me, and I knew we were okay.

But not my mother.

She lifted her head from the windowsill she was scrubbing. "Sky, you poor thing, I'm so sorry you had to live like this. Olivia, why didn't you clean?" She punctuated her sentences with heavy sighs.

I pretended she was talking to the scrub brush, but Sky was polite. "Mrs. Gesso, it's fine. You really don't have to do that."

"Oh, it's nothing, honey. No reason not to leave it spotless for the next people. You should always be thinking of what's coming next, right?"

"Of course, Mrs. Gesso," Sky agreed.

"But I don't have to tell you that, you smart girl, getting that scholarship to Rome. Your parents must be so proud." I winced like she was scraping my skin with the metallic bristles.

"I'm going to help Dad with my room," I interjected before she could draw me into the conversation and start talking about medical school.

My dad let me slam things in boxes for at least 15 minutes before he spoke. "She just wants what's best for you, Liv. We both do. You're all we have."

"I know, Dad. I know." He patted my shoulder and hoisted a box out of the room.

By late afternoon, we were all too tired to worry about the future. Sky and I made one last sweep of our digs. She neatly folded her floral sheets and I rolled up my purple sleeping bag, and just like that, our dorm looked as though we had never been there.

"It feels empty. You okay on your own?" I asked her.

"My parents fly in tonight. I'll crash their hotel."

"Can you believe—"

"Call me," Sky said and wrapped her arms around me before I could say anything to make us cry.

"Of course."

And that is how we ended four years of life-altering academic and social education. When there's too much to say, sometimes it's easier to be quiet.

With my diploma in hand, I headed to Texas. I landed in Austin late at night and woke up the next morning to an insurmountable to-do list that included things like finding an apartment and leasing a car. Before I could worry about navigating the for-profit world of beepers, cell phones and software code, I had to set up a new life in a different state. To help its new hires, Kava Tech had made "arrangements" with apartment complexes and car dealers who would accept my employment offer letter as insurance that I would be able to make the monthly payments on whatever I bought or rented.

The Kava-sponsored apartment complex was unlike anything I'd ever seen up north, and I understood immediately what Sky had been talking about when she said I'd be better off living in Austin. In New York City, you rented a room on a street clogged with cranky people and trash bags. A city building had "character" because it was built in 1903, which really meant that you walked up six flights of steps to get to your one-room apartment, your steam pipe heat clanked on at 4 a.m., and your shower dripped. If you liked the urban look of exposed brick, you just looked out your window because that was the only view you could afford.

To the contrary, here, everything was new and expansive. The pristine apartments boasted rustic brickwork, vaulted ceilings, and porches that opened to breathtaking views of Austin's rolling hills, flush with oak and cedar trees. Each bathroom had deep tubs and closets. Kitchens had dishwashers and laundry. There were even ceiling fans and a stone fireplace with a wooden mantle. And it was a paradise I could afford and still save money every month. I signed the lease immediately and wrote a check for two months' rent, which was most of the money I had.

The digs were a deal, but I soon discovered that buying one thing precipitated an unavoidable chain reaction of consumerism. Got an apartment? You'll need a bed. Got a bed? You'll need sheets. And I still had to find a car, which meant insurance, and then gas money, and on and on it went. I found out fast that setting up as a professionally employed adult was expensive. Saving money was going to be harder than I thought, and I still needed everything from pillows to toilet paper.

The next day, after searching for things like shower curtains and soap, I came home to a package from my parents. While they still weren't over me quitting the med school path, they were pleased I was at least earning a decent salary at what I assured them was an up-and-coming company. Still, explaining software to middle-aged parents who owned a rotary phone and didn't trust ATMs was exhausting. Their note read, "Good luck and since you are trying new things ..." and from the box, I pulled a pair of roller blades. My mom and dad were trying, and I needed to try too. I promised myself I'd help them get an AOL account they could use at the local library.

I was grateful for something to do that didn't involve my wallet. I put my hair in pigtails like the fierce roller derby girls and strapped on the skates. But in the parking lot, instead of tough, I felt more like a baby giraffe trying to find its legs for the first time. I wobbled. I tripped. I spilled. But I discovered that if I put one foot over the other, I could pick up speed. I circled the periphery of the blacktop, once, then twice, faster and faster until the gates to the apartment complex swung open. A silver BMW rolled in front of me, and though the car was barely moving, I had no idea how to stop. I plowed into the side of the hood and rolled over the front. I landed in a heap. A car door opened. I heard music. When I focused my eyes, a guy hovered over me.

"Oh my gosh. Are you okay?" His head blocked the sun, but rays of light extended from beyond his hair like a wild golden halo. The breath came back to my lungs in gasps. "Did you hit your head?" He reached out but stopped short of touching me.

"It's okay. I'm okay." I sat up slowly. I was too stunned and too embarrassed to cry.

"Do you want to get up?" When I didn't answer, he sat down on the curb, the engine of his car still humming, the stereo blasting through the open door.

"Just want to sit." I righted myself and inched towards the curb. "Really. I'm okay. You should park." My elbows were bleeding. He watched as I checked my knees, which were fine because I landed on my back. I rubbed my neck and head, which had a bump, but everything seemed in place. The guy stared wide-eyed.

"Never hit anybody before?" I joked for my sake and his.

"You're my first. But I'd say that you hit me."

"Fair enough."

"A Band-Aid? You want a Band-Aid?"

I stretched out my arms to check them again. "How about a box of Band-Aids?"

"I just moved in, but I have a first aid kit. I'm Christopher." He stuck out a hand and I gingerly took it. It was long, pale, and thin like the rest of him. Wire rimmed glasses hugged his giant blue eyes, and together they took up most of his narrow face. His sandy hair stuck out in every direction.

"I'm Olivia. Is that a new toy then?" I glanced at the shiny, latest-model Roadster whining about its open door.

"Are those?" He pointed to my feet.

"How could you tell?" I laughed and winced.

"Oh, come on. I even have Tylenol. You don't happen to be working for Kava Tech? A lot of their employees live here." He helped me to my feet.

"I start next week."

Christopher smiled. "Me too."

"Did they hook you up with that?" I wondered if I had made the wrong deal on my Nissan Sentra.

"Signing bonus."

"Yeah, me too." I pointed to my roller blades, and he laughed. "So ... you're a developer, then?" Only a coder would get a signing bonus big enough to buy a car like that.

"Yeah, from Harvey Mudd. And you ..." he looked

me over, "are a recruiter?"

I shook my head and then remembered the lump. "How'd you guess?"

"Same way you guessed I was a developer." He gave me a wry smile and insisted I come to his place for help.

Christopher's apartment was laid out just like mine, however spaces normally outfitted with furniture were full of electronic and music equipment. And books. And magazines. Piled everywhere. He turned on his stereo, which was hooked up to two speakers each as big as a bay window.

"I just got this. You have to hear it." He plugged in the sound system and fiddled with the amp that doubled as a coffee table. "Country music okay? It's the only thing you can listen to in every state. I just drove cross-country." Bonnie Raitt sounded like she was in the room, and he picked up a guitar and started playing along. He was pretty good, and I could see him driving and singing in his tiny sports car.

"You sing better than you drive."

He stopped strumming like something bit him. He dropped the guitar and disappeared into the bathroom. He returned a minute later, tripped over a cord and dropped everything in his hands. We picked up the Band-Aids that scattered everywhere and I sat at his table to patch my arms back together. Christopher's story sounded like Willy Chang's—a highly recruited comp sci major who decided between starting his own company, the big tech giants, and start-ups like Kava.

"Why'd you pick Kava?" I asked.

"Why did you?"

"I want to make a lot of money, fast," I admitted.

"Honest. You're honest."

"Sort of. Your turn."

He handed me another Band-Aid. "I came because it felt like everything I didn't get in college. Friends. Girls who talk to me. Parties. Community."

"You came to party?" I asked.

"I came to belong. I can make the same money anywhere. But at Kava, everyone is like me, and likes me. I'm not just the guy whose problem-set answers you want to borrow."

"You were that guy at Harvey Mudd?" I whistled. "Kava's lucky."

"So, what are you going to do now?" he asked.

"Well, I don't think anything's broken." I wiggled my fingers.

"No, like with the rest of the day."

"Oh. I don't know. Buy a first aid kit? And a mattress. I've been sleeping on the floor."

"Want company?" He looked hopeful when he asked.

"Can you drive? I mean, you did mow down one person already today." I held up my scraped hands.

"You hit my car. My new car. I should sue." He pushed his glasses up his nose to his bright blue eyes and crossed his arms playfully.

"It'd be your word against mine." I rubbed my head, pouted my lip.

"Typical recruiter. Pretty face gets you everything."

"So they say. Your car then?"

He grabbed his keys. "Where to?"

"I have no clue where anything is. Bed?"

"That was fast." He pointed to the room behind him. "See? Kava was the right choice."

I laughed. "That came out way wrong. Mattress store. Can we put the top down?"

"You got it."

That night, thanks to same-day delivery services, I lay on my bare, extra plush Serta. Like every night, I thought about what it would be like to work at Kava Tech, and when I might see Marion again, and if all that flirtation would amount to anything. And then I wondered if the seeds would last a year. They were safely stored now, in an O.B. tampon box. It was the centerpiece—the only piece—on my fireplace mantle.

More Culture

My first day of work felt like the first day of seventh grade. I worried. Would I know anyone? Who would I sit with at lunch? Did I look alright? A country's natural heritage and my parents' goodwill depended on me being good at this job. I gently rattled the feminine hygiene maraca on my mantle. The seeds sounded fine. Then I put on my nice jeans with the stitched pockets. The floor to ceiling bathroom mirror that I never had in college told me they weren't that nice.

"The worse your clothes, the smarter people will think you are," is what Sky had told me about dressing for tech. Instead of monied, I looked underwhelming at best, ill-prepared at worst. I thought about my nail biter of a lab partner, the boys at the info session, and the nose picker at dinner. What would they wear today? Star Trek t-shirts. What were they worrying about on their first day? It sure as hell wasn't the pockets on their jeans. I was too nervous to eat.

The confidence I summoned blasting my stereo fizzled when I pulled into campus. The parking lot was a ZZ Top video. Leggy blondes in short flowery sundresses climbed out of a cherry red Audi. On the sidewalk, scruffy guys stared and parted for them to pass. A black Beamer rolled in, top down, stereo up. The driver bummed the door shut, balancing on high wedge sandals, a clutch under her arm. Didn't spill an ounce of her Starbucks. The cars said executives. The clothes said socialites.

"So much for techies in sweatpants," I said to my Sentra. I slung my backpack over my shoulder, walked across the parking lot, and cleaved through the doors of my future. The frosted glass was heavy. You had to really want to move through it. On the inside, the parking lot socialites stood out like hibiscus flowers in a landscape of boys wearing burnt sienna and khaki. I filtered into the mass of people all my age, all talking loudly, and I looked for someone I might know. A few minutes in, I found William and Viola. They felt like long-lost friends.

"You came!" We bellowed over the din. There were hugs. And then stories about the end of school, where we were living, and how we moved. From the lobby, we trickled into a room inadequately stocked with folding tables and metal chairs. Some took the creaky seats, others sat around the perimeter on the thin wall-to-wall, navy carpeting. Like the engineers' wardrobe, the cheap furniture made a statement about company priorities. Appearances didn't matter if you were brilliant, if you produced—I watched a hibiscus adjust her skirt as she sat on the edge of the metal–if you were a guy.

Up front, I recognized Levi. He stood next to a tiny woman in a smart blazer and jeans. She used his shoulder to climb on top of a folding table. She megaphoned her hands and yelled in a voice much too loud and too deep for her petite frame.

"Can you hear me?" She waved her arms. "Welcome to Kava Tech!" She raised her fists like a boxing champ. We clapped and cheered. "As you know, we're not fans of formality, so let's get going. I'm Mora Morris, but around here people just call me More. I'm the Director of Corporate Culture and Human Resources, and I have the best job in the world. I recruit amazing people like you and I make sure they have the most awesome time ever working for Kava." Someone had scribbled "More! CultHR!" on the whiteboard next to her. She pointed to it. "That's right people, when you need more culture you come see me." She put both thumbs on her chest. "Any kind of problem at all, really, don't be afraid to come to HR."

"And this," she pointed at the group standing below her, "this is your leadership. Levi, needs no intro. Marty Krauss, CTO. Brian Anderson, CFO, Robert White, COO." They waved when she called their names. More didn't mention the other woman that stood up front, but off to the side. She was the only one dressed like an adult. Pencil skirt, heels, and a serious bob cut to her angular chin. Dark red manicured nails. She toyed with her phone, didn't look for an introduction, didn't look up when the others were introduced.

"Vi, who's that?" I pointed to the suit.

"Melissa Burge."

"Who?"

"Known as 'The Closer.' Leads technical sales. Closed the last three deals Kava made."

"Oh." Melissa looked like the kind of animal best watched from a distance. Any nearer and you might lose a body part, or worse.

More boomed. "Now you know who we are. Let me tell you who you are. The best. The brightest. You are the next generation of Kava Techies." We clapped and she cupped her ear. "I can't hear you!" We cheered louder. "There it is. You feel that energy? That's Kava energy." She pumped her fist. I made my eyes big and looked at Viola, who laughed. This was my boss. "I brought you all here because you're fabulous people, and you're going to make this company even greater. Get to be friends, learn from one another. You are now Kava Tech family." More opened her arms wide towards us and smiled at Levi. He gave her a hokey thumbs-up, and then he took the floor.

Former Wall Street powerhouse. Island hippie. Idiosyncratic coder. I'd met the latter, and we didn't quite hit it off. "Thanks More," our CEO said smoothly. Levi was dressed for the beach, but he owned the room. "You're all here because you're brilliant ... and ... we thought you were pretty cool. I hope you feel welcome and free to explore your potential. Exploit the opportunities Kava gives you. Nothing here is predetermined. It's up to you to write your own destiny, in code, of course." People chuckled.

"Nobody thought we'd revolutionize the industry. 'A bunch of kids,' they called my company. I won't say what they called me. But it didn't matter, because we were the smartest people in the room. We persevered, through a lot. And we partied ... maybe just a little." He pinched his fingers together. "And then we landed a deal, and then another, and another." He looked at Melissa, and she gave him a tight smile. "You know how the story goes, and you're here to write Kava's next chapter. You're the company's funnel for the next generation of products. How far will you go? What will you make?"

More, still standing on the table, yelled again. "Get! Excited! People! What's the next great Kava Tech product? Do you have an idea? Are you going to create it? Will you lead it? What will it be?"

I thought these were just loud rhetorical questions. But then, from the back of the room, a familiar voice answered.

"Let's revolutionize beer distribution." I turned, along with 250 other people, to see that it was Christopher who had answered.

Without pause, Levi hollered back. "Love it. Get a team together and do it." Nobody moved, they just turned their heads from Christopher to Levi and back again.

Levi challenged the silence, "And if you have a demo by the end of September, I'll buy you—and all the members of your team—any car you want."

Christopher stood there blinking. People clambered to him.

More glanced at Levi, then taunted us. "Now you get it? I think you do. Risk and reward. We're serious, people." We looked at one another for assurance that what just happened, happened. We shifted, shuffled, and murmured over a chorus of squeaking metal chairs.

More was unphased, like this was just any other day at Kava Tech, and she moved the presentation along. "Not only will you create new products for Kava, but you will become experts in Kava's business space. In your welcome folders, there's a required reading list. It's 60 books long. The library is on the third floor and book club meets twice a week. Attendance is mandatory. Start with *The New New Thing* by Lewis. After that, read *Built to Last* by Collins and Porras and so on." Papers shuffled. People chattered.

"Quiet down! You too, beer people in the back." The group around Christopher was now substantial and they had not stopped talking.

"There's a fully stocked pantry on every floor, so you never need to go out for food unless you want to. We'll cater breakfast, lunch, and dinner. Focus on your work, and we will take care of everything else. Every Friday night we have a happy hour. If you're in town, attendance is also mandatory. That's right people, we have mandatory parties and they rock. Work hard, play hard. It's what we do.

That's it for now. Open your welcome folders. Fill out the HR paperwork, find your groups, and get started. Recruiters, you report to the War Room." I half expected her to do a cheerleading flip into Levi's arms. Instead, More pounced down and high-fived the C-suite standing in front of the table.

The show was over, and the room was an instant frenzy. Welcome speeches were short at this company. The message was, "Get to work." I wished William and Viola good luck and waved at Christopher. Then I went to meet my colleagues in the War Room, whatever that was.

Mr. America

The War Room was a Miss America pageant holding tank. I recognized the girls from the parking lot. Everyone else looked just like them—or better. In a pitch of tropical wildflowers, I felt like a mushroom. More parted the meadow. She strode to the front of the room and sat on a table. Perhaps chairs in this company were considered too formal? But she didn't need formality or a stage or a microphone. More was the feature presentation, a wisp of a woman with a gigantic personality rivaled only by her lung capacity. She clapped her hands, wrists stiff, to get everyone's attention. We fell in line immediately.

"What a room full of people." She took us in, her doughy eyes wide with parental pride. "Now this is a dream team. And have we got some big goals to hit this year. I'm gonna lay it out for you, short and sweet, my people. The reason we hired so many of you," she pointed at us Uncle Sam-style, "is because, this year, we have to triple the amount of them." She pointed towards the room from which we had come. "You heard me; we're going to triple the size of this company in 365 days."

People whispered and shuffled in their seats, feeding a current of excitement and anxiety.

"Levi wants to make a statement this year. He wants big growth, and therefore, we need human capacity. But we don't want just anybody," More cautioned. "We want the top people from the top places. You will find them, and you will sign them. But your job won't stop there. Oh no. You will be college recruiters hitting hiring numbers, but you will also be the beating heart of this company, the lifeforce flowing through Kava. Recruiters are our social glue, the bond between Kava Techies. You will be everything to everyone, all the time—the guiding light that brings Kava Techies here and the energy that sustains them. You will recruit and you will retain." More clasped her hands together in front of her chest and lowered her gaze.

We applauded on cue until she interrupted to ask that we think of a slogan for the daunting task of tripling the company's size in a year. "Come on, call out some ideas," More urged. "Recruiters aren't shy." A couple of people blurted catchphrases until More pointed at a girl with her hand raised. "What's your name and where are you from?"

"Amara Young. Julliard."

"What do you say Amara?" More asked.

"How 'bout ... size matters?" The room erupted into laughter.

"Cheeky. Perfect," More clapped. "Size matters. Our new mantra for tripling Kava."

I leaned against the wall and watched Amara. In a room full of pretty, she was astounding. Artsy. Stylish. Short shorts, a lace cardigan, and fire engine red lipstick made sense on her. She made me think of Marion, that same kind of beauty that draws you in and keeps you staring.

While I gawked at Amara, More had moved on from the loaded slogan. "... the risk of growing the company this fast is real, but Levi believes if we get the right people, the best people, that we can be crazy profitable." When she started talking money, More got my undivided attention. "Levi promises serious bonuses for recruiters that hit their numbers and that will be on top of any other windfalls for hitting the triple. Work hard. Play hard. Earn big. Because size matters.

Oh, and another thing. What did you all think about Levi offering cars to the beer people if they make that product? Any car they wanted. I thought that was pretty cool. But you know what? We're gonna work hard too. I think, the team that brings in the most recruits, weighed of course to university size, should get an all-expenses paid trip ... to somewhere ..." More looked around. "Where do you want to go?"

"Paris," somebody called out before I could open my mouth.

"Great. How's that for some friendly in-house competition? The team that hires the most wins a trip to Paris. Go now. Find your partners and get on task."

The room disbanded into chatter and chaos. Luxury cars, trips to Europe, bonuses. I was so going to make it all happen. I flipped through another welcome folder of instructions and set off to find cube number M043, my new office space.

I walked through a maze of whiteboards and cushioned desk partitions dotted by thousands of rainbow-colored pushpins. Private offices along the perimeter were appointed with folding tables, rollaway chairs, and computers connected by tangles of cables.

When I got to M043, I dropped my backpack down on the particleboard under the gold-plated number. The strap bumped a Styrofoam cup, which tipped and oozed brown goop onto the desk like a murder scene from a 1950s horror movie. A guy barreled over from behind me. "Shit. Get a paper towel. That's dip." He hurried to sop up the nicotine-laced spit that covered the desk and threatened the carpet.

I clutched my backpack. "You were dipping ... here?" I checked to make sure I had the right cube number.

"I'm trying to quit smoking. Not so easy. I didn't want to waste time and go outside. We have so much to do." He looked for a trashcan, a wad of disgusting paper towels in his hand. He paced to the left and then to the right without committing to go anywhere.

"It's under the desk. What do you mean, 'we'?" I asked.

"Well, aren't you Olivia? You look like your picture." He wiped his palms on his jeans.

"I am. Olivia. Gesso." I extended a hand but,

remembering the paper towels, retracted it into a wave before he could shake it.

"I'm Jeremy Kolin. We're a team."

"We are?" I asked.

"Sure. It says so right here." He shuffled papers, scattering them all over the desk.

"It's okay. I believe you."

"You can call me Skoals. Everyone does." He was still fidgeting with the papers, losing some to the floor.

"Skoals, like the dip?" This is my partner? He didn't fit the bill of tall leggy blonde or bombshell brunet. Jeremy was offensive lineman large, and in jeans, hiking boots, and a flannel shirt, he looked ready to wrestle a bear in the wild. I stepped back. "You might want to move those." Dip-spit fused the papers to the desk.

"Oh, right." Jeremy picked up the pile and scratched the stuck paper with a fingernail.

"Sorry, I didn't realize the cup was full of——"

"Fine. Fine. Fine. All fine. Here, sit down. We have so much work to do." He rolled another chair next to his. I didn't move. He sat down. He stood up. "Did you see? We have the best schools. You and me. We have MIT and Harvard. Boston. You're going to Boston."

"I am?" I took a paper from him.

"We're going to be a great team." Jeremy looked left and then right, like a nervous antelope sniffing for a lion in high grass.

"That's great. That's a great assignment for us."

Jeremy stepped towards me. "We should get to know one another. That's what the schedule says we should do. Let's go somewhere and talk." A step back. "Should we sit here? Is here okay, to, uhm, talk?" A step forward.

"How about we go out on the patio?"

A hunter's bullet dropped the lion and the antelope sagged with relief. "I knew I was going to like you. We're going to be the best team here."

A few solid drags on a quality cigarette, and Jeremy was a different person. Calm, almost, and very motivated, "stoked" to borrow his own word, "to hit the triple."

"You already read our assignment manual?" I asked in amazement.

"I asked for an advanced copy," Jeremy said, taking a long drag.

"So, how does it work?"

"We're like a tag team. You'll recruit in Boston and I'll man the ship here. Our schools are so important, they gave us a floater."

"A floater?"

"Extra help. She'll support other teams too. She'll have her own numbers to hit, but we'll all work together."

"Who is she?"

"Avery Stone. She's out of Duke. Another pedigree, like you."

"Isn't everyone here a pedigree?"

"The developers and tech people, for sure. But recruiters, not necessarily. We'll hit the big state schools, the business schools, and the money schools, like Middlebury and Southern Methodist, where the rich daddies send their sweethearts. It takes a certain type to recruit a certain type, if you know what I mean." That explained the parking lot, I thought. "You'll be good for the nerds out of MIT, for sure."

"I will?" I looked down at my jeans.

"You have that salt-of-the-earth thing going on, but it's cute. And you're an Ivy Leaguer. They'll respect that. Won't eat you up."

"Thanks?"

"Don't mention it."

"Where'd you go to school?"

"University of Texas. Hook 'em horns. I'm a local. I know everything about Austin. You wine and dine 'em up north and I'll seal the deal in Texas."

"Very collaborative." I smiled at Jeremy.

"It will be." He stubbed out his smoke.

"How did you end up in recruiting? You don't exactly fit the description of—"

"No shit. Totally. I was creeping around a UT career fair dressed in a t-shirt and shorts. Everyone else in suits."

"I hate suits," I offered.

"Yeah, so I saw Laurie in a tight pair of jeans at the Kava Tech booth and thought, first, that she was hot and, second, I should probably go talk to her because she also wasn't wearing a suit. We got to chatting, and that was that. I know how to have a good time. This is totally the job for me. Plus, we hit those numbers, and well, it'll be good."

"I want to make those numbers too. We have the most important thing in common." I slid the smoking ashtray further away.

Later, I introduced myself to our floater, Avery Stone. The other recruiters I met were warm, ebullient personalities. They could coax a rock into a conversation. Avery was the rock. Cold, smooth, and still. A handshake as firm as her expression. She was the only recruiter I wanted to look away from. Actually, I wanted to run.

My hand still in her grip, she glanced distastefully at my clothes. Her stare lingered on my dirty backpack long enough that I too looked down. "Where'd you go to school?" she asked.

"Dartmouth." I forced myself to make eye contact.

"Oh good. At least you aren't a state school bimbo communications major or hot mess wealthy wannabe. Your team just might get something done." She brushed her bangs away from her forehead, curling her fingers like she had a roll of cash in her palm. "I went to Duke."

"Uhm, yeah. I heard."

Avery leaned in, her voice barely louder than a purr. "Look, between us, I was meant for marketing, but Levi begged me to help out with recruiting, with the expansion and all. They needed someone smart enough to sign the real talent from the real schools. So here I am. It had better be worth it." She looked beyond me, maybe to where the marketing people sat. I wasn't sure.

"It'll be fine," I said, more for my benefit than hers.

"We'll see. Hit your numbers, Dartmouth. And this will work out." She disappeared into the cubicle maze.

"I intend to," I said to her back. Then I ran to Jeremy and cornered him against his spittoon for a debrief.

"Yeah, I met her too. We're going to have to work around that. Doesn't matter. We'll be unstoppable." He glanced at his watch. "Damn! We need to get our goods. Come on, you want the newest stuff?" he called over his shoulder, already jogging.

"I totally forgot." I ran behind my own personal lineman to a dark room in the back of the building. A line formed down the hall. It led to a pale, acne-ridden and possibly malnourished man who checked our identification and handed out tech equipment.

I tapped Jeremy. "Does he live in that closet full of electronics?"

He giggled. "Vitamin D deficiency? I heard it's a real problem with these tech types."

"Shut up. It's not."

"They never see the sun. Scurvy? Somebody get him an orange."

"That's so mean. We're terrible. Stop it." I laughed.

By the end of the day, thanks to the man who lived in the server room, I was ready for 24-7 connectivity. I had a beeper, which I clipped to the waist of my pants like every important person did; a cell phone sized like a six-inch hoagie with an antenna; and my first laptop, which was like carrying around a microwave in a padded bag. And Kava Tech paid for it all.

Close to midnight, I sprawled on my bed surrounded by a battlefield of black electronic devices, ethernet cords, and beeping battery packs, all charging my self-importance.

Risk

The first couple of 12-hour days were my shortest. Regular hours were 8 a.m. to midnight. It wasn't mandatory, but it was expected. Some worked longer. Since Kava Tech provided everything I could ever need during this stretch of time, I never wanted to leave the office. Even during breaks when I played ping-pong with Willy or sat with Viola in one of the strategically placed massage chairs, I talked about Kava Tech or something work related. Besides the provision of break-room entertainment, the kitchens were fully stocked with everything imaginable thing from candy bars to lunchmeat.

While I'm sure our productivity waxed and waned throughout the day, it never ceased. We were young, energetic, and unattached. Everyone was happy for this office nirvana. Best of all, I didn't spend a dime on food, and hardly anything on apartment utilities.

A week or so later, I sat with Jeremy, both of us

nursing giant, steaming cups of coffee. Our laptops sat unopened on the desk.

"What time did you go home?" I asked.

"One." he said. "You?"

"Just after. Does Jolt Cola make eye drops?" I asked.

"Start-up idea," he replied.

The office was quiet, but More used a megaphone anyway. She walked through the cubicles shouting. "All employees report to the parking lot. Leave your computers now."

"There had better be a fire."

"No way, they want us to leave the laptops," Jeremy smirked.

Prompted by the relentless megaphone, some 200 people made their way outside. In the bright Texan sun, we squinted like bats forced from a cave, squirming on the broiling blacktop.

"Today we'll learn about risk. We're going skydiving. Sign the waiver. Buses are waiting," More said.

"Olivia?" Jeremy asked.

"Yeah?"

"This is fucking crazy." Jeremy looked off into the distance, shaking his head.

I handed him a copy of the waiver making its way through the crowd. "Come on, let's go learn about risk."

We were among the many who boarded the buses for a first-hand tutorial in risk-taking, a main tenet in Levi's business philosophy, and something I guessed the best employees embraced. I saw More writing down the names of who went. I hoped it was for bonus points or something, and not a way to cross reference for anyone who didn't come back.

We drove for almost an hour, to what felt like the middle of Texas. Off the main highway, a dirt road led us to a dingy, metal hanger. A few rusty planes sat on a faded cement air strip that cut into the middle of an endless dry, grassy field. Cows dotted the barren landscape, grazing in the blazing sun.

"Who needs caffeine when you can jump out of a plane built during the Cold War?" I said to Jeremy. He put his forehead in his hand.

We were sent inside the hanger for basic training. The temperature was easily 95 degrees. I sweated through my clothes in minutes. Towards the end of the hour-long session, the instructor handed us another release to sign, which freed him from any liability if we "pancaked." Then he gave each of us a bright yellow strip of paper with the five most important rules for first-time jumpers. In bold type, it reminded us to, "Eat a healthy breakfast!", "Breathe!", "Open your eyes!", "Take photos!", and "Have fun!".

With that, we were assigned tandems—the person attached to your back who deploys the chute and prevents inexperienced jumpers from freaking out and dying. My tandem, the man in charge of my life, smelled like old whiskey, cigarettes, and body odor. He grinned at me without teeth, or at least without the front ones, and stroked a long, nicotine-stained goatee. Once on the small plane, I nestled into his lap so that he could tether his front tightly to my rear. I stayed as still as possible.

"Yah nervous?" He yelled into my ear as we ascended.

I nodded.

"Don't worry, we got an emergency chute." He patted something on his back. "And yah know what they say?"

I didn't answer.

"If in doubt, whip it out." He cackled himself into a convulsive, emphysematous coughing fit against the back of my head.

"Please don't whip it out," I repeated into the engine drone.

My heart pounded through my chest and my throat had gone dry at take-off. On Tandem Man's command, we crawled doggie-style towards the front of the plane. He yelled over the engine roar, "Get ready to have yar first air-gasm!" I was too terrified to even roll my eyes.

Then he told me to move, "Foh-wad!" And my legs went weak. But it didn't matter. They were dangling out the plane door. Cold wind lashed against them.

I felt Tandem Man yell but didn't hear him. Then, without warning, we were falling. Air roared across my face, but I could not breathe. Sky then ground, then clouds then grass streaked past. My senses were too scrambled to know if I would die. The confusion, the terror, it exploded. The detonation in my ears yanked my heart from my chest. Then, silence. A gentle breeze. A view for angels. The chute had opened. We floated down, but I stayed high on a tonic of relief and adrenaline, hardly aware of my tether.

When we landed, Tandem Man detached without any shortage of "pulling out early" jokes. I walked a distance from the building on shaky legs and sat on a patch of grass. Hands in the dry earth, eyes closed, I heard the cry of a distant hawk, cows mooing, and the steady sound of my breath. I turned my face towards the sun and thought that only chancing death could yield that deep of an appreciation for life. Take the biggest risks to experience the greatest rewards—if that was Kava Tech's lesson today, I had learned it.

War

That was risk. Next, Kava taught us about war. I learned why it was called the War Room, and we assembled there daily for instruction replete with dick references.

"We aren't just crafting a hiring strategy," More warned. "We're planning *balls out* war against our competition. Do you understand?" We nodded, grasping the gravity of our task. "And we won't, we cannot lose." She waved a stiff finger at the end of a stiff arm. The unwavering finger pointed to a list of competitors scribbled on a whiteboard.

"Each of these is a battle target. But, here is the evil empire. *Numero uno.* Pegasus Systems. They are the Death Star we must destroy. You will go h*ead to head* with a Pegasus recruiter on every one of your campuses. They have money to spend. They play our game and they are good. But you will be better. They are conniving, but you will out craft them." More's finger was resolute.

Balls out. Head to head. Size matters ... I giggled to myself and started thinking about Marion. I wanted to see him again. I worked with all women, all day, except for my lip-dipped partner. When I wasn't with them, I hung with Viola, Christopher, William, and their nerd herds. But Marion didn't work here, and I couldn't bring myself to call him. That he hadn't contacted me, it said something, didn't it? I looked around the room of beautiful faces. Maybe he wasn't single at all. The thought made me fidget. Besides, I came here to make money and save a species from extinction, not to chase boys.

"As recruiters, you're going to win great battles, not with brawn and blood, but with careful psychology and artfully calculated maneuvers," More instructed. "You're going to infiltrate your university campuses and learn everything about the culture of the college and the mentality of its students. Within that, you're going to know everything about each candidate. I don't care that there are going to be thousands. You will remember each of their favorite colors and their favorite foods. You're to be able to tell me their most treasured aspirations and their greatest fears. Then you will use this information to design individualized sell strategies for each candidate.

That you're all fresh out of college, essentially students yourselves, is a weapon to be forged. Your youth and your understanding of what it is to be a senior in college faced with tough life decisions will engender friendships with your candidates. Recruits will identify with you, confide in you, and when you have established this rapport, you'll be able to sell them on coming to work for us. They will trust you and take your advice to heart. Advise them to come here.

Your youthful disregard for old-school rules and stuffy corporate culture is more firepower when it comes to recruiting against other companies. Your work–life balance includes skydiving and crazy bar tabs. You wear flip-flops to work. The established corporate giants can't compete with this, so use it. Flaunt it. Market it. You need to show your candidates that this company is beyond anything anyone else can offer them. You need to sell a vision of a lifestyle that no new college graduate can refuse. You need to be that vision."

The CFO interrupted Recruiting Psych 101. He carried a black cardboard box.

"And this," More said, "is how you will pay for everything you do."

The CFO handed each recruiter an American Express Platinum Card.

"What's the limit on the card?" somebody asked.

"$100,000. Monthly," the CFO answered.

"What are the rules for spending?"

More said, "We trust you. Do what you have to do, but don't do what you don't need to do. Expenses are approved after the fact. Don't lose your receipts. Make sense?"

"Clear as mud," I whispered to Jeremy. "I'm 23 years old and my monthly credit limit is more than twice my annual salary."

"Crazy," he agreed. "But that card's gonna feel really good in your wallet."

And it did.

The Big O

Risk-taking and psychological warfare were integral parts of company culture. So was binge drinking. Regular companies had a water cooler around which employees gossiped. We had a kegerator. Grabbing a cold one here and there, throughout the day, was encouraged. While midweek beers were optional, attendance at Friday happy hours was a must. By the end of the week, most of us had worked 80 hours and were quite ready for quality stress relief. This meant drinking ourselves beyond sloppy before going bar hopping and dancing. It felt like the end of finals week at college—five days of searing pressure to perform and little sleep relieved by full-on fraternity-style excess— every Friday night.

The last happy hour ended with a $8,000 bar tab at a speakeasy downtown. Levi circulated correspondence congratulating the company on the achievement. A follow-up email said that our next get-together would have a 70s theme. There would be a DJ, a costume contest, and a lip-sync contest. It would be a banner week for thrift shop sales in Austin.

On Friday, Jeremy and I started drinking at 4 p.m. Later, I fumbled in the bathroom with my costume, a tight pair of brown paisley pants and an orange and yellow-striped polyester, button-down shirt. I pinned down a pink Jackson 5-style wig and smeared glitter everywhere.

"Go big or go home," I told myself in the mirror.

Happy hour was in full swing when I arrived. Some people already danced on the patio walls, and dance remixes drubbed the speakers. I stopped inside the glass doors to watch the spectacle. The patio was crowded, my colleagues an unrecognizable blob of brightly colored synthetic material.

But not everyone. Statuesque, like a beacon of corporate sanity, Marion stood at the center of it all. A gaggle of women hung on his every word. I strained on my stilettos for a better view. He had an arm draped around Melissa Burge, the legendary tech sales queen with the blunt cut bob. Her red silk shirt was tucked into a tight gray pencil skirt. She leaned into him, head tilted to hear what he was saying. She looked relaxed, like Marion had disarmed, even charmed, her ferocity. Amara Young, the theater major turned recruiter, and Avery Stone, my floater, stared starry-eyed at him. None were in costume.

"Come on, Olivia. Go get him. Those girls are no fun," I said to myself and pushed the heavy glass door.

"Don't." The voice was authoritative. "You're

wearing a clown wig. It will end badly."

It was Viola. Standing behind me, watching me watch him. She pulled the door shut.

"Vi, I wasn't going——"

"Oh yes, you were."

"What are you wearing?" She had on a purple wig, fluorescent yellow pants, and a Wonder Woman cape. "Your eyelashes are longer than mine."

"I win," she winked.

"You do," I sighed and let go of the door.

Last week, over a turkey sandwich in a massage chair, I had told Viola all about what happened with Marion during my recruitment weekend. She was sympathetic that he hadn't come looking for me. "Don't be like a love-sick puppy. Let him come to you."

"Vi ... look at us. We're at a mandatory work function."

"Yup. Now let's go get more drinks." I followed her into the crowd, and we met William at one of the kegs. His shirt unbuttoned to his navel showed off fake hair glued to his impish chest.

I gave him a hug and smeared a mutton chop-shaped sideburn. "Did you use a dry-erase marker? On your face?"

"But check out my chest hair. You know you love it." He hugged me back, spilling beer down my shirt.

We played beer pong. We ran the keg-themed obstacle course. We did keg stands. The lip-sync competition started later. Levi, as drunk as the rest of us, jumped on stage and then crowd surfed, a beer in hand. He landed awkwardly next to me on the pavement. I tried to help him up, but he pulled me down to him and yelled, "Chug!" On our knees, the CEO of Kava Tech and I raced to finish our beers. The crowd chanted "Go! Go! Go!" Levi buried me. I was still drinking, beer running down my neck while he celebrated and stumbled off into the crowd. I sopped my dripping chin with a rayon sleeve, and William, pink and slurring, tugged me to my feet. My lip-sync group had started, and they were looking for me.

I danced up the makeshift stage screaming Gloria Gaynor lyrics into a fake mic. My part of the act put me on the shoulders of our tallest member. And above it all, when I pointed to the crowd, you know, because I was a 70s rock star, there he was front and center, my Marion. I winked my glitter-glued eyelashes.

After our second song, I stumbled down from the stage into the welcoming high-fives of my colleagues. Somebody put another plastic cup of beer in my hand and then somebody else made me chug it. I spilled most of it. It took a while, but I tottered through the party to Marion. I went to hug him, and he gently stiff-armed my shoulders, a hand on each.

"Easy there." He steadied me with a cocky smile. "Nice eyelashes."

I pouted and winked. "I thought I would've seen you by now."

"I work too, sweetheart," he said.

"Well, I've been busy, jumping out of planes and stuff." I put a defiant hand on my hip, missing it the first time, like an uncoordinated, petulant child. "You coming dancing tonight? At Polyesters?" I felt ridiculous as soon as the words were out of my mouth.

"Not tonight," he replied coolly.

"Well, you should——" Before I could argue why he should come out with a bunch of drunk kids in costumes, something heavy hit my ribs.

"Livia! L-train! La vida loca! The Big O ... Oh ... Oh ... Ohhh ... Ohhh ... Livia!" Jeremy wrapped his giant arms around my waist and hoisted me over his shoulder. I was paralyzed, upside-down in the grip of my monster partner.

Mars looked at Jeremy indifferently. "I like the Big O," he said casually.

"Whoop! I'm having the Big O! The Big O is mine!" Jeremy hollered and ran off with me bent over his shoulder. He stumbled up the stone steps.

"What the hell are you doing. I was networking." I screamed into his back, "Put me down."

He eased me off his shoulder just inside the glass doors. "My ass. I was afraid he was going to eat you, looking at you like that. Or maybe you were going to eat him. Besides, you need a nickname."

"Seriously," I hissed. "If you ever pick me up again ... I will end your existence."

"You will what?" He flexed his biceps. He was dressed like a pimp, massive gold chains dangling from his thick neck. He had glued on a blonde handlebar mustache, like Hulk Hogan had. I yanked it off his upper lip. He shrieked like an injured kitten.

"What the hell are you two doing?" Viola and Willy found us.

"I'm showing Sloth over here who's in charge of

this operation." Jeremy dabbed at a red patch of skin that was now missing real hair.

"Whatever. We're headed downtown to the bar. The cabs are here. You wanna go with us?" Willy asked.

"Let's get out of here."

Before I could turn to go, Jeremy picked me up again, laughing hysterically. He carried me like a dumbbell over his head, out the front doors. Then he orgasmed my name—over and over—in front of a hundred plus colleagues out front waiting for cabs.

"The Big O ... Oh ... Oh ... Ohhh ... Ohhh ... Livia!" This time he added a dramatic pause before bringing my last name into his rapturous finish. He exhaled, "Ge ... sss ... Ohhh."

One hand on my hip and the other on my shoulder, Jeremy kept me suspended above his head, pumping me up and down. It caught on quickly. Before he reached the curb, company drunkards were orgasming my name in unison.

"Fucking, thank you," I said, when he put me down. Jeremy snorted with laughter. He had won. I was christened "Big O" by the Kava mob.

Roulette

A couple hundred of us took taxis to go downtown and drink more on Kava Tech's dime. We squeezed into the taproom of an old Irish pub, upending tables and sliding chairs to climb on the carved mahogany bar to dance.

A guy tugged on the bellbottoms of the girl next to me. "Come here, pretty," he said. Her legs opened like butterfly wings and he leaned between her knees. She dropped lower still, bobbing to the music until she lay supine on the bar. He licked limed salt off the curve of her neck and lifted her shirt to slurp tequila out of her navel. She squealed with laughter when he ran his tongue along her ribs, stopping at the lace of her bra. She rolled off the bar giggling into his arms, and they both fell to the floor.

Rounds of shots, beers, shots in beers, and wide-mouthed martini glasses sloshed in endless succession through our hands. We ran out of places to put the empty glasses. They littered the floor, shattered glass crackling under our dancing feet. The servers couldn't keep up, so we bought them drinks and trashed their order pads. The bartender dunked his head, washed his hair under the tap, and left it running for anyone else who wanted to take an open-mouthed dip.

Later, when the spouts were dry and there was nothing left to serve, More hollered, "Credit card roulette!" Levi waved over a waitress who brought the bill and a hat, like she'd seen this before. Soaked with liquored sweat, we jostled to watch what was happening.

Levi held up the limp piece of paper with the total circled in red pen at the bottom. "You don't wanna know," he said. He dropped his credit card into the hat and gave it to More. She did the same and handed it somebody else. Anyone brave enough to gamble on footing the entire night's bar tab put a card in the hat. I took a step back as it came towards me, but people leaning to see bumped me forward, and then somebody orgasmed my name. It spread like an STD through the sticky crowd, "O ... Oh ... Oh ... Ohhh ... Ohhh ... Livia ... Ge ... sss ... Ohhh." They chanted, "Go! Big O! Go! Big O!"

More looked at me and said, "They love you. You're one of us, right? Let's go recruiter, throw in." I shook my head. "Come on, show 'em what HR is made of." More winked at me, and I knew it was all a show. A game. Besides, I couldn't say no to my boss in front of all these cheering people. I dropped my corporate Amex into the hat, because my personal card was maxed out.

"That's my girl," More said and cheered for recruiting.

The game began when the waitress shook the hat. She fished the first card out and read the name. "Garrett Sanders. Not tonight's winner." She handed the card back to the guy who had first interviewed me on campus. He pumped his fist, celebrating his loss. One by one the cards came out, and we hemmed and hawed as their owners cheered not having to cover the tab.

The waitress announced when there were three cards left. I found myself standing in the middle of it all with Levi and More, the only two people here who could afford the bill. They taunted one another like old friends at the end of a wild night. The waitress pulled a card. She cradled it and read the name, "Lev――"

Levi grabbed his card from her before she got to his last name. He pointed at More and I, and he said, "Drinks on one of you." The richest man I'd ever met just told me that I might be buying a Friday night out for his entire company. This was a game, right? Surely he didn't mean it. I turned to More, who was looking at the waitress, who already had the next card in her hand. It wasn't silver, it wasn't mine.

"Olivia Gesso wins." The waitress said, reading my name off the last card in the hat, before she disappeared into the crowd with my Amex. Didn't she know it was a show? That I wasn't going to pay for it all?

People celebrated me. They hugged, thanked, and high-fived me. "Drinks on the Big O," somebody yelled and hoisted me up. I crowd surfed like a mascot at a Big

Ten football game until I landed on the other side of the room where the waitress waited for me to sign the receipt. She cracked her gum and handed me a pen.

I steadied myself on the bar. Under my Amex card, the total read $10,351.07. I cackled at the ridiculous number. Of course the company would reimburse me. That's why I had the company card in the first place, right? That's why More winked. I scribbled my name like a $10,000 bar tab was no big deal and smashed the receipt in my purse. The waitress rolled her eyes.

I needed space to breath, to be sure of what happened, to stop my head from spinning. I pushed my way through people toasting my "win". I looked for a bathroom and stumbled into a musty, dark hall. The corridor was quiet, cool, and empty, and I leaned against a door marked utility. I heard people still calling for the Big O through the wall. What an insane game, I thought. I checked my beeper, a new habit, but the glowing numbers blurred on the screen. I threw it back in my bag and fumbled with the stuck zipper.

"I've never seen a recruiter play credit card roulette."

Startled, my hand flew to my chest, and I dropped my purse. "Marion?" I never saw him at the crowded, sloppy bar.

He picked up my bag off the floor. "You still want to hang out tonight?" he asked, his voice silken, barely audible over the raucous.

I nodded.

"Come then." I took the hand he offered. We walked out the emergency door and into the darkness of a side street. We didn't make it far before his arms were around me, the back of my neck pressed against the cold stone of the building. His mouth on mine; warm whiskey and sweet peppermint. It was the kiss I had wanted at the salsa club, the kiss I'd imagined for months. Minted fire on my lips, his hands up in my hair.

In the cab to my place I climbed onto his lap, and the driver slammed the partition shut, cursing, and turning up the music. "You are trouble." Marion drew out the words, trailing kisses across my shoulder, up my neck, and nibbling his way back to my lips.

"But I'm worth it," I murmured into his mouth.

"Show me," he said, pulling my hips to his.

I don't know how we got in my apartment door. It opened, like the rest of me, inviting him, hustling him inside. My body said faster. What I wanted, coming in moments. But he said, "No." With deep certainty, "Like this, baby." And he slowed. The pace of everything. Achingly patient, almost torturous. His fingertips tracing my stomach, my lower back, my inner thighs, my ankles. Tender but hungry. His mouth teasing through my clothes until they were damp, irrelevant piles on the floor. I didn't try to lead, didn't need to. I let him take me apart. Deconstruction, one piece at a time.

Later, tucked under one of his arms, the hazy world, the bed fell away. I floated, my cheek against his chest.

"Mars?"

"Yeah, baby?"

I ran my fingers through the thin line of hair under his navel. "Is this a mistake?" I took him into my hand.

He exhaled and fluttered his eyes closed. "Do you really care?" he asked, easing himself onto me one more time.

"No," I whispered between shallow breaths.

I woke up the next day and peeked out of one eye. I hadn't dreamt it. He was lying next to me. I opened the other eye to be sure. He was fiddling with his phone, the covers low around his waist. The night came back in hot flashes. The bar, the credit card game, him, us.

He realized I was awake. "Okay?" he asked, dropping the phone and turning to me.

I groaned a yes and buried my face in the pillow. My breath smelled of dead things. "Water? Please," I mumbled into the pillow. He went to the kitchen, and I crept to the bathroom. In the mirror, my face was a Picasso of smeared glitter and eyeliner. I smudged some makeup off, gargled, and padded to the living room couch, the only piece of furniture besides a bed I owned.

"I love what you've done with the place," he said, handing me a plastic cup of water. I laughed at the bare apartment. "I mean, you've even decorated with a box of tampons." On the mantle, my prize possession. The seeds safely stored.

"Don't touch that."

"Wasn't planning on it. You not staying long or

does the company need to pay you more to buy, I don't know where to start. Glass glasses? A chair? There's this amazing place called Ikea, you should check it out."

"Stop it." I smiled and put my cup on the floor. "I just haven't gotten around to it cause I'm going to be traveling to Boston all the time. What's the point?" I patted the cushion next to me. Marion sat down close. "Besides, when you don't have furniture, you can use the whole place for whatever you want."

He twirled a length of my wild hair around his finger and tugged it. I slipped down between his knees.

The Whale

It was easy to get lost in my thoughts about that night. My brain had new feelings, pleasures, to wrap itself around and to coddle. I plotted how I'd see him again. Don't get attached, my head warned. No, definitely not. Marion needed to be a plaything. After all, I was a traveling recruiter, and he was a traveling investor. Plus, the seeds. I'd be clear across the world in a year, hopefully. But still. How come, I lamented, every time a girl opens her legs, she also opens her heart, even if just a little?

My email dinged and brought me back to reality. I opened a message from More. I had written to ask her how to get the bar tab reimbursed. Her message read:

Congrats on taking a gamble, Olivia. So proud of you, but it wasn't a game. The stakes were real. Kava will pay the tab upfront and you can pay us back in installments out of your salary every month.

So glad you're on the team—M

Monthly installments? I buried my face in my hands. My email kept dinging while I hyperventilated at my desk. When I looked up at the screen, it was full of congratulatory messages for the "Big O" who "won credit card roulette for the company's most expensive happy hour yet." Overnight, I had become a company celebrity, albeit a very poor one.

There was a message from Christopher, chiding me.

WTF? I thought you came to make money, not blow it. Big O? I'll save the jokes for later. Let's hang soon, Christopher

I put my head down again. What had I done?

"Olivia," Jeremy demanded.

I jumped in my seat. "Nothing. Sorry, just thinking. What do you need?"

"We have to practice our pitches in the War Room. Remember the meeting?" Pitches were the speeches we'd make on campus to students at information sessions, in elevators, on the street, and everywhere else. We needed to perfect them.

"We do? Yes. We do. I'm ready for that," I lied. "Let me get my notebook." I rooted around our cube, a catastrophe of cups, cords, and papers.

"We have to do something about this desk. These cups are everywhere. And they scare me."

Jeremy tutted. "I know. Feel free."

"I'm not your maid." I pulled my notebook out from underneath a stack of other files and knocked several post-its off the wall. Thumbtacks scattered on the floor. I left them there. Before we reached the War

Room, we ran into a wall of cheering Kava Techies.

"What's happening?" I asked. Jeremy shrugged.

"Vegas! Vegas! Vegas!" Some yelled, while others chanted "Whale! Whale! Whale!" The sound of champagne bottles and beer cans popping echoed down the hall to the meeting room where they were all headed.

Jeremy and I looked at one another and then followed the flow. We saw Levi and Melissa Burge and other executives in front of the packed conference room. They were all uncharacteristically dressed in suits. Levi loosened his tie and then threw it on the floor. He climbed on one of the flimsy folding chairs, cupped his hands around his mouth and hollered. "We just landed the whale! The fucking whale! Pack your bags. We're going to Vegas to celebrate."

The chanting grew louder. People queued to shake Melissa's hand. Champagne sprayed everywhere. Jeremy looked at me. "The whale was a $75 million dollar deal. Melissa Burge was the account lead. Do you know what this means?"

"I think we're about to find out," I said.

Kava Tech chartered three airplanes to take the entire company to Vegas to celebrate the deal. We boarded early the next morning. Some people were still drunk from the night before, upper-level management among them, while others ordered drinks the moment they stowed their overhead luggage. I sat next to William and Viola, who took turns making drink napkins into paper airplanes. Before take-off, they argued the physics behind which design was superior.

To prove her point, Viola doused her plane in her drink and threw the sopping wet napkin. It stuck to Willy's forehead. I wondered if the celery garnish in my Bloody Mary counted as a breakfast food.

Levi rented a couple of floors at the Bellagio, Vegas' newest hotel casino. We changed into swimsuits and headed down to the expansive pools to play in the water. Nobody cared that it was summer in the desert. We drank, then dunked ourselves, then drank some more. Viola wore her giant sun hat and a black one-piece. She dangled her long white legs over the side of a lounge chair and toyed with the olives in her drink. Willy looked like her annoying kid, in neon orange swim trunks, white zinc oxide smeared on his nose. He floated on a frog-shaped inner-tube sipping something garnished with a pink umbrella.

"At least you embrace your inner dork, Willy," Viola said from somewhere under her hat. He splashed at her.

"I can't believe I'm sitting here, right now, doing this. Is this really my job? How is any of this a job?" I asked, crunching an ice cube.

"Why not? This is what it's all for. Wait until we go public. There's gonna be so much money, this'll be a cute memory," William said.

"Levi loves his cult," Viola said. "If everybody's all-in, if everybody celebrates, then everybody will do it again—make another product, close the next deal. More money for him and us."

"I'm totally in," William said.

"I went out with Christopher the other night for

dinner, and he told me HereBeer is moving fast. They're going to try and roll out as soon as possible," I said.

"HereBeer? That's what they're calling it?" Viola asked.

I nodded. "It's great, right?"

"Wait, you went on a date with Christopher?" William asked.

"Jealous, Willy?" Viola laughed.

"He's my neighbor. We hang out."

"Why him when you could have all this?" William rubbed his man-child body with his palm.

"I'm gonna be sick." Viola pulled her hat down, and I giggled.

"Willy, I'm not dating anybody in this company. Ever." Marion didn't count, because he didn't technically work at Kava.

"Why not? We're all hot and making a killer living." He tweaked his tiny nipple.

"It's way too close," Viola agreed. "Plus, look at the selection," William gave her the finger. "But, you know people are already hooking up." She lifted her hat.

"It has to involve recruiting. They're the only women here," I said. "Besides, you."

"Of course it does," Viola said.

"Who's hooking up?" William leaned and fell off his float.

"He needs those inflatable arm bands," I said to Viola. "Kava Tech feels like a social experiment, where they put a handful of hot women in a beer bottle with a bunch of socially backward men. Shake it up and then see what happens."

Viola sighed. "It's a total netherworld, where the loser in your high school is the it-man at Kava."

"I'm the it-man?" William asked.

"Oh yes," she said suggestively, "a total dweeb, but such a computer stud." She blew him a kiss.

"There's nothing sexier than a man illuminated only by the light of his laptop," William agreed.

"Enough about you two. What about me?" I asked.

"What about you?" William asked.

"You two at least get to be the comp sci stars. I'm the cheap entertainment, a company ornament. What would Kava Tech nights out be without recruiters?"

Viola said, "Sausage fests."

"Recruiters are the reason the rounds keep getting bought. We're the bedrock of Kava's party culture. It's our job to perpetuate it. That's a weird job," I said.

"Hell yeah, it's your job," William said. "What's the only thing a tech genius still can't get in this job market?"

"What?"

"A girlfriend. And that's where you come in." William pointed at me.

"I'm not anyone's girlfriend," I said.

"But, you're the *illusion* of a girlfriend." William traced an hourglass shape in the air. "These geeks, trust me I should know, don't get the attention of girls like you—ever. A hot recruiter? Yeah, I'm gonna talk to her. She wants to buy me dinner? Take me dancing? I'll even interview with her company. And there you go."

"You're a high-tech geisha," Viola said.

"Exactly." William pointed at Vi but looked at me.

"You entertain. You tease. You cajole. You sell us nerds a future we can't refuse. Private limo service, surf and turf, top-shelf vodka at the hottest nightclub in town. And most of all, time with you," William said. "Fuck the money. Money's the low hanging fruit. You're the cherry at the top of the tree."

"So, I'm bait?" I asked.

"You're the boat. Kava Tech wants the fish to jump in the boat and stay there." I scrunched my nose. "Come on, Liv, this can't be news to you. Why do you think the recruiting department looks the way it does?"

"You're not alone, Liv," Viola said, "It's not all that different for me. Doesn't matter that I can out-code any dude I work with, including you Willy—"

"Doubt it," he said.

"If you have these," Viola grabbed her breasts, "people assume you're a plaything or that you played with a thing to get where you are. Doesn't matter where we work, women drag around a ball and chain of assumptions."

"Well, sometimes I feel like recruiters have the biggest balls. And, you know what they say in my department?" I asked.

"What?"

"Size matters." William looked at his crotch. Viola laughed, and we bumped our drinks.

Choices

Levi's exultant mood was not to be underestimated. That night he invited the entire company to a sushi feast. I had been drinking in the Vegas sun all day, and after the pool, Viola and I went looking for dresses to wear to dinner. I didn't want to spend the money, especially since I accidently bought a happy hour out for the entire company, but I felt loose and comfortably buzzed. It was a celebration, after all. Viola picked something with an empire waist that showed a lot of leg. I found a backless slip that tied at the neck with a string of feathers. Later, we teetered to the dinner on Vegas-style stilettoes.

There were long tables in the banquet room adorned with ice sculptures and flowers. I examined the orchids, spotted purple and white. Rodrigues had a few rare varieties of the flower, and I remembered climbing with ropes up steep boulders to get a glimpse of them. They were a shade species, beautiful but always hiding and so hard to find. I plucked one of the flowers from the table arrangement and put it in my hair.

We weren't sitting five minutes when an army of waitstaff brought rounds of beer and sake, for sake bombs. A couple hundred of us dropped the shots into the frosty ale and chugged the brimming foam. We toasted the company's success like this, over and over. In between the rounds of drinks, the servers presented wooden boats overflowing with sashimi and sushi. By the end of dinner, the floor was littered with rice, fish, flowers, and a few people who couldn't stay upright. A sticky film of sake spume coated the rug, the chairs, and most of us. The intricate ice statues of fish leaping from the water, now puddles of slush, were pushed to the table edges to make room for piles of uneaten, real fish.

The dinner bill topped $60,000, but we were just getting started.

Somebody staggered into the room and announced, "I have a roulette wheel!" The ones who could stand followed him out of the banquet room to the casino floor.

The game was simple. He explained, "There are 38 pockets on the roulette wheel. Bet two paychecks on a number. Whoever's number comes up takes home everyone else's salary for two months."

I was paying off a $10,000 bar tab. If I won, my sake-bombed head reasoned, I could be out of that hole and fly the seeds back to Rodrigues tomorrow. I touched the orchid still resting behind my ear. And if I lost? It would be another crushing blow, the bar tab plus regular bills to pay and no salary to do it. I listened to the people around me doing hazy math, the excitement palpable. When was I ever going to have these odds to make this much money this fast? We all knew the answer and quickly took the numbers.

"I want 21." Viola yelled from behind me, pushing forward. With two left, I took number 11. I felt the rush, like when I rode the wakeboard, jumped out of the plane, and when I dropped my Amex into the hat. I shook out my hands, savoring the high. Minutes later, 38 of us gathered around the wheel, a rowdy pack cheering behind us.

I heard my pulse in my ears. Strangers stopped to watch. The dealer released the ball. It spun the circle several times, and I held my breath. It slowed, 25. Skipped, 33. Dribbled, 14. Another skip, 28. Slower now, 30. Slower still, 11—*stay*. It took one last jump, 17. The ball stopped on 17.

"Ghadir Alami! Ghadir! She won!" Everyone turned to celebrate the winner.

My feathery dress felt like a steel cage, the weight pulling on my shoulders. Two months of salary gone in seconds, while Ghadir had won an ungodly amount of money. The tears welled in my eyes. I raised my wrist to dab my face. Risk was only fun when your chute opened, and you landed on your feet. I pushed my way out of the crowd and ran into Levi.

He grabbed my arm. "Risk is always worth it, don't you see?" He smashed five one-hundred-dollar bills into my palm and moved to the next person. People realized what he was doing and surrounded him. When the crowd got too thick, he threw the money in the air—handfuls of one-hundred-dollar bills. Colleagues and strangers dove for the cash that floated down behind him. Levi didn't bother to turn around. He meandered through the casino floor making his own kind of ticker tape parade.

Viola and William found me wiping my eyes and clutching Levi's generosity. "Forget it Liv. You'll earn it back in bonuses. You know you will. Let's go dancing and blow it all off," Vi said. I shoved the cash in my purse, and all but ran from the casino floor with my friends. From there, my night liquified like the ice sculptures. It became a dripping mess of flashing disco lights, club music, and then nothingness. Silent and black.

The next morning, the sheets felt cool against my bare chest, the hum of full force hotel air conditioning filled the dark room. I rolled to pull the covers closer and bumped an arm. A hairy arm. Inches from me in bed. A flood of panic triggered a scream from the pit of my stomach, and I jumped from the mattress with no idea where I was, how I had gotten there, or who was in the bed. Tangled in the blankets, I fell backwards off the side of the mattress, my dress wrapped low around my waist. The cold air grabbed my bare breasts.

"Holy shit, Olivia. Stop it."

It was a familiar voice, but a man's voice. I kept screaming and struggled to get away, kicking at the covers. On my knees I reached and pulled the blackout curtains, flooding the room with sun and blinding myself.

"It's me!"

Christopher, fully clothed, sat up in bed shielding his eyes from the light.

"What the hell are you doing in my bed?" I screamed. I grabbed the water glass off the desk and threw it against the wall, just missing his head.

"Stop it! You were sick! I took care of you!" he screamed back, protecting himself with a pillow.

My chest heaved. My chest! I pulled my dress to cover my breasts. My head pounded as my eyes adjusted.

"What did you do? Did you touch me?" My voice broke.

"No! No." His voice was sharp, sincere. "You undressed yourself. I tried not to look. Okay, I looked. But I didn't touch you. Nothing happened. Honest. Look at me, I'm dressed. Please, calm down. I'll leave right now. Do you want me to leave?" He cowered behind the pillow.

"Turn around," I snapped. Christopher did as I asked. He swung his legs over the opposite side of the bed and faced the wall. I slipped my arms back into the dress and knotted the feathers.

"It's okay now."

"You sure?" He held the pillow over the back of his neck.

"I'm sure."

"Olivia, I didn't touch you."

"Okay. It's okay." I sat on the floor at the foot of the bed, my head in my hands. "Tell me what happened." I felt quieter now, my hangover beating down the adrenaline.

"You want some water first?" Christopher asked sheepishly.

Another morning. Another guy offering me hangover water. "Please." I hugged a pillow on the floor. He came back from the bathroom with a glass and sat down on the bed above me. He talked. I drank.

"Liv, you blacked out or something at the club downstairs. I was walking by and saw you. Viola was a mess and William was trying to help her. Actually, I wasn't really sure what was going on with those two, but anyway, I took you back to your room. By the time we got up here, you threw up ... on my shoes. They're outside the door, if you don't believe me."

"I'm so sorry." I kept my face buried in the pillow.

"I carried you inside, and I was going to leave, but you got sick again. Go look at the trashcan."

"I can smell it," I muttered.

"I was afraid to leave you ... that you might choke or something. So, I stayed. You were so drunk you started undressing yourself. You kept saying something about wanting to take a shower. I tried to stop you, but you weren't listening. You untied your dress and passed out on the bed. I tucked you in, sort of."

"I'm so embarrassed. I can never look at you again." Tears wet the pillowcase.

"It's okay. You might owe me a pair of shoes. But you've got great boobs, so it made up for it."

I glanced at Christopher's quirky smile. I couldn't help but smile back, and when he laughed, I threw the pillow. "Stop, really, I'm mortified. I'm sorry I thought the worst." I wiped my nose and eyes. "I don't remember any of it."

"I'm gonna go. I can't take the smell in here, though I could stick around if you still want help in the shower." He grinned again.

"Go." I crawled over to him, put my hands on his knees, and used them to help myself stand. He looked up at me and I hugged the top of his head. "Thank you. I owe you more than new shoes." I mussed up his hair.

In the afternoon, I rolled myself out of bed and went solo to the pool. I camped under a large umbrella and ordered a cheeseburger and two bottles of water from the bar. I pulled my baseball hat low over my sunglasses and buried my nose in a ratty copy of *The World According to Garp*. I nodded off in the afternoon sun, reading less than a chapter.

I woke sometime later to cool raindrops falling on my feet. The book was on my chest, my neck stiff from sleeping upright. Christopher stood in front of me blocking the sun and dripping onto my chair. He was so pale and thin, the light shone through him. His Teva sandals velcroed over his swim socks.

"Why do I keep waking up to find you staring at me?" I asked, putting the book down. "And, why are you wearing socks to a pool?"

"I saw you sitting here alone, and thought I should check on you," he said.

"I'm fine. Recovering. You want to sit down?" I motioned to the empty lounge chair next to me.

"Sure. You like Irving?"

I handed him the novel. "He makes me laugh, but

I like the politics too. Cider House Rules is one of my favorites."

"Abortion is a tough topic." Christopher knew Irving's writing and we started talking about the books, which led to the next subject, and the next. Soon, the sun was setting and the desert air cooled. We swaddled ourselves in extra towels and ordered more food from the bar.

"What are doing you tonight?" he asked.

"I thought I would dance topless for money and ruin some shoes." I covered my face and peeked at him through my fingers. "No really. This is it."

"You wanna be my date on our last big night in Vegas? Shuffleboard?" He pointed to an outdoor area across from the pool.

"You're kidding. What, are we 60?" I laughed. "Your socks will be fashionable."

"Come on." He pulled a shirt over his lanky frame.

I followed him to the shuffleboard court. Palm trees wrapped in white Christmas lights lit the court. I put my hand on one, its bark smooth like its distant, extinct cousin. What had I done, losing all that money last night? I felt like crying again.

"You okay?" Christopher asked. "You know the rules?"

"Prepare to be crushed," I said and grabbed a cue so he wouldn't see my face.

He slid the first weight. I went second and knocked his off the end of the platform. We traded rounds back and forth, and after a while it looked as though I would take the game. My headache finally fading, I sang and danced to Barry Manilow to distract him from his final shot, and his last chance at winning. Christopher looked at me, shook his head and threw the last weight. I leaned against him to watch it slide down the lane. When I turned to celebrate, he bent down for a kiss. I felt it happening. I let it happen, and I kissed him back, his thin, soft lips under mine. He put his hand on the small of my back, to hold me closer, but I stepped away.

He pushed his glasses up the bridge of his nose and then didn't know where to put his hands.

"I'm sorry," he stammered and flushed.

"It was sweet." I put a hand on his shoulder to make him look at me. "But this isn't a good idea ..." I fished for the right thing to say, my feelings a jumbled mess. "Christopher, I can't. Not now. There is ... I leave for Boston soon. I have so much work. And so do you. I mean, you *are* HereBeer. And this company, it's way too small. I appreciate what you did last night, but——"

Christopher was looking over my shoulder at something, or rather someone. "Do you know him?"

On the other side of the pool was Marion. Watching. Brooding? His posture tight, his hand balled up at his side. A duffle bag lay crumpled at his feet.

"Shit."

"I got it." Christopher looked down at his feet. "I should go."

I let him walk away. Christopher was a nice guy, and I was grateful for his friendship, and what he did the other night, but a relationship was the last thing I needed. Yet, I found myself walking over to Marion to try and save one. Sin City had made my life way messier than I ever intended.

Marion's fist wasn't balled up. He was holding his cell phone. I stood in front of him.

"You're here." I said.

"I am."

"I didn't think you would be."

"Obviously."

I looked down. He was wearing loafers; the kind rich men wore on yachts. "It's not what you think."

"You don't know what I think."

"Tell me." I searched his face.

"You're going to make a great recruiter."

"Work? You're thinking about work?"

"And that you should come out with me tonight."

"You came all the way to Vegas to take me out?" And this was how I greeted him.

"Among other things. Unless you prefer ... who was that?"

"Christopher." Marion looked at me blankly. "The HereBeer guy."

"Oh, yes. Unless you prefer the beer guy. I heard he's bright."

I shook my head. "I'm sorry you had to see that."

"You don't need to apologize." If he was angry, hurt, or disappointed, I couldn't tell. Business Marion was matter of fact. He picked up his bag. "Meet me at the Heavyweight. 9:30ish. It's a dressier club. At least, we'll start there." He nudged my chin and smiled. "See you later, pretty. Go get cleaned up."

I fished the feather dress off the floor and sent it to laundry for emergency vomit removal. I tried Vi and William, but they weren't answering. Probably still sleeping it off. I ate dinner in my room, took a nap, took more aspirin, and drank a lot of water. Later, I looked ready, but I couldn't wrap my head around whether it was good or bad that Marion didn't seem to care about Christopher kissing me. Did he understand that it meant nothing? That stuff just happens? Or did he not care enough about me to care what I was doing? But he'd come all the way here. Part of me wished he had been overwhelmingly jealous and stormed over. Stupid girl, stop it. Marion isn't some college boy.

My dress was missing a feather or two, so I tied it together to hide the missing plumage. I felt the way I always did when I thought I'd see Marion. It was involuntary. Some parts of my body tightened, others loosened. It was way worse since we'd slept together.

"You're perfect." He looked happy to see me. I felt relief, then angst. Why wasn't he angry? I twirled in my boa and returned the compliment. "A drink?"

"Of course."

I looked around the club and didn't recognized anyone from Kava, though the booths with bottle service were quite private. I sat on the soft chaise and ordered a vodka soda. It was a space large enough for a group, but oddly it was only the two of us.

Like he read my mind. "I have a friend."

"I'm sure you do." I sipped my drink though my body said not to. It had had enough. "About today ..."

"Liv, you're a big girl. You do what you want."

"Well that's grown up. But I feel like I owe you an explanation."

"I'm not interested. You're here now. Doesn't that say everything?"

"I hope so." I took another hard swallow and winced when it went down. I looked around the space at the empty chairs. "So, is this like a date?"

His dimples flashed. "Did you eat dinner?"

"Room service. Was I supposed to wait? It's almost 10."

"No." He fished something out of his pocket, a finger-sized vile. Inside were tiny blue pills with a mermaid stamped on one side and an "S" on the other. "Ready?"

"Ready for what?"

"There's a party I want to take you to. But this will make it more fun."

"What is it?"

"A cocktail. Dulls the edges but sharpens the senses." I stiffened. I'd never taken more than an over-the-counter pain killer. When I didn't reach for the mermaids, he put them in his mouth. He took my hand and started kissing my wrist. "Liv. Listen to me."

"You have my attention." I murmured. I closed my eyes against the warmth of his lips, the tip of his tongue dancing up my arm.

He slipped his hand under my dress, between my legs, pressing into the wet that was already waiting, ready. He whispered into my mouth. "Remember the way I felt in you?" His fingers pushed inside of me, "Remember?" and when my breath hitched, the pill slid from his tongue to mine. "This is even better." I swallowed it. "Good girl. Let me show you, now." He pulled me onto his lap.

It didn't take long for the room to blur away. For

me to be aware only of where his skin brushed mine. The waitress came to collect the drinks, but it was like she wasn't really there. She looked like a smudge on the other side of window glass. "Mars, why can't I see?"

"You can see, but you don't need to. Just feel." My arm in his, we were walking. Floating? Was he carrying me? The hall was a kaleidoscope of colors. My skin celebrated everything it touched. The rub of my dress, the lace of my panties. In the elevator, the shiny silver walls waved like wheat. We hung suspended by cables. I hung suspended by him. His mouth on mine, the rest of me vanished. "I told you, sweetheart."

After, the doors dinged open to a cavernous room. Pristine white couches reflected off giant black windows. The zebra print rug moved like a swimming pool. "Mars. Mars, I need to lay down." The couch leather felt cool against my cheek. My eyelids tickled when I closed them.

When I opened them, the lighting had changed to a hazy purple. I sat up. The people next to me were a moving Dalí, dreamlike, contorted but connected and fluid. They passed through one another, a body with three heads. Nipples hard and pink. In his mouth, under his hands. Elbows, knees knotted together. His face came through jots of hair. A river of hair. I knew him. The round of his nose, the curve of his face, the sound of his voice, urging them on. I knew him. I stood over them, squinting through the haze.

"I know you," I said, pointing. The three-headed snake couldn't hear me. But it was close enough to touch. I said it louder.

"Drink this."

The voice put something slimy in my hand. "No." The glass shattered when it hit the tile floor.

"Let's get you home."

"I know him." I pointed again. I felt hands on me. They were smooth and cool. "Mars?"

"Yeah, baby?"

"I don't feel good."

"I know."

I woke up in my room. I was clean, taken care of, and in my pajamas. I wasn't hungover, at least not in the usual way. Instead I felt sad, empty like I had lost something or someone special. The shower stopped running.

"Marion?" He stepped out of the steam. Towel tucked around his waist. Fingernail marks streaked his shoulder, his lower back. "Your back. Did I do that ... in the elevator?" I couldn't remember much else. I looked at my hands, my unmanicured nails too short to ever bother with. He twisted, trying to see the scratches in the mirror. "What happened last night?" I asked.

"Too much candy. Cut the party short for you." He was still trying to see behind him.

"Whose party?"

"C-suite."

"Who?"

"Execs I know, high profile people."

"Levi? Did my CEO see me like that?"

"No, he never goes. Not his scene."

"But important people like him?" I couldn't

imagine what I'd said or the impression I'd made.

"You could say that."

"Why did you take me there, like that?"

Marion sat down on the bed. "Don't worry about it. You were a hit."

"I was?"

"No. You were asleep. It's okay. It happens." He patted my leg.

"I can't remember. I had weird dreams, uhm, from whatever that was. A mermaid?"

"Too much. Next time, half a mermaid. Okay?"

"I don't want a next time. I feel unhappy."

"It'll go away. It's a different kind of hangover."

"The dreams. I saw people I knew, I think." I looked at my hands again. "Did I know them?"

He threw on a t-shirt, sat on the edge of the bed, and stroked my cheek. "They were dreams, baby. I'm sorry. It won't happen again. It's not your thing."

Alpha Wolves

The parts of Vegas I could remember, I had made terrible decisions—gambling and partying to dysfunction. Why? I had blacked out twice and woken up two different days with two different guys in my bed. It was like I was making up for all those years I ran track instead of acting like a rebellious teenager. What was I doing? Trying to fit in? The best Kava techies could handle the drink, the wager, and the work. I couldn't keep up. And I'd racked up an absurd amount of debt, when the only thing I was supposed to be doing was saving. I apologized to my tampon box on the mantle. I promised it I'd do better, that I'd earn it all back.

While I came back from Vegas, hungover, confused, and further in debt, Kava Tech's leadership came back and announced they had successfully filed to take the company public. Employees could buy stock options.

"Another gamble?" I asked, when I saw the email.

"No. This is a sure thing. The market is raging. The

stock price will go through the roof," Jeremy said.

"When can we sell the shares?"

"Who cares? A year, a year and a half? No insider trading," he said.

"That's a long time."

"Not really. I'm going to hold this baby for a while. Cash out big in the long run. I'm ponying up at least five. Maybe more if I want to cut my family in."

That night, I called the one person I knew who had spare cash and loved inside information. I pitched the idea as a strategic alliance and deal of a lifetime.

Sky was excited. "For real? Are you kidding? A red-hot tech IPO? I'm totally in."

"There's nothing to lose. I'll pay you back with interest when we sell," I told her, praying this would fix my mistakes.

"How much are you thinking?" she asked.

"Five thousand? Total initial investment between the two of us with you covering my $2,500, just for now, until I can pay you back."

"I'll mail you a check."

"You won't regret it."

I wanted to cry to Sky about the mess of everything I'd made so far, but I didn't want to scare her out of investing. Instead, I told her about jumping out of a plane and everything I was learning. And I listened to what her life was like in Italy. There were cafes, museums, and men named Marco who pined for her, and of course side trips for couture shopping in Milan. I thought, if I could fix my mistakes, on my way to Rodrigues, I'd fly through Rome and see her. Maybe I could be the one doing the expensive shopping and lending her a dress.

At work, I swore off the distractions, specifically the men in my life, minus the one I had to work with every day.

"We can't call our hiring strategy 'The Lemming'." I was resolute.

"Why not? It's perfect." Jeremy held his ground. "When the best kids come all the others will follow, like lemmings off a cliff."

"It's offensive."

"To who?"

"Our candidates? The lemmings? They don't even do that cliff suicide thing."

"Big O, don't make me dip."

"Put that shit away." When he pulled out the tin and shook it, I changed tactics. "How about we call it 'Alpha Wolf'?"

"I'm listening." He tapped the tin.

"Our best kids are pack leaders. They're influencers. Others see value in their decisions. If we hire the alpha wolves, the strongest candidates, then the pack will follow them here. It's your concept, but packaged differently."

"I like it."

"Prove it," I said. He put the dip back in his pocket. "Okay, so who are the alpha wolves?"

"Easy. The top three are Conor, James, and Julia. They're the holy trinity of candidates. Smarter than God."

"James is the top of Course 6 at MIT, so yes, he's

an alpha. But why Julia? She's just his girlfriend. She doesn't even code."

Jeremy raised his finger. "I did the research. First, she is a brilliant writer. Her fiction has been published in several journals already. She is an alpha in her field. Second, she has a perfect GPA, and we could totally hire her to do something here. And third, she is James' girl."

"And that matters why?"

"Because while James can get a software development job anywhere, he'll never get another girl like Julia. We have to recruit them together."

"Fine. And why Conor ... what's his last name ... Walsh? We haven't even seen his resume. He never answers emails or phone calls. How do we know his credentials are more than a whisper campaign?"

"Again, I did my homework. For the last four years, Conor has won every major collegiate computer science competition worth mentioning, in the US and internationally. In certain strange circles, he is a total celebrity."

"James, Julia, and Conor are our top alphas? If they come, everyone comes?"

"Don't forget about the car and the ski trip," Jeremy said.

"Right. Those are huge." To get attention on campus, we bought a car to give away. It wasn't just any car. We bought the *Back to the Future* time travel car. A refurbished, silver DeLorean DMC-12, worth about $50,000. "Give Us a Resume, and We'll Give You the Future." Our slogan was brilliant. What geek could resist the chance to win that car for doing nothing more than giving us a piece a paper? Once we picked the other alphas from our pool, we would close them on an exclusive ski trip in Telluride, Colorado. "And what about Avery, our floater?" I asked.

"What about her? She'll help out."

"She worries me."

Beantown

Kava Tech paid for me to live at the Cambridge Marriott. When I wasn't hunched over my laptop eating room service, I was out scouting event venues and shoring up reservations. Sometimes it was easy. I'd mention Kava Tech and they knew immediately how much money I'd be spending.

"We don't normally take reservations, but for you Ms. Gesso and Kava Tech, you may certainly book the entire top floor of our restaurant on a Saturday night."

But when places didn't know Kava, it was way harder. First, I had to convince them that I was old enough to purchase a beer, and then that I would like to put a $15,000 deposit on my American Express card in anticipation of a party I would throw for 22-year-old kids that also didn't look legal.

I also went to career fairs. My first was on the MIT campus, where I would be up against hundreds of other company reps scouting the same talent. Like

More had taught us, I prepared for battle. I wore the Kava Tech recruiter uniform of tight jeans, a company t-shirt, and sneakers. After a full pot of 5 a.m. coffee, I dragged a dozen 50-pound boxes containing a booth, tables, banners, t-shirts, and company logoed tchotchkes from my room to the lobby. The elevator beeped incessantly, annoyed at me having propped its doors open. The Marriott's Ghanaian doorman, and my new best friend, took pity.

"Big day?" Kwaku asked, smashing a box into the trunk of the cab waiting out front.

"My first career fair. And I almost forgot ...", In addition to a large cash tip, I pulled out a handful of light-up bouncy balls (with company logo) and handed them to him. "For your children. There are three, right?" I asked.

He flashed a bright white smile and shoved everything into his coat pocket. "Thank you. They will love these. When I go home, you know, really home, Olivia, I will bring you something from Africa."

"I'd like that."

On campus, Kwaku was not there to help me unload. The cabbie avoided eye contact, not that he could see me in the backseat over the boxes. I slid them, one at a time, across endless sidewalks and up the steps into a vast gymnasium. From the mangled cardboard, I assembled a 10x10 booth frame, snapping colorful motivational panels to the metal bars. In the middle I hung a picture of the DeLorean with our futuristic slogan advertising the giveaway. An eternity of boxes later, I had turned an empty exhibition space into a vibrant nook of Kava Tech marketing gimmicks.

Representatives from hundreds of companies, some next to me, like Goldman Sachs, Morgan Stanley, NASA, and the diamond company DeBeers, had done the same. In every direction, rows upon rows of logoed key chains, whistles, pens, squishy stress balls, and t-shirts offered students a cornucopia of corporate junk. Polished recruiters in suits ran demos on laptops and buzzed like flies to the complimentary offerings of pasty bagels and tepid boxed coffee. Some shook hands and exchanged company trinkets, an introductory currency; others crouched behind their motivational panels and warily assessed the competition. I wiped my sweaty palms on my jeans and rehearsed FAQ answers.

A gentleman with clear blue eyes and hair gelled beyond casual interrupted my pitch practice. He took a stress ball off my table. The white stripe on his fourth finger where the ring used to be stood out against his tanning booth-colored skin. He looked around my space and then offered me an introductory handshake. "Price Johnson."

"Olivia Gesso. Kava Tech." I glanced over my shoulder. "As if you couldn't tell."

"Pegasus," he replied. I let go of the handshake. "A DeLorean?" he asked. "Good move."

"Thank you."

"Plans all set for the year then?"

A woman answered for me. "Ahhhh, hellllloooo, Price." Avery Stone's voice, like nails on a chalkboard. I spun on my heel. "I see you've met Olivia."

"Hello, Avery," he said with certain familiarity.

Neither offered the other a handshake, but my in-house nemesis and my biggest external competitor stood close enough to suggest a history.

"You know one another?" I asked.

"Price did his best to bring me to Pegasus last year." Avery had yet to look at me, her eyes locked on his. "He did his very best."

"Good luck today, Avery. Olivia." Price nodded and walked away with the squishy ball.

"Uhm, that was weird. What are you doing here?" I asked.

"I'm the floater for MIT. Did you forget?"

She had paired pearls, low pumps and a suit jacket with jeans and a t-shirt. The outfit screamed "Trust me, I'm hip!" She sipped a steaming cup of Starbucks.

"I didn't ask for floater help at this event," I reminded her.

"I'm here to sign the best kids. I've got numbers to hit too, you know."

On paper we were teammates working towards the same goal. There was no reason she couldn't be here, especially under the guise of supporting our team. And she wasn't entirely wrong, there could be candidates for her in the mix, extra recruits I wanted help with. But it was my job to identify them and give them to her. She wasn't supposed to be here poaching them.

"Well, why don't you set up over there." I gestured to the other side of the booth.

"I think I'll work the front." She sipped her coffee. "You should've really stopped for one of these, so much better than the sludge they have here."

The sweat marks under my pits from setting up the booth had just dried, and I didn't want to sully myself by strangling her. Plus, there wasn't time. The gym clocks in their wire cages struck 9 a.m. and students filtered through the heavy double doors. Many, in suits but carrying backpacks, took a direct path to our booth. In 15 minutes, the queue of candidates waiting to talk to us grew to 20-deep. When word got out about the DeLorean, the wait grew exponentially and the line wrapped around our row. It didn't matter where Avery or I stood, we were inundated.

For the next six hours, with no break for lunch, I gave the same pitch and answered the same basic questions from every student that waited to speak with me. When kids made a good first impression, I marked their resume with a star. When they annoyed me or didn't seem qualified, I put a check. I felt a deranged sort of power when I checked yet another resume. That's life, I thought, your future decided by a 30-second conversation with me. At least you get a free t-shirt and a bouncy ball.

Many students, when they realized we were going to give away a car for a resume, skipped the wait for an introductory conversation and just dropped a resume in our box. The DeLorean was working.

When James and Julia—my MIT alpha wolves— rolled up, I abandoned my station. We had already exchanged so many emails that I felt like we were old friends. We huddled behind the table for a more private conversation, and I invited them to dinner that night. It was a restaurant I knew they had gone to for an anniversary last year. I also asked about Conor, the third part of the "holy trinity" and lynchpin to our alpha wolf strategy.

"Yeah, we know him. We have class today," James replied. "Not that he ever goes, but he aces everything anyway."

"If you see him, why don't you invite him out with us tonight?" I asked. Julia gave me a look that said no thanks, but they agreed to it anyway. When they left my booth, I watched them stop at DeBeers. I wondered if they were serious enough to be talking about a diamond or if he was just looking at the geo-engineering opportunities. I didn't have time to think more of it. The candidates kept coming.

Several exhausting hours later, my voice wrecked, the doors to the gym closed and the last of the students left the building. Avery handed me the box of resumes and grabbed her bag to leave. Thankfully, we hadn't interacted all day.

"Wait, Avery," I croaked. "Can I see the resumes in your bag?" She froze, and I knew I had caught her off guard. I'd seen her slipping CVs from our collective box into her giant alligator purse.

"Oh, you wouldn't be interested, they're all misfit kids. I did you a favor because now you have fewer resumes to comb through." She turned again to go, and I stepped in front of her.

"Really then, no big deal to let me see them. I can go through them quickly, right now." I took a step towards her, and she covered her purse like I was going to snatch it.

"I told you. I'll give you them later." She brushed past my shoulder, bumping me with the edge of her bag.

I watched her walk away with who-knows how many of my best candidates. "Bitch," I whispered under my breath. "Thanks for helping me pack up." I sat on the table, my back to the gym, and called Jeremy to tell him what happened. Those were his candidates too.

"Don't worry about it, Liv. The qualified resumes will be entered in the drawing for the DeLorean. Maybe she'll contact the kids first, but we'll get to see them, eventually. Our candidates won't want to deal with her. Did you meet the alphas?"

"Sort of," I said wearily. "I met everyone we've been emailing with. I talked to Julia and James. They're great kids. I'm taking them out to dinner tonight. But I didn't meet Conor."

"You still can." A voice startled me. How long had the student been standing there, listening to my conversation?

"Jeremy, I have to go. Call you later," I said, clicking off the phone.

"Can I help you?" I hopped off the table. The student was shorter than me, even with three inches of crazy red hair sticking up off his head.

"I'm Conor Walsh. You can meet me." He crossed his arms over the logo on his black t-shirt.

"Olivia Gesso. I was hoping to see you today. You're a hard guy to track down."

"That's on purpose."

"I understand." Conor didn't try to shake my hand

or show any interest in making a proper introduction. "I'm glad you're here. Better late than never." I tried to sound recruiter-grade cheery despite my cracking voice. "I'm taking Julia and James from your class out to dinner tonight. Want to join us?"

"Nah. I'll pass on dinner with Romeo and Juliet." Conor smirked and ran a hand through his wild hair. His eyes looked golden under his thick, auburn eyelashes. With his slight build, fiery coloring, and casual indifference, he reminded me very much of a feral cat—a beautiful, agile creature that was also incredibly destructive. I'd seen them decimate wild bird populations for dinner and swat butterflies for sport. On the islands, we trapped and euthanized the moggies, just like the rats.

"Another time then." I didn't want to come off as eager, but I needed to get him into the interview process. It felt like I was trying to get a date with a guy who wasn't into me. I didn't want to be desperate and scare him, but I needed to let him know just how interested I was, but then, he probably already knew that. I stuck to the basics. "Did you want to drop a resume? I mean, we are giving away a DeLor——"

"I don't have a resume."

"No?"

"Never needed one."

"At all?" I marveled at his confidence.

"Nope."

"Uhm, okay. Conor, are you interested in Kava Tech? I mean, you did come by," I pointed out, not sure what else to say to a kid that stopped by my career fair booth without a resume and who didn't want to be treated to dinner. And my throat was killing me. "Are there any questions I can answer for you? I'd love to have you interview, but I'll need your resume."

"Is Avery Stone here?"

"You know Avery?"

"Kinda." Maybe he'd seen her info plastered around campus. "Is it true what they say?" he asked.

"Say about what?" I leaned against the table, my feet hurting as much as my throat.

"About Kava. The parties and other *stuff*." He lingered on the word "stuff," and I instinctively crossed my arms. I reached for my auto-pitch.

"Kava Tech is a work hard, play hard kind of place. We take only the best people, who also fit our culture. And we like to have fun, while revolutionizing software-as-a-service. Here's my card." I pulled one off the display and handed it to him. "You can call me anytime to set up an interview. Whenever you're ready."

He inspected it and put it in his pocket. "Avery said I didn't need to interview."

"When did you talk to Avery?" Stealing a few career fair candidates was one thing, but poaching my alpha wolf was an act of war.

"A while ago," he shrugged. I wondered how she got his phone number. I had sent so many emails that went unanswered. "I came by to see her."

"You did? What'd she tell you?"

"Since I already have a standing offer with Pegasus, she said I didn't need to bother interviewing. That Kava Tech knew I was qualified."

Pegasus was that far ahead of me already? I couldn't believe that Avery knew all of this and didn't tell me. "Can you tell me about their offer? I'm sure we can beat them."

"I already went through all of this with Avery," he said petulantly and took a step away.

I backed off. It would be better to deal with Avery than irritate Conor. "Got it. You have my card. Call me whenever you want."

I let him leave with no handshake, no resume, and no rapport. I watched him pick his way across the other recruiters taking down their booths. He didn't stop to speak with anyone else.

The Green Belt

After a month of living in hotels and talking non-stop about Kava Tech to every student with ears, I was ready to go home. I needed to stop dancing the recruiter beat, to stop chasing alpha wolves, and to take a break from trying to outwit Avery. On the flight home, the situation I had pushed to the far corner of my mind roared back like a jet engine. Vegas. I hadn't spoken to Christopher since he kissed me, and minus a few late-night phone calls, Marion was nearly as distant.

I arrived home in time to catch the end of happy hour, the grackle birds chatting in the cedar woods. I went right for one of the plastic buckets and opened a Shiner Bock. Jeremy found me after my second sip.

"Welcome home," I heard through a spine-crushing hug.

"One day you're going to kill me like Lennie did to that mouse," I said, straightening my clothes.

"You'll be better off having experienced this much

man." He was drunk. It was Friday night.

"Looks like I'm behind."

"Big O, I have so much to tell you." He leaned in, lowered his voice, and raised his eyebrows. I laughed. My, he was ridiculous.

"Why are you whispering?" I took another swig of beer.

"Come over here and sit down," Jeremy said, glancing around. I followed him to the outskirts of the party. "The Julliard girl?" he asked.

"Amara Young. What about her?"

"Gone."

"What do you mean, gone?"

"Fired."

"For what? She was the hottest recruiter here." I was starting to sound like everyone else at Kava Tech. "They sent her to the big state schools. I'm sure she was a hit."

"Oh, she was a huge hit. Threw four massive parties. All at bars. Lost control of the last one. Cops got called. Some kids, underage, bought a bottle of Clase Azul on her Amex."

"What's that?" I asked.

"A $1,500 bottle of tequila."

I laughed. "We bought a $50,000 car. We're still here."

"Yeah, well, I guess they're waiting to see what we do with it. Amara's $1,500 went to an underage kid."

"Students get drivers licenses at 17. We're good." I sipped my beer. "It's a shame though, sounds like she was just doing what we've all been told to do."

"Yeah, bigger is better. More risk, more reward. It's all good, except when it isn't. And it got her fired. How are we supposed to know where that line is?" Jeremy asked.

"No clue. You sound paranoid. You need a smoke or something?" Jeremy looked spooked. "We're fine," I reassured. "You should be more worried about Avery."

Jeremy scoffed at her name, but he wasn't done talking about Amara. "Want to hear the best bit? *Techie Now Magazine* is doing an article on Kava Tech's college recruiting machine."

"Really? That's incredible. We'll be famous. Why don't you look happy?"

"Amara Young was the last person they interviewed for the article. The weekend before she got fired."

A lot had happened while I was in Boston. "So what? As long as the magazine doesn't get wind of it, it won't make the article. It'll be awesome press we can totally use," I said.

My phone rang, and I left Jeremy to his paranoid delusions.

"It's been too long," I sighed.

"It's about time you came back," Mars said. He sounded drunk too. "My place. Tonight?"

After the stretch I'd had in Boston, I didn't hesitate. Marion felt like a reward. "Now?"

"Later. I'll be home later. Let yourself in. Wait for me."

It was a booty call, and after weeks away, I didn't care. I hung out at happy hour as long as I could, listening to Jeremy's conspiracy theories on why

Amara was fired and how the *Techie Now Magazine* article might impact us on campus. Later I grabbed a cab to Marion's and left a trail of my clothes from his entry, up his steps, and to his bed. Then I promptly fell asleep.

I woke up to heaving, like a retching wildebeest was trapped in the bathroom. The clock glowed 5 a.m.

"Mars?" I asked, setting my feet down out of his bed. "Mars, you okay?" I walked towards the bathroom door, but he closed it, I presumed to spare me the horror. I heard him vomit again.

"Go," he mumbled through the door. Or maybe he said, "No," but I couldn't tell.

I stayed. I went downstairs, picking up my clothes along the way, and pulled a Gatorade from his fridge. I left it outside the bathroom door and went back to bed. When I woke up hours later, the bottle was half empty, the door was open, and Marion was passed out on the tile floor, his long legs scrunched against the wall, his head next to the splattered toilet. There was no waking him, so I got him a blanket, shoved a pillow under his head, and called myself a cab.

I was miffed he drank that much knowing I was waiting for him, and after not having seen me since that crazy night in Vegas. At home, I checked on the seeds. They reminded me to look out the window and remember that there was a big beautiful world out there beyond Kava Tech. I decided to spend my first free day in a long time out hiking.

I called Viola to see if she would go with, but she was away on a sales mission in Michigan. I thought she'd become the next big deal-closer. Next was William, who told me he didn't really go outside, but that he had to work anyway. I knew Jeremy was probably as hungover as Marion. So I called Christopher. I wasn't sure if it would be awkward, but I took a chance. He'd probably be working anyway.

When he answered the phone, he lied to his team. "Hey guys, I have to take this call. It's important." I held my breath.

"Hi, Liv." I heard a door close behind him. "You around?"

"You want to go hiking on the Green Belt? I can't make myself go into the office today. It's Saturday. I need a break. And it's beautiful out." Neither of us brought up Vegas. Some things were just easier to avoid.

"I'll meet you there."

"You sure? You can leave work, like, now?"

"Yeah. I'll see you there."

Christopher stood next to his car waiting for me at the entrance to the Green Belt, just off the highway. He had on a fly-fishing hat and had shoved a bottle of water in his cargo shorts pocket.

"I can't believe you beat me here. Need to get away?" I walked into his open arms and gave him a hug. Just like that, the weirdness I expected to feel vanished, and I was again with my friend.

"You have no idea. I've been in that room with that team for an eternity. Code for the product is moving. We've got to get customers interested and signed to pilot it, and people doing the right stuff to get a launch together."

"Sounds like a lot."

"It's ridiculous."

"Well, I spent the last month courting 22-year-olds and battling my own teammate for candidates. And a recruiter got fired." We set off on the trail, and I told him about everything that had happened while I was traveling.

He was quick on the crumbled shale path, his long legs easily outpacing mine. Months of boozing and restaurant food and copious amounts of sitting were killing my fitness. I worked to keep up while we exchanged battle stories from the office. We strategized about how to deal with one another's problems. I regretted having kept my distance since Vegas.

As the sun rose overhead, the temperature shot up fast and the scraggly trees along the trail offered no shade. We took a break where the path opened to a wide stream. The water ran gently around sun-bleached boulders and pooled at the bottom of an old growth oak. A tire swing dangled from a thick, low branch.

I dropped my backpack under the tree and took off my shoes and socks. I waded out into the swimming hole and climbed onto one of the boulders. I laid in the sun, my toes dipped in the faint current, and watched swallows dart over the water. Christopher sat on the shore, his feet in the stream.

I stretched out on the rock. "You know, I lived in a place where I felt like this every day." I told him.

"Felt how?"

"Peaceful. Happy? It was the most beautiful place

on Earth, until a hurricane decimated it. I haven't been back since."

"Where's that?"

"Rodrigues. A tiny island in the middle of the Indian Ocean."

"I didn't know that about you."

"There's a lot people here don't know about me."

"I know one thing."

"Yeah?"

"You're dating that board member. The one that's always at happy hour, that showed up in Vegas."

I sat up on the rock. "We're not dating."

"What are you doing then? What's his name? Marion?"

I sighed. "Do you hate me?"

"Why would I hate you?" he asked.

"I don't know." I shielded my face from the sun with my arm.

"How did it start? Do you really like him?"

I couldn't tell if Christopher was asking because he'd heard something or was just curious. "It doesn't matter. Can you just leave it be?" You got into Dartmouth because you ran track. You got a job at Kava because a board member thought you were hot. I didn't want to deal with it.

We stopped talking for the first time since we had started on the trail. Christopher skipped rocks across the water, wading in deeper to look for flat stones. After a while, he threw one that bounced into my foot. "Sorry," he said.

"It's okay." I rolled over to look at him.

"We should've brought swimsuits." He splashed water on his face and hair and took his glasses off to wipe them on the front of his shirt.

"I didn't think it would get this hot. But you know ... there isn't anybody here." He looked up at me. I don't know if I felt bad that he knew about Marion or if I just wanted his attention, but I stood up and unsnapped my shorts. "Why not?" I wiggled out of my pants, leaving them in a twisted pile on the rock. I threw my t-shirt on top and jumped into the cool water. I popped my head above the surface just in time to see Christopher, fully clothed, cannonball off the tire swing.

Like school kids, we took turns catapulting into the water. We tried to catch the iridescent dragonflies that buzzed our heads and splashed the birds that zipped out to eat them. I ignored my cell phone when it rang from my backpack, again and again. But it kept ringing, and I worried there was some emergency. I waded to the shore to check my caller ID. I shivered in the shade of the tree; the wet lace of my underwear stuck to my skin. Christopher watched from the stream.

The phone said I had missed 17 calls from Jeremy. I listened to a couple of frantic voicemails and pieced together that Conor Walsh was coming to Austin that night. How that had happened I had no idea, but it didn't matter. We had to put together a sell night, now. I threw the phone back in my bag.

"Christopher, I have to get back. I have an important candidate unexpectedly coming in tonight."

"It's okay. I should get back too. My team is probably freaking out that I'm not there." Christopher walked out of the water and stood close to me. I looked up at his hopeful face. He touched my cheek with the back of his fingers. "I really like you, Liv." He rested his hand on my shoulder and looked at me as though asking permission. "I know what you said, what you've got going on, but there's something that fills the space between us. I like the way it pulls me. Time with you feels right."

I needed to tell him 'no,' but I didn't have to. The voices of a hundred screaming children echoed up the trail, and someone yelled after them to wait.

"Shit." I ran through the water to the rock and scrambled on top. The kids neared, and I forced myself into my burning shirt and shorts. My damp foot got caught on the material, and I fell off the rock and into the water. I made it to shore, dressed and drenched, just as the Boy Scout troop swarmed the tire swing.

Christopher laughed from behind the tree and handed me my backpack. "Serves you right."

We talked the whole way back but never about Vegas and certainly not about Marion. What Christopher said wasn't wrong. I felt that pull too.

Cabs and Pigeon Shit

I found Jeremy dipping in our cube.

"How did this happen?" he demanded when he saw me. "Travel called and said he was coming. Who referred him?"

"Obviously Avery. The kid barely spoke to me at the career fair and hasn't responded since." I sat down next to Jeremy.

"Avery's not even supposed to be in town this weekend. Is she here? He's not her candidate." Jeremy packed more dip in his lip. "Doesn't matter. He's coming, and we have to do something about it."

We brainstormed a solution that involved piggybacking on some of the other recruiters' Saturday night plans. A lot of the state schools had resumed earlier than ours, so the candidates had already gone through on-campus interviews and moved on to on-site assessments and sell weekends. We expanded on the reservations already made, which involved a typical night of an expensive dinner and drinks, a show, and then dancing. There was no time to get a booking at a more exclusive restaurant or to get on the calendar of one of our top executives. It was not the night we would have put together for Conor, had we had any warning he was coming.

I went home to get my game face on for dinner. Instead of my usual jeans, I pulled one of Sky's pieces out of the closet. It was a jumpsuit with colorful embroidery along the neckline and spaghetti straps. It was unique, casual, and classy—an outfit that said this is what a future in Austin looks like. I rattled the tampon box for luck. I told the seeds I was going to the best seafood place in town.

At the restaurant, I looked for Conor among a big group of unfamiliar recruits. I wondered if he would show or if this was just a game to him, or maybe to Avery. My phone rang. It was Marion. I was still miffed about last night, but it didn't stop my stomach from twisting into a knot of hope and anticipation that I'd see him. I stepped outside, away from the noise.

He apologized for last night and offered to meet for dinner.

"You missed your chance. I'm at a sell dinner. An important one."

"Already? I didn't realize you'd be selling this fast."

"Me either. This one's out of order. Can I call you after?"

"Look forward to it."

"Me too."

Back inside, I paced the restaurant one more time, but still saw no sign of Conor. Just lots of fish frying in butter. I mingled with the recruits, made polite conversation, and got the drinks flowing. It was a big group, and I knew the other recruiters appreciated the help. When we sat for dinner, I had the staff put a reserved card in front of the seat next to mine.

Conor arrived with the main course. He looked freshly showered, his hair wet but combed back. He had on jeans, a white t-shirt, and a leather jacket. James Dean, without the cigarette. Instead of smoke, he reeked of Old Spice.

I stood to say hello and pulled his chair. With so many people talking at the table, his arrival went unnoticed. He looked around like he was waiting to be greeted by the other candidates. I wondered if he usually got recognized, like a celebrity in his nerdy tech circles. But not here, and Conor looked disappointed.

I got right to the point. "Jeremy and I didn't know you were coming until the last minute. How did that happen? We would've done things differently." I motioned to the large group and couldn't believe I was tacitly apologizing for taking him to a five-star restaurant.

"Avery invited me. I just met with her and Levi." He read the expression on my face and grinned.

"Are you interested in coming to Kava?" I asked, keeping a neutral face.

"Not sure what I want to do," he said. "Can I get a drink?"

I left for the bar, where I could seethe in private, even if just for a minute. Avery had stamped herself all over this hire, and fast, because I hadn't been aggressive enough. I had been cut out of the important stuff, like a meeting with Levi, but was here doing the entertaining. I came back with two gin and tonics. I clinked his glass and watched him gulp the cocktail. Five minutes later, he asked me to fetch another.

"Why don't we wait for the waitress. I'm sure she'll be around. Are there any questions I can answer for you, about Austin maybe? Or even the company? Or maybe you're hungry?" He had pushed a plate of surf and turf to the top of his setting.

"I already asked Levi the tech questions you won't be able to answer. And I know the recruiting towline. Avery made sure of that."

I took a sip of my drink, swallowing more pride with the liquor. I reasoned that if this kid came, I might still get some credit for the hire because I was here serving him and, after all, he was a star recruit. Even if I didn't, he would draw in others, alpha wolf style, and wasn't that the strategy? There were good reasons for me to keep at it.

Conor toyed with his cup of butter and eventually started eating. He dipped the steak in the grease and ate the lobster plain. I let him be and talked to the other candidates around me. After a while, he pointed out that I said the same things over and over.

"Most candidates have the same questions and

concerns," I shrugged. At least he'd been listening. Maybe it would be recruitment by osmosis with him— or brainwashing. I chuckled to myself about that and wondered if I was brainwashing candidates by telling them the same things repeatedly until they believed me. I was telling them the truth, wasn't I?

"What else do you do?" Conor asked. He leaned an elbow on the table and looked at me. "Besides answer the same four or five FAQs."

It was a weird question, but then again, this was a weird candidate. I pitched. "I'm hiring the next generation of geniuses, like you, to grow this incredible company. Recruiting is the lifeline of Kava Tech."

"But, like, is this it?"

"Is what it?"

"You go out to dinner every night?" I wondered if he was asking me this because Avery had commandeered his interview and offer process, but here I was buying his drinks and dinner.

"Often, yes. But it's more complicated than that. You interested in being a recruiter?" I flashed my brightest recruiter smile.

"Maybe I'm interested in being *with* a recruiter." He laughed the "Just Kidding" laugh.

And so did I, pretending to enjoy a joke I'd heard before. And then I got back to business. "So, with the right offer would you come here?"

Conor leaned back in his chair and looked confused. "I have an offer."

"Excuse me?"

"Levi made one tonight."

How had Avery not only skipped the interview process but also gotten Levi to make him an offer? Why didn't Jeremy and I think of doing that? Not only had she poached my star candidate, but she did it with the blessing of the founder. And she knew that if Conor came down, Jeremy and I would jump right in to take care of all the details—the hotel, dinner, and entertainment, which didn't matter that much because he'd already met with the damn CEO. But maybe all wasn't lost, I thought, if I could be the one to get him to sign the offer. That would turn the tables.

"Are you happy with the offer?" I fished. "Do you like what you see?" I sipped my drink and leaned in, "... of the company?"

"Honestly, this place seems like a bunch of Levi-worshiping zealots." He took another big gulp of what I thought was his third cocktail.

Conor was cocky, but this was a new level of rude. Maybe he was just using the Kava Tech offer for leverage to get other companies to offer him more? It was dating game psychology again—tell one lover you have another, and they'll want you more. It was possible he had no interest whatsoever in coming to Kava Tech. But then again, I could see the kid's point. Our company was kind of cultish.

I jabbed back to see what he would do. "Levi is buying you those drinks." I shook the ice in my glass.

"You know, maybe I do have some questions," he replied, his eyes everywhere but my face.

"Like?"

"Like, why did William Chang and the rest of that

MIT Course 6 class come here? Did they really want to make software-as-a-service? What's the fascination? Why not start their own companies? There must be *something* else."

He fixated on my cleavage, unabashedly staring. Unlike at the career fair, I didn't cross my arms. Is this what it's going to take, I wondered? I remembered what More had said about selling a vision of a future that couldn't be refused. Were my breasts really that vision? And, so what, I reasoned, if this little punk wanted to look, as long as he didn't touch me.

I reached for my drink, giving him a full view. "There is something else." Conor looked at me wide-eyed, waiting to be let in on a secret. I said it quietly, because the most important things are whispered, "Guys like William come because it's like nothing else they've ever experienced." Avery might have gotten him an offer, but I was going to sign him.

Conor looked from my chest to my eyes and back again. Then he retreated to his comfort zone. "I've got a company offering me more. More than Kava Tech or Pegasus."

Money was a game I could play. "Yeah? Who?"

"You wouldn't know them."

"Why not?"

"They're cutting edge. Totally private. They don't need tech cheerleaders."

"Tech cheerleaders?"

"Recruiters."

I bit my lower lip and let it slide through my teeth. "So where is this magical opportunity?"

"Boston."

I laughed. "So ... it's a couple of your friends hiding in a basement on Mass Ave writing secret code?"

"It's a serious company."

"In a freezing, over-priced, and traffic-choked city."

"I'm from Boston," Conor snapped.

"Whatever. It's stuffed with cabs and pigeon shit. The traffic sucks."

"My dad drives a cab!"

I shrugged. "If I were you, I'd take my chances here, with the Levi zealots and his bountiful cheerleaders."

Conor spent the rest of dinner with his back to me, talking to the candidate next to him. After dinner, we went to Ester's Follies, a downtown comedy gig. By the end of the show, I regretted what I'd said, and on the walk to the nightclub I thought about how to fix the situation. I dropped back from the group to call Jeremy. He didn't answer.

At the club door, I handed my ID to the bouncer in exchange for admission and a handstamp. As usual, the company had a private area roped off for the evening. Club dancers in Daisy Duke cut-offs and bra tops bounced around our lounge. We had our own servers and a couple of velour couches. I skipped by all of it, went straight to the bar, and ordered a double martini. I sipped and watched the candidates pound shots. I had seen only two female prospects all night, both of whom smartly decided to go home after the comedy show. There were now 30 dudes out on the town—a sex ratio only Kava Tech's recruiting department could balance.

Candidates started to dance with one another, which was my prompt to rejoin the group. I plastered on a smile and looked for the little shit I was supposed to be wooing, but I couldn't find him. Instead, another group of recruits I met at dinner danced their way to me. They made a tight, drunk, rhythmless circle. This was it. My job. I let them play the part of killer whales, grabbing, tossing, and toying with me, their limp seal. They high-fived and sloshed their drinks above my head, raining sticky pink Cosmo on my hair, shoulders, and chest.

The night only got sloppier. While the recruits partied, random people from the club befriended our open bar. They crowded the private lounge, the strobe lights illuminating their faces. Hands without bodies reached through the pulses of light, grabbing without accountability. It got hard to move, and I still hadn't found Conor. I bobbed my way towards the lounge chairs but got stuck again between dancing recruits. One grabbed my hips. He must have climbed over the couch, because there was no other way in. His arms around me, his jeans quickly becoming too thin a barrier between us.

I stared at the disco ball, as though up was a way out. I thought about elbowing the candidate off me, but I had already messed up with Conor and I couldn't ruin somebody else's hire. There was just no room to passively bump him off. I slipped my hand under his to pry his thumb loose. Then, I twisted in the tight space, his chest bouncing against mine. At least now I could face the problem. But he took this move the wrong way and pulled me closer, fish breath on my neck. I held onto his thumb with my fist. I just needed to get his other hand off my ass, and then I could make a go for the couch. Maybe I could pretend to fall, if I could just get his other hand off my ...

The recruit abruptly pulled away on his own. He looked at me, confused and then lurched forward. His forehead cracked my collar bone, a sharp, immobilizing pain. Hot chunks of half-digested seafood and tequila tumbled onto my breasts, seeping into my bra and dripping down my stomach. I two-handed shoved him backwards onto the couch and scrambled over the cushions. My heel punctured the velour and snagged on a coil, stranding me in a straddle, one leg over the vomiting recruit, another dangling over the back of the chair. I yanked hard. My heel snapped, and I tumbled to the floor behind the couch. I bounced up and smeared my way through the packed dance floor. In the bathroom, I vomited too, on the outside of the stall door.

There was no recovering, not with the unabsorbent cardboard rectangles that public restrooms call paper towels. I wiggled my shoulder in the mirror. My collar bone wasn't broken, just bruised. I held a swampy paper towel over the rising welt, but it didn't help. After a while, I limped back to Kava Tech's VIP area. Stinking like shark chum, at least people gave me space. I rooted in the couch for my purse stashed between two seedy cushions. On the way out, I finally saw Conor. He gave me a friendly wave and a triumphant smile from the bar stools overlooking the VIP area. He had a hand on the shoulder of the guy who had just hurled on me. Conor raised his drink giving me distant cheers. I stormed out the door.

I gimped towards Congress Avenue. There, I reasoned, hailing a cab would be faster than waiting for the one I called. But one look at me, and the drivers rolled up their windows and kept moving. Thirty minutes later, after promising I wouldn't vomit in his backseat, somebody agreed to take me home.

I called Jeremy, again, to tell him what happened. Maybe he could go to the club and save the Conor situation.

This time he answered, slurring my nickname. "Big O Gesssoh." I didn't have a chance to tell him anything. "Liv, you won't believe it. I just got a blow job from the waitress at——"

I screamed and threw the phone into the cab's partition. The driver kicked me out. It took an eternity, but I hailed another cab for home, took a hot shower, and then went to Marion's. His loft was all grey tile, right angles, and mirrors. His bed, pillows, and duvet were immaculate hotel white. They smelled of clean, and after my night, of sanctuary.

When I opened my eyes the next morning, Marion teased that I had finally earned my nickname, Big O.

"Stop it." I hid my head under the covers. "You were my outlet."

"Anytime sweetheart. You can do this." He encouraged.

"Do what? You?"

He tutted. "No. Hire these kids," he said. "Hire that kid. Last night was a blip."

I touched the lump on my collar bone. "Don't you stop thinking about this company? I don't want to talk about it," I said.

"Nope. It's all I think about. And don't you have a flight to catch?"

"Don't remind me." In a couple of hours, I would fly back to Boston for another month. I rolled out of bed and put on my undergarments. I couldn't find my t-shirt. I flopped back on the downy pillows and asked to borrow one. I watched Marion get out of bed. No shirt, pajama bottoms hanging off his hips. Every muscle an iron chain running under baby soft skin. I considered following him into the closet and making love on the floor, but he came out before I could commit to moving. He threw me a small, pink t-shirt.

I held it up. "Your girlfriend's?" I asked.

"No, but did you think you were my first?"

"I'm not wearing this." I threw it back at him.

"I thought you'd want something that fits," he said defensively.

"Can't I just I borrow one of yours?"

He put both palms up to show he would oblige. He handed me another shirt, and then went to check his phone.

Later, it wasn't just the flight, everything felt up in the air.

A Madam

One month on campus turned into another and then another. First-round interviews, introductory dinners, information sessions, career days, open houses, and career fairs packed my schedule. Marion, the seeds, Christopher, the tropical warmth of Rodrigues, when I did think of them, felt like a sideshow of indulgences that didn't fit into the world in which I was now immersed.

The constant travel improved my financial situation. Everything I consumed was expensed to the company, a company that had very successfully gone public. In Boston I missed all the fanfare, the ringing of the bell and the celebrations, but I didn't care because my shares were already worth $15,000. It was almost enough to cover both roulette games I'd played, though it would be a long time before I could sell. I emailed Sky updates on our investment.

With the market on the uptick, the company also

looked to launch HereBeer, and I knew the pressure was all on Christopher. I gave him the space I thought he needed, and that, maybe, I needed too, to focus on work. I also had to deal with Avery. After what happened with Conor, Jeremy and I agreed to let him air out and sit on the offer. There would be other opportunities to fix the damage, and we opted for patience. At least he hadn't turned us down, but Avery still had one of our star candidates in her pocket.

It made haggling with her over campus events that much harder, and we ended up agreeing to hold the DeLorean giveaway on Harvard's campus. We acquiesced because Avery booked the venue, the Hasty Pudding, without telling us, and losing the deposit would have attracted negative attention from management. It was well known in the recruiting department that we had a strained working relationship with Avery, and anything that jeopardized team goals was frowned upon.

Jeremy and I did our best to make lemonade from lemons, and I had to admit that the Hasty Pudding was pretty cool. It billed itself as America's oldest social club, having hosted the likes of John Quincy Adams, Theodore and Franklin D. Roosevelt, and John F. Kennedy, among many others of similar notoriety. While its list of prestigious members was as long as the club was old, this coming Friday night we would be its newest stars—the company that gave away a DeLorean. We micromanaged every detail, from the car's delivery (with a bow) to the impossible task of getting a panel full of Kava Tech's top executives, including Levi, in the same place, at the same time, to speak.

The advertisement for the car attracted thousands of resumes, but we only invited 200 of our most qualified candidates to the event. The Hasty Pudding was as small as it was exclusive, and this was the right message to send. We only wanted the best. This made candidates want us to want them. Funny, I thought, how that psychology works in both relationships and business. When I wasn't filtering stacks of resumes and haggling with Avery over which candidates to invite to the Pudding, I thought about that pink t-shirt and how much more I wanted Marion because of it.

I scheduled interviews every day of the week leading up to the event. A crescendo of brilliance, I saved my best kids from Harvard for Friday. My stars would interview by day and possibly win a car that night.

I set up shop for weeks at the Charles Hotel in Harvard Square. Unlike the Cambridge Marriott, my other home away from home, the Charles was a small, independently owned establishment. Nightly I slept on a down pillow top, wrapped myself in oversized chenille robes, and pocketed the tiny carved soaps and chocolates left by housekeeping. I indulged in the hotel's $50-a-person brunch of hearth-baked breads, lox, fresh-squeezed juices, and New England clam chowder. I eavesdropped from behind the *New York Times* on conversations about kids at Harvard, houses in the Vineyard, and decorators gone rogue.

I loved the Charles Hotel. And I imagined they loved me, or at least Kava Tech, which would spend some $100,000 on rooms this recruitment season alone. I had reserved five for the last couple of weeks. Three housed me and my two interviewers, and the two large suites I used for first-round interviews. I used to marvel at my monthly Amex bills, thinking I could rebuild all of Rodrigues for what this company spent on hotels alone. But it didn't take long to grow numb to the gross excess in which I worked, to forget I had friends and family sleeping in shelters. I no longer so much as glanced at my bills. I just tucked the receipts into my purse for reimbursement later.

I ran my interview process from the lobby. Ten hours a day I greeted nervous candidates, and told them what to expect.

"They're going to ask you object-oriented programming questions based on your C++ and Java knowledge. Are you ready for that?"

They would always nod.

"Also, there may be questions on distributed systems, client–server technologies, databases, and core Windows tech like OLE, MFC and DCOM. Sound okay?"

Again, they would nod. Some would flush. Others would pull notes from binders.

"But have fun," I'd say cheerily. "Kava Tech is about having a great time, while thinking your hardest. The best questions, I think, are always on artificial intelligence and application design. You might also discuss internationalization and compilers."

Truthfully, I had no idea what I was talking about. I memorized the pitch, which made recruits think even the recruiters at Kava Tech were brilliant. Some candidates looked determined. Others looked like they forgot to study for an exam. I marched them all the same up the elevators to the suite, where they would meet whatever techie interviewer I managed to have with me that day.

When the interviewer called me, 45 minutes later, I would guide the exhausted, red-faced, and sometimes sweaty or even teary-eyed recruit to a lobby chair for a quick debrief. I offered them a cool sip of water, got an idea of how they thought they did, and discussed follow-up protocol for possible on-site interviews in Austin. Then I sent them on their way and received the next round of kids.

For this final day of first-rounds, I pried William and Viola from their work in Austin to interview for me at the Charles. I looked forward to spending time with my friends, a rarity in Boston, and showing them what I had accomplished.

That Friday morning I dressed for evening. There would be no time to change between the end of the interviews at the Charles and the event at the Hasty Pudding. I wore a fitted gray dress and a string of pearls that would transition well from day to evening wear. I usually worked in flats, but instead opted for a pair of sharp, 3-inch, black patent leather heels. I put on a lot of makeup. Dark lipstick, eyeliner, and mascara. Too much for the sunny, gold striped wallpaper of the Charles lobby, but later it would look great on stage at the Pudding.

By midday we had interviewed half of the day's recruits. I treated Willy and Viola to a quick lunch, and we returned within the hour to meet the next crop of candidates. We had made it ten heel-clicks into the lobby when the hotel manager, accompanied by a security guard, stopped us.

"Olivia Gesso." He addressed me, his little gold badge reflecting the afternoon sun.

"Yes?"

"You need to conclude your affairs at this hotel," he said sternly.

"I'm sorry?"

"We need you and your associates to cease your activities in this establishment and leave. Immediately." The security guard took a step forward, looking at Willy and Viola.

"What?" I shifted the weight of my laptop bag from one shoulder to the other. "There must be some confus——"

"We have been observing you for weeks. We will not tolerate any such business at our hotel."

"What business? What are you talking about? I have 12 more recruit——"

"Hi, Olivia." My first candidates of the afternoon arrived, their hair wet from a recent shower. They looked eager. "We can't wait for tonight." William, Viola, and I shook their hands, and turned back to the men who eyed the recruits and glanced at one another.

"Are these Harvard students?" the manager asked.

"Yes. Of course they are," I said.

"I'm sure the University wants no part of this. If you don't leave immediately, we will be forced to involve University authorities."

"Excuse me gentleman, but I have no idea what you're talking about. I have interviews to run, for my company, Kava Tech." I motioned to the candidates and to Willy and Viola. "I paid for the use of this hotel, in advance. I do not appreciate this unwelcome interruption to our business, which I remind you spends quite a sum at this establishment. Now if you would like to tell me what——"

The manager turned to the security guard. "Do we need to phone campus police?"

"What on Earth for?" I demanded.

"This hotel will *not* be party to this *service* you are running. We will not tolerate illicit proceedings on our premise."

"*Service*? What do you think I'm doing here?" People in the lobby took notice of the unfolding confrontation. The manager suggested we step into a conference room. We followed him through a heavy wooden door to a long wooden table.

"We aren't sure what you're doing," the hotel manager gestured to our group, "but we have watched you ferry young adults to and from privately rented rooms for 45-minute intervals all day, every day. Enough is enough. We want nothing to do with such affairs."

It made sense from their perspective. Here I was, a young woman wearing a ton of makeup and sharp heels, scuttling students to hotel rooms for "quickies" with other young people who I changed out every day. I had new interviewers all the time, men and women. My prospects looked nervous when they arrived and a sweaty mess when they left. I laughed aloud when I realized what the hotel was worried about.

"I am not running a prostitution ring," I said. "We're a start-up technology company conducting campus interviews." I looked at the recruits. "Isn't that right?" They peeped yes and stayed pressed to the wall. "Show them what you brought. They have resumes and computer science notes with them. Not the things you bring to a paid sexual encounter." Everyone in the room blushed, and William stifled a snicker. "The university knows us. They know me. We're always presenting at career services and running campus events. Call career services, they'll tell you."

"If you like, I can certainly call and involve them, or even the Boston police, if that is preferable. Though I doubt anyone here wants that kind of attention," the manager said.

"Willy, Vi, show him your company badges. These are my interviewers. They aren't prostitutes. And I am not a madam. Your accusations are offensive and absurd." William pulled out his badge with a smirk.

The manger didn't budge. "Ms. Gesso, we have many distinguished guests at this hotel. We do not permit corporations to run unsanctioned events from our lobby. At the very least, your operations are disruptive, or have the appearance of disruption. You are loitering in the lobby, excessively. This is a violation of hotel policy."

"But I paid——"

"The hotel will refund you for the unused reservations. Do not book with us again."

"You will regret this."

"I sincerely doubt it. You have an hour to vacate or we will involve additional authorities." The manager glanced at the stone-faced security guard.

I left the conference room with Willy, Viola, and the two recruits in tow, who I had to send home. The manager was right, I didn't need negative press, or want the involvement of the police. Even if everything got resolved, I'd be late to the Pudding. I imagined being detained at a police station for prostitution while Avery presented on stage next to Levi.

An hour later, William, Viola, and I schlepped our luggage to the Border Cafe, a Mexican restaurant down the street. The candidates that I could reach on the phone interviewed against the backdrop of multi-colored Christmas lights and telenovelas. The ones I couldn't reach got stood up in the hotel lobby. I fretted over what the front desk told my best kids when they asked for my whereabouts. I spent all afternoon sending apology messages and trying to reschedule my star interviewees for later. It was a mess.

By evening, at least I had scored us rooms at the Cambridge Marriott. On the cab ride over, I rested my head in my hands. Viola patted my back.

"It's okay," she assured.

"You know Liv, this trip is such a gift. Thank you for that," William said quietly.

I sat back and looked at him. "How's that, Willy?"

"Big O Prostitution Ring Shattered." He waved his hands, palms open, displaying the fictitious headline. "Wait until the company hears about this."

He was laughing hysterically. "Big O Gesso, the Madam of Harvard Square. A new way to improve your Big O algorithm performance." Viola snorted.

"It's not funny, William. They almost called the police. Imagine."

"But they didn't. Come on, Liv. Or should I say, *Madam O*. It's hilarious." William persisted. Viola was still laughing. I put my forehead back down on the cab's partition.

When we got to the hotel, I apologized and handed Viola the key to the room we would share. "There were only two rooms available on such short notice," I told her.

"Liv, it's okay." She handed the key back to me.

"What do mean? Where're you going to stay?" I asked.

Viola looked at William, who looked at his feet.

"You're kidding me?"

"I was going to tell you," Viola insisted.

"How long's this been going on?"

"Vegas. But we'd appreciate it if, you know, you kept it on the down low," William said.

I looked at him and narrowed my eyes. "If I hear one word about a Madam O prostitution ring, your secret will be frontpage company news. Got it?"

William shook my hand. "Deal, but you know you could join us, Madam O, for a threesome, like later, if you——"

Viola slapped the back of his head.

Hasty Pudding

I stashed my luggage in my room and went back to the lobby for a complimentary cup of coffee. I nursed the caffeine in a cushy lobby chair and stared out the large glass entrance. A small army of hotel workers hung Christmas decorations out front. The day wasn't over, I thought, but I had another break coming. Soon my campuses would turn into holiday ghost towns. Through February we would give kids the space to take exams, go home for winter recess, and start their last semester. Maybe we would send some thoughtful holiday gifts.

A black Mercedes pulled into the hotel roundabout and a tall, suited man, his back to me, opened the door for a lady. They stood kissing, leaving the bellhop unsure if he should greet them or look away. When the couple turned to come through the open door, I spat my coffee back in the cup and hid in the chair. Price Johnson, the Pegasus recruiter, was mugging

Avery Stone. He kissed her one last time, before she hurried, head down, rollaway luggage behind her, to the elevators.

As soon as they were gone, I grabbed a cab and called Jeremy on my way to the Hasty Pudding.

"She's sleeping with the enemy," I told him.

"But what does it mean?" Jeremy asked.

"I don't know if she is playing us or him. No way to tell," I said.

"Maybe both."

"What do we do?"

"No idea. She'd deny it. Your word against hers. We don't want that mess," he cautioned.

We didn't have time to speculate further. My cab dropped me at the Pudding. Avery arrived 20 minutes later. I greeted her at the door.

"Hey, Avery. I didn't realize we were both staying at the Marriott. I would have offered to share a cab, but I didn't want to interrupt."

"I thought you were at the Charles," she said, stuffing her gloves in her pockets.

"Last-minute switch. It was hectic, but everything is fine. You looked, uhm, busy, when you arrived." Avery stood motionless. "You haven't spoken to Conor, have you? I asked him if he was coming tonight, but I haven't heard back. No surprise there. Such a difficult candidate. What does he think of his offer? Thanks for helping with that."

Avery cleared her throat and brushed her bangs out of her eyes. "I haven't heard from him."

"Well, I wonder if he's still considering Pegasus.

Maybe you could use your connections to find out." Avery's cheeks flushed. "But now," I said, "we should focus on tonight."

I left her standing at the door and cheerily commissioned the Pudding staff to set up. They brought me a box of company literature I had planned to give candidates as they arrived. I stacked the navy folders on the entry tables and flipped one open to inspect the marketing materials. The first headline, reprinted on heavy cardstock, was the *Techie Now Magazine* article. It was titled, 'Sirens on the Rocks.' They'd published it a few days ago, and I guessed Jeremy had gotten copies for the folders.

The feature opened with a group shot, Amara Young in the center. She sat on a stool, with Kava Tech executives standing around her, looking ambitious. Marion was in it too, his arm draped around her shoulder. She smiled at him like they were sharing a private joke while the others looked at the camera. The caption read, "Kava Tech's founding members support recruiting any way they can."

Marion had never said anything to me about being in the magazine article. Plus, he wasn't a founding member or even an employee. But, I thought, why wouldn't Kava feature the prettiest people possible. And who could blame him for wanting to be in the hippest tech magazine in America. Or, and the thought soured my mood, maybe he wanted to be next to her, Amara.

I skimmed the article. It oozed standard company propaganda. All our buzzwords—young, hip, stocked kitchens, massage chairs, parties. On the next page was another photo. Amara in a white string bikini, posed on the helm of a Kava Tech speed boat, Marion at the wheel. Behind him on the bench sat three recruits, gawking at her. The caption read, "Kava Tech's Amara Young is the ultimate human resource."

I jumped to the text below the photo. "...Kava Tech is battling to hire the best software developers in the country. And no other company can match their 'military' might—an army of bombshells in bikinis on boats also known as college recruiters. While these babes don't have to be the smartest, they certainly have to hire the smartest, and they are doing just that. Kava recruiters find and sign top talent by showing their candidates the best of their company's crazy, high-risk, high-reward culture."

The candidates were arriving. I skipped to the next paragraph, "... nerds with unlimited venture cash, the company is a camaraderie of tech geniuses who love to party; who love their cult-like brotherhood; and of course, who love their babes on boats."

I snapped the folder shut and threw it on top of the pile. How hard had I worked to have my job trivialized to a string bikini? *Babes on boats?* I had read all 60 books in my welcome folder. I'd studied psychology, communications, and marketing since coming to Kava Tech to get good at recruiting. I'd learned and perfected public speaking. I had crafted individualized sell strategies for hundreds of candidates from my campuses. And my department was full of women just like me, Amara included. What about the fact that she had studied theater at Julliard? Why didn't they talk about her credentials for doing this job? Instead, we had to read about her damn bathing suit.

I graduated the Ivy League. "They don't have to be the smartest ...?" Why did we only hear about how brilliant the software developers were? Kava used the same standards for hiring recruiters as it did its coders. We were top graduates too, even if it wasn't in computer science. But nobody wanted to see us as academic powerhouses. Was it because our skillsets went beyond the letters and numbers of a keyboard? Was it because we were attractive women?

I was not a madam building a "cult-like brotherhood." Kava was a bunch of crazy geeks, for sure, but they were my friends. Willy, Christopher, Viola, Jeremy—they were my best friends. Maybe they got a little wild sometimes, but they cared about this company and they cared about me. And I was trying to hire more people like them. Candidates started arriving in earnest.

I took a deep breath and uncrossed my arms. I channeled my recruiter autopilot; she was in there somewhere. Company executives and prospects had to arrive to smiles, hugs, and firm handshakes. I handed the folders out, greeting everyone who came. "I'm thrilled you made it ... So thankful you're here ... Come, let me get you a drink." Two hundred invitees filled the room quickly. "Have you met the CTO? Or maybe you'd like some time chatting with the CFO?" A hello, an introduction, and a hand-off, as fast as possible.

I stayed by the door. James and Julia came. I brought them to Avery who brought them to Levi. Conor never showed. Some of my Harvard kids from today were also missing. It didn't matter, the scallops were sizzling in their bacon. The party was bumping. Like a wedding, months of planning unfolded in minutes. In a room filled beyond capacity, I made my bridal rounds thanking each guest again for coming.

Redundant conversations tangled into a dull roar.

"Offer."

"Market."

"Solutions."

"Can I get you more wine?"

"Paradigm."

"Engine."

"Growth."

The drinks were sweating in their palms.

"Sales."

"Innovative."

"Destiny."

The flower arrangements stood tall and resolute.

"Bonus."

"IPO."

"Network."

"Future."

"The pigs in a blanket are delicious."

Avery silenced it. She called the leadership to the stage. She handed me the mic for the welcome, and I was ready, my jokes rehearsed. I should have been nervous, but I felt hollow. 'Sirens on the Rocks.' Angry. No matter what that article said, I was so much more than a pretty face in a string bikini. We all were. I picked up my chin and looked out over the school of fish that were supposed to jump in my boat.

"Good evening. And thank you for coming. I know most of you so well, it's like you're old friends, if not family. That's what happens when you spend too much time drinking together. Kava Tech's leadership can attest." I glanced at the executives behind me. Everyone chuckled. "But this company is more than a family—it's a *brotherhood*. *Techie Now Magazine* saw this when it featured us in this month's issue." I spun the press. Papers rustled.

"In a few short months, you will all start your careers, somewhere. Last year, when I was in your position, a senior graduating the Ivy League, I wanted to save the world. But instead, Kava Tech saved me. I was a biology major and I thought I was going to travel the globe saving endangered species, like one of those crazy National Geographic types. Because you know, that sort of work pays really well." I got another laugh out of the crowd.

"And then I met a recruiter from Kava Tech. And I learned how this fast-paced company was revolutionizing everything from dress code to source code. How it was driving global industry, putting software-as-a-service at the core of the future. And I saw an opportunity, a chance to make a different kind of impact, to support a company that's creating efficiencies, and well, let's be honest, creating wealth. I'm sure you've read about our IPO. Ideals are important, but you have to eat. Did I mention Kava Tech has fully stocked kitchens?" The room gave me another hearty giggle.

"At Kava Tech, I wouldn't be pursuing some youthful, naïve ideal that—somehow and for no money—I was going to be a do-gooder and save the environment. Instead, I would help build a team, a network of the smartest people in the world, who would change the global economy with the very products they created. I realized that making the planet a better place didn't have to be a zero-sum game. At Kava Tech, I could have it all—an incredible network of colleagues that felt like family, an impactful and important job, all while participating in incredible wealth generation opportunities. We make products that make people's lives better—so they can get the things they need and want faster and more efficiently. When companies do better, people do better.

So here I am, barely a year out of college, fulfilling my dreams in ways I never imagined possible, thanks to Kava Tech. I am a highly valued member of a company built around a high risk, high reward—work hard, play hard—mentality. We'd like for you to join us. As I turn the floor over to the people you really want to hear from, I encourage you to listen to their fascinating stories. I hope you see Kava Tech for what it is. Thank you."

The crowd erupted into applause, and I gave them a gracious smile. I handed the mic back to Avery and returned to my chair on stage. I sat, attentively, not listening to anything anyone said. I stood on cue when Levi pulled the winning resume. An excited young man in a suit tripped up the steps to receive the keys. Out front, in the brisk Boston wind, we huddled around the car for a photoshoot.

Later, the Harvard Crimson headline read, "Kava Tech Gives Lucky Engineer Keys to the Future."

It's Just Business

We rang in 1999 like that Prince song said we should. So did the stock market. These days, Atlas had bull horns, not shoulders, and Kava Tech was the matador. Analysts predicted that Kava would be the world's leading SaaS provider. Plus, eight months after he called out his idea on our first day of work, Christopher launched HereBeer. To signal the strength of its position to the industry's shareholders and investors, Kava Tech spared no expense throwing lavish HereBeer launch parties on both coasts, and of course, at its corporate home base in Texas.

For me, the HereBeer launch party in Austin was a chance to reconnect with Marion and to congratulate Christopher. While I welcomed any move on the company's part to boost its valuation, I also looked forward to attending a black-tie affair that I didn't organize, and for which I was not the servile entertainment. And it was good to be home in Texas. I never thought I'd say that.

I pulled a little black dress from my closet, another hand-me-down from my fashion-forward college roommate before she left for her European shopping spree she called a Fulbright. The dress label read Emilio Pucci, whoever that was. I remembered asking Sky why she didn't want to keep a black dress—something practical that never goes out of style.

"Because angular cuts are over. Next season will be all soft curves," she explained.

Her reasoning was lost on me. I never looked at the dress to figure out what she meant, just shoved it in my closet. But now, I understood. Mr. Pucci must have liked triangles. A V-shaped cutout plunged below my breasts in the front, the material barely wide enough to cover my girls on either side. The back was similarly cut, which made it impossible to wear panties, a bra, or stockings. Mr. Pucci made getting dressed easy. The only thing I had to do—the only thing I could do—was pull the hidden zipper and hope my lady parts remained hidden too.

I arrived at Austin's Driskill Hotel solo and commando. Built in the late 1800s, it was the city's oldest establishment and was rumored to be haunted. Inside, massive longhorn taxidermy, cowhide rugs, and leather chairs warmed cold expanses of marble and Texas-sized chandeliers. Blazing medieval fireplaces lit heavy oak adornments, and firelight danced up the grand staircase. I looked but didn't see any ghosts. Instead, I found the entire company dressed in formal wear mingling with the Texas business community. I moved through the rooms greeting colleagues who were hard to recognize with combed hair and shiny close-toed shoes.

More waved me over.

"Olivia, this is Bill Watts," she said, expecting me to know.

"Uhm? Oh. Hello." I remembered he was the founder of a medicinal herbs mail-order company called Congo Scripts headquartered out in San Jose, California. The business had blown up big and Bill Watts was already very rich like Levi.

More said to Watts, "Olivia is a star recruiter who will definitely help launch the product."

Launch what product, I wondered. Did she mean HereBeer? I pretended to understand.

"Well you've all certainly made headlines," Watts said. "And it's a product we would certainly consider using."

"Thank you," I said, and that was that. I didn't get to ask why a medicinal herb company was interested in the HereBeer product before More led him away to talk to someone else. I took my cue to move on and went looking for the bar. Planted there, no surprise, I found William, Viola, and Jeremy sharing a drink.

"I met Bill Watts," I announced. "My second billionaire, if I count Levi."

"Killer dress, Liv."

"You too." I hugged Viola.

"The Big O." Jeremy held a beer. "Looking good."

"Madam." William grinned and hugged me.

"I didn't think we could all pull this off—the entire company looking so adult," I said, toasting my friends. We took our drinks to a standing table in the corner, prime real estate for people-watching. Jeremy started talking recruiting at MIT with William. Viola and I had a contest to see who could identify the most men under 30 worth over $20 million.

I conceded. "Fine, you win. I know college seniors; you know real people."

"I heard Matthew McConaughey and Sandra Bullock were invited," Viola said.

"I know who they are. I'll introduce you when I see them."

"The hell you will. I'll introduce myself," Vi said. "Besides, there's Christopher, the real star of the night."

In a tuxedo, Christopher looked like a man. The cut of his jacket filled out his shoulders. The thick black material hid what I knew were skinny arms toned to type on a keyboard. But, looking at him tonight, his hair slicked back, he looked elegant.

"That's surprising," I said.

"He cleans up nice," Viola agreed and looked at me in that way.

"Oh no," I said quickly. "Absolutely no."

"Why not?" Viola pressed.

"Because. You know why not."

"Marion?" She snarked his name.

"Because. He's my friend. Have you seen Marion?" I asked, hopeful.

Viola shook her head. "You haven't either?"

"We're in touch, but it's been a while," I admitted.

"What happened?"

"Nothing. I travel. He travels. It's not like he's my boyfriend. I just ..."

"You just what?"

"Nothing. We've both been super busy."

"That's your excuse?"

"There's more," I admitted and told her about the pink t-shirt. I didn't mention the *Techie Now Magazine* article, how Amara gazed up at him in that photo. It was stupid to feel the way I did. She didn't even work for Kava Tech anymore.

"So?" Vi shrugged.

"I don't know. Something felt off, all of a sudden." I shook my drink ice. "I'm ridiculous."

"I'm sure you'll see him tonight, if you want to."

"Or how about right now?" I pointed to Marion, who walked over to greet Christopher and the small group of people around him.

Vi sighed.

"I know."

"He's like a black hole," Vi said. "Attracts all the energy in the room, a vortex of hotness. If Christopher is tonight's star, Marion swallowed him whole."

"He's definitely got a celestial body," I joked, and she laughed. "Mars burns hot."

"Actually, Mars is really cold. Temperature can drop to——"

"What's she doing here?" I interrupted.

"Who?"

"Amara Young. Wasn't she fired?" Jeremy and William were now paying attention.

Jeremy answered. "Modeling."

"What?" I spat.

"Rumor is that she was going to call *Techie Now Magazine* to re-interview after she got fired. So Kava Tech offered her a new position to keep her happy and quiet. She's now the face of HereBeer. Willy, grab that." Jeremy pointed to a brochure on a nearby table. Willy handed Jeremy a tri-fold marketing brochure that featured Amara leaning against the wall, holding a sweaty beer to her chest. "They're using her for all the Kava marketing materials. At least that's what I heard," Jeremy said.

I looked from the brochure to the real thing, standing across the room. A rose-colored slip of a dress clung to her slender curves as she cat-walked over to Marion and Christopher. Christopher greeted her and quickly put his hands in his pockets. Marion kissed her cheek and spoke in her ear. She giggled and put her hand on his elbow. He introduced her to the others in the group. They took turns ogling, all eyes, all attention on her.

"She's the other black hole," I said to Viola. "What happens when two black holes collide?"

"They eat each other. And become one giant black hole."

We finished another round of drinks before I excused myself to congratulate Christopher. I pulled him away from a group of developers and gave him a hug.

"You look amazing," he said, holding my shoulders.

"You too. You've come a long way since running

me over with your car. Has it all been worth it?"

"Hitting you or launching HereBeer?"

"Both," I said.

"Yes, and yes, so far anyway. But we'll see how things go," he winked, "and wait till you see the car Levi's buying me." He pushed his glasses up his nose, grinning proudly. "You'll never get out of the way of that one."

"Dance?" Christopher didn't budge. "Come on, dance with me. Can't be worse than your driving." I grabbed his hand and he gave in, following me to a space in front of the band. I put his hand on my lower back. "Like this."

"Got it." He looked down at his feet.

"I'm better looking than your shoes."

He looked up, embarrassed. "For sure."

"So, tell me. What's there left to do? Your code is all written and your product launched into outer space. You lounging around eating Cheetos?"

"Oh Liv, as if. Nobody's talking about how the product barely functions."

"For real?"

"It's okay, but there are a million things to fix. So many weak spots, like jokes written into the code."

"That's hilarious."

"No, it's not."

"Well, when all my geniuses sign on, you can recruit a few to work on your team."

"That'd be good. Levi put Melissa Burge on sales, so things are going to start moving fast."

"Spin me. Like this." I took his hand and twirled

myself out the length of his arm. He pulled me back to his chest.

"I like it when you're closer," he said.

"I heard Melissa is super intense."

"But she's really good. She already got distributors signed on for a trial."

"You sure it wasn't the photos of Amara straddling the kegs that got them to sign?"

Christopher laughed. "I'm sure it didn't hurt. Christ, she's hot. We all watched that photoshoot. I still can't get those images out of my head. That photographer had quite a good time splaying her all over the place. We used the tamer pictures for the brochure. I mean, we're a reputable product, not a music video."

"The dev team was there?"

"They wanted a few pictures of the HereBeer team too, you know, to hide in the back of something somewhere. But we all just sat around drooling over Amara."

I couldn't explain the annoyance that welled from my gut to my ears and drowned out the jazz. I'd had enough of Amara Young, in pictures and in conversation. "You know what? I'm sorry, but I didn't get a chance to say hi to Marion."

I jerked my hand out of Christopher's and briskly sidestepped the couples around us. I heard him call out my name, but I didn't turn around. I weaved my way faster through the crowd. In another room, at the bar, I found Mars. I caught him alone, sipping Scotch. He put his drink down when he saw me coming. And I knew from the way he looked at me, and my dress that was barely there, that I could have whatever I wanted.

"Won't you offer a lady a drink?" I asked, breathing in his cologne when he kissed my cheek.

"I would, if the lady would ever make the time to talk to me." His dimples danced.

"A gentleman should come to her."

"I'm no gentleman." He motioned to the bartender to serve a second drink.

"No, you certainly aren't."

"But I do know how to show a girl a good time, especially when she looks as gorgeous as you." He traced the edge of my dress near my collarbone, and I felt the inescapable pull of the black hole, my own gravity no longer holding me in place.

"It's been so long I've forgotten," I lied.

"Maybe tonight I can remind you, if you're free." He lifted his chin towards something behind me. Christopher.

"Oh, Jesus," I said.

"Liv, what was *that* about?" Christopher demanded.

"Hi, Chris. You know Mars."

"Yeah." Christopher didn't offer a handshake. He spoke to me. "Look, I was telling you that ... she's hot, but I'm ..."

"It's fine." I held up my palm, Jerry Springer Show-style to interrupt him. "I'm in the middle of something. Can we catch up later? Please."

Christopher looked from Marion to me. He walked away muttering and shaking his head.

"Your drink." Marion handed me a Scotch. "Got

the star developer wrapped around your finger?"

"Please, Mars. He's a friend."

"Have you told him that?"

"What? No."

"No?" He raised his eyebrows.

"I didn't think I had to."

A group of guys in tuxedos joined us at the bar. They looked like one another. Young, well-groomed, and monied, but lesser versions of Marion. They came up burly, chiding each other, and quickly enveloped Marion in their gang. From their jokes, I realized he had played golf with them earlier that day. They were lawyers or bankers or something. Mars leaned down to my ear and whispered, "Excuse me for now, but I'm serious about later."

I spent the rest of the night dancing with company friends. When I saw Christopher again, it was his turn to hold up a palm. I tried to feed him some explanation of why I needed to talk to Marion, but he was curt.

"Liv, I don't know what your issue is, but it's fine. I don't care. You don't owe me anything."

After that, I left him alone. Later, as the party wound down, I saw Viola and William sneak out the door within 30 seconds of one another. I went to get my shawl from the coat check, wondering if I should end my night by finding and apologizing to Christopher or by hunting down Marion. I didn't have to choose. I ran into Marion and his entourage of tuxedos, visibly drunk, in the tiny coat check room.

Marion put a heavy arm around my shoulders, pulling me to his chest. "Gentleman, may I introduce

Olivia Gesso? Our best recruiter. Handpicked by me."
He gave me a squeeze and waved a Vanna White arm
towards the group. "Olivia, these gentlemen are good
friends of the company."

This time, I shook their sweaty palms.

"I saw the *Techie Now Magazine* article. Heard a lot
about recruiting," one tuxedo said.

"We're making a name for ourselves," I agreed.

"Why don't you come with us, you know, to an
after-party?" another asked. He had, I assumed, his
girlfriend with him. She looked too drunk to stand
on her own. I wondered if he wanted to bring me as
company for her.

I glanced at Marion who shrugged a "Sure, why
not?"

"Come with us," the tuxedos urged.

Marion handed me my shawl, and I followed the
group out of the hotel. A driver opened the front door
to a SUV waiting on the street. I rode quietly up front
while the boys in the back cracked jokes and poured
more whiskey, passing me a glass over the console.

Fifteen minutes north of downtown, we took a
roundabout off the highway and drove for another
few minutes down a road devoid of street lights. The
driver stopped in front of what looked like a stucco
box air-dropped onto a square of superbly manicured
property in the middle of Texas nothingness. The plush
green grass that surrounded the building cut straight
lines into the dry prairie grass and shale pebbles that
were everywhere else. The boys left the other girl
passed out in the back of the car and told the driver

to wait with her. We walked down a brick sidewalk to a dark entrance hidden behind sculpted shrubs.

"Is this the part where you all strangle me?" I joked.

The men laughed. Mars gave me a sideways smirk and put his finger to his lips—shush.

At the door, an enormous man dressed in a tight, white button-down shirt greeted Marion by name. I could see multiple tattoos through the thin material that hugged his arms. He escorted us into a room full of red velour seating, heavily polished, dark walnut tables—and strippers.

"You're cool, right?" Marion murmured to me as women in flower-shaped nipple pasties and G-strings pulled plush chairs for us to sit.

"Of course." But it felt like the first time I saw people sniffing cocaine off a bathroom sink at a university party. I was vastly uncomfortable, but I knew the rules from college: act like you've been there. I leaned back in my chair confidently and looked at the men. They were friends of the company, after all, here for Christopher's product. And then I felt badly for how I had treated my friend. Did I ruin Christopher's night? Could I make it up to him, somehow, by helping here with these guys? Talk up his product? One more reason to be cool. Why was I so prickly about Amara? I didn't even know her. Plus, now, I was surrounded by 30 naked Amaras. One leaned in to take my drink order. Her sweet perfume lingered through the thick cigar smoke.

I ordered like the guys. "Chivas. Neat." I tried not

to stare, and instead, stole glances around the room. Bouncers, sized and dressed like the one at the door, stood vigilantly at the perimeter. The tables were set spaciously apart, except for near the stage which jutted outward, dividing the room in half. Along its edge, naked girls swung with uncommon strength from poles anchored to the ceiling. Men in suits, ties loosened at the neck, stared at them or at televisions. There were almost as many screens as dancers, each airing a different sporting event. One table over, a girl gave a patron a lap dance. Some with him watched, while others checked the burn on their cigars. The client slid a thick roll of bills into her panties.

Marion called my attention back to the table when the drinks arrived. "To HereBeer."

"To Kava Tech," said a tuxedo. And we threw back our tumblers. A barmaid refilled the drinks. A long rope of faux diamonds swung when she reached for their glasses, but her remarkable breasts did not move. His chair behind mine at the circular table, Mars watched me watch. The tuxedos chatted, distracted by the endless parade of service.

"I've opened and closed a lot of business here," Mars said in my ear.

I leaned close to hear him over the stage music. "It's a man's world," I said.

"It is, but really, we're all suffering here." He sipped his drink, but I nearly choked mine back into the glass laughing.

"Clearly. I can see you all writhing in pain."

"We're damned to want what we can't have. Look,

but don't touch the girl. Or the multi-million-dollar deal that's just out of reach. These girls know how to give a glimpse of what's possible. They make you smell it, get so close you can taste it. You can't help but imagine how it will feel to sink all the way in. You'll do anything, pay anything to get it."

"I'm sure for enough money, you could have anything here you wanted," I said.

"Exactly. For enough money, you *can* have anything in business, here or anywhere. It's about making them, he motioned to the tuxedos, want it bad enough to pay your price."

"This is the art of the deal?" I asked.

"Works every time. You should know, Ms. Recruiter."

I stiffened at his insinuation. "I would never——"

"Never what? Tease somebody? Paint a picture of how good the future could look, feel, and taste? To get them to sign on the dotted line?" Mars ran his finger from my elbow to my wrist. "It's who you are. It's what you do."

"That's way different," I protested.

A tuxedo took notice of us talking close. "Hey Mars, share the wealth, would yah?" As if there wasn't enough ass available. "Whatcha talkin' about?" His Texas drawl was thick with Bourbon.

"Business," I said, sitting up.

He tutted. "What does a purdy thang like you know about business? Where I'm from, in Dallas——"

I didn't wait to hear what he'd say about Dallas. "I'm hiring the next team of developers to grow HereBeer, for starters."

Mars backed me up. "Liv scouts out of MIT and Harvard."

"I'll bet you do," Dallas said, looking me over.

I ignored him. "The guy who developed HereBeer, Christopher, is the smartest person I've ever met. I should know since I graduated Dartmouth." I sipped my drink. It burned without ice. "But the candidates I'm recruiting," I whistled, "they've won every international coding contest the planet has to offer. Everybody wants them, but they'll come to Kava Tech. I'll make sure of it. I'm hiring 30 Christophers. I can't imagine what they'll make next. Today's valuation will look like a quaint joke."

I had their attention until Dallas slapped his heavy hand down on the table in front of me. "Well, shit, recruiter."

"Olivia," I corrected.

He smiled at my impertinence. "Kava Tech hires 'em feisty, eh? Well, how 'bout you show me how you get them geniuses to sign? Come over here." I didn't jerk my wrist away when he grabbed it or fight him when he pulled me onto his lap. I could handle some drunk investment banker.

"Recruiter, you wanna dance?" He asked over a gulp of whiskey. I shook my head no, thinking he was joking about me getting on stage. Instead, he waved a hundred-dollar bill in the air. Two girls in stilettos materialized in front of us. They posed and asked him to choose.

"Aww hell, ladies. It ain't for me, but my friend here. And she wants both of ya'll." ✦

The others watched, amused by Dallas' antics. He took both my wrists in his meaty hands, centering me on his lap with a leg between my thighs—holding me the way the strippers would never allow. The girls danced closer and I leaned away, back against his chest. I felt him grow underneath the thin satin of my dress.

"Relax darlin ... you're as stiff as me," he laughed.

Like vanilla-scented snakes plucked from the pages of a Victoria's Secret catalogue, the girls wound around us. The girl behind Dallas put her hands through his hair and into mine. She tipped my head back against his shoulder and brushed her breasts along my cheek and his. I closed my eyes but shot them open when the stripper in front pinched my thighs open wider. She circled her ass slowly downwards, grinding me harder each time into Dallas' lap. He groaned when she pressed herself against me, and me fully into him. She relented, for a second, only to turn, face me, and wrap her long legs around us and the chair, her body weaving circles against mine. Dallas pulled hard on my wrists, his whiskey-soaked breath bathing my neck. When I thought the material on my dress might give, the girls scattered like glitter.

The tuxedos howled their approval and Dallas let go of me to stuff panties full of cash. I slipped over to my seat, my face burning, and fixed the triangles of my dress over my breasts. I rubbed the top of my hand where Dallas' wedding ring had left a red dent.

The girls circled the table one last time. Marion slipped a bill to one, and, in a muffled voice, said to me, "Nice show."

"Damn, recruiter, you give quite a ride. No wonder those geeks can't say no. Hell, I'd come too." Dallas guffawed and winked.

I winked back, but he was no longer looking at me. Instead, he rooted through the jacket hanging on the back of his chair. From the inside coat pocket, he fished out a few Cubans and a book of matches. Later, when everybody was chewing on the ends of stogies and watching the stage through halos of smoke, I excused myself to the bathroom.

Marion knew. He mouthed the words, "Call me later." I bolted from the table and asked a bouncer for the ladies' room.

"Up the stairs, back of the hall." He pointed with a massive arm.

I walked past rooms, each closed door black-lacquered and gold-lettered. I wondered what sort of thing went on in the "Heavenly Sweet." I was sure, in comparison, my little lap dance was no big deal. But away from the tuxedos, and all at once, I felt embarrassed, and then something else, fiercer—disappointment and then, anger. Who did that jerk think he was, grabbing me like that? Why didn't I make a scene? Should I go back there now and say something? I stopped walking. What good would it do? You were supposed to punish a dog right when it was shitting on the floor, not after.

I watched the stage from the upstairs hall. A new set of girls dropped their feather boas one at a time to the floor. They weren't mad or shamed. They were impassively doing their job. Doing what they needed to do to get paid. Wasn't that what Marion was trying to tell me? It was just business after all, wasn't it? Lure them in and make them pay. I'd played the game, but I wasn't sure if I'd won or lost. I drew a deep breath, held it, and let it go.

In the bathroom, I washed Dallas' cologne off my skin and rinsed the whiskey out of my mouth. I rubbed the spot on my hand, though the mark was long gone. I stared at the water running needlessly. I thought about the strippers, a two-headed boa constrictor pinning me to Dallas. It was like that tangle of people at the C-suite party in Vegas, after Mars gave me the 'mermaid.'

And crystal clear like the water running through my fingers, I realized who the man was from that night, the one fucking those girls on the chaise next to me. I knew I hadn't dreamt it. "I know you." Chef. It was Chef's accent that I had heard. Chef's round face coming through the girls' hair, his slippery mouth tugging on their nipples. I remembered what he'd said to Marion when I met him at his restaurant. "I'd like to see her again. Enjoy her." The water scalded my hands and I jumped away from the sink.

"Fuck." I needed to go home.

I made it half a step out of the bathroom and froze on the threshold. At the other end of the hall, a bunch of guys in tuxedos from the Driskill stood talking to Melissa Burge, like they were still socializing at the launch party, not a gentlemen's club. She made a joke, animatedly waved her hands, and they all laughed. Then she held one of the black doors open and followed them into the room with the confidence of a lion. The heavy door slammed behind her.

I crept down the empty hall and stopped in front of the "Lovers' Lounge." I didn't know what I was going to do, what I should do. I put my hand on the handle, but I didn't turn the knob. The most powerful woman in our company, the closer, didn't need my help. She would know how to handle herself. She would know how to handle them. I was the one who couldn't deal. I scurried down the steps and out the front door. I called a cab and waited behind one of the carved bushes, which I realized was shaped like a naked woman.

Later, Marion left a message on my phone. "Wow, did they love you. More money coming in for a new product. I knew you'd be great."

I didn't know what he was talking about and I didn't ask.

Taco Tuesday

On Tuesday, I went to see Christopher. He shared an "office" with several developers on his team. They crowded around several folding tables buckling under the weight of screens, hard drives, and extension cords. The dark room smelled of stale soy sauce, dry-erase markers, and foot odor. I knocked on the open door and everyone looked up from their keyboards at once.

"Hi, guys," I said. "Sorry to disturb."

"Big O." The calamitous orgasm of my name followed. "Gessssooooh."

"Hi. Uhm, thanks for that. Have you seen Christopher?" One of the guys pointed to the cube behind me. "Oh, hey. I didn't hear you."

"How could you over all the groaning?" Christopher said.

"You want to grab lunch? Uhm, outside the building?" I looked back at the dev room. "Do they let you out of the building?"

He smiled. "They do. Once a week, to get extra soda."

"Taco truck? It's on me," I offered. It was the least I could do after the way I'd left things at the launch party.

"Bring us back something," they hollered from the computer cave.

We drove to the south side of the city where a mobile taco truck called Vestitos parked on a blacktop corner lot. Its service window opened to red metal picnic tables and umbrellas, never enough to seat its long line of lunch patrons. The only thing more famous than Vestitos' food was the homeless cross-dresser who lived in a tent behind the lot. He often rode a rusty 1960s-style bicycle around the city. Today it leaned against his makeshift dwelling, a tutu and a t-shirt drying on the handlebars. If the vagabond was around, the unwritten rule was to buy him a vegetarian taco and a soda.

When we finally sat down to eat, I got right to it. "Chris, about the launch party. My behavior, it wasn't okay." I handed him a lemonade from our shared tray.

"Is there an 'I'm sorry' somewhere in there?" he prodded, taking the drink.

"The closest you'll get." I shot him a smile. "That's if you'll accept it?"

He thought about it, chewing on a taco. The sauce dripped down his wrist. I handed him a napkin.

"It's okay. I shouldn't have been talking to you like you were ..." he searched for the right word, "a guy."

"You talked to me like a friend. You can tell me

anything." He looked skeptical. "And I have no place being jealous of Amara Young or anyone. There's just something about her that rubs me wrong, but it's stupid. I don't even know her."

"I didn't mean to make you uncomfortable."

"You didn't. I worried that I ruined your night."

"I've been to three launch parties, so no, you didn't wreck my senior prom. Actually, someone else did that."

"Wrecked your launch party?"

"No, the prom."

"Oh. High school sucks for everyone."

"Some more than others."

"True. So, if I didn't mess things up, what did you do after? Anything?" I asked the question that I wanted him to ask me.

"The team went out for a few beers after, nothing really. Could only get them to stay in tuxes so long. What about you?"

I blurted the truth. "I went to a strip club."

"After the Driskill?" Christopher's expression was somewhere between amused and surprised. "Classy. Make any money?" he chided, smudging sauce on his glasses.

"Stop it. I didn't dance. Really, I couldn't possibly hold myself on a pole like that. That part was incredible. You ever been?"

"Yeah. Every guy has been to a strip club."

"Like a bachelor party or something?" I asked.

"Something." I let him play cool. "Why'd you go?" he asked.

"I didn't really know I was going. I hopped in a SUV with Marion and his business associates. Oh, and one of their girlfriends." As though the drunk girl made the story easier for him to hear.

"Liv, that guy ..." He shook his head.

"What about him?" I sounded defensive.

"It's useless."

"What's useless?"

"Trying to explain. He irks me the way Amara irks you. Were the girls hot?" I wasn't sure if he asked because I brought up Marion or because he was truly curious.

"Crazy hot. It was like being at the Amara photo shoot, except she's naked and there were 50 of her walking around, also naked." My honesty, the image, made us both laugh. The tension eased. I kept talking. "It was some private club I guess, higher-end clientele and women. But it was so weird, a lot of guys smoked, or watched TV instead of the girls."

"Fifty naked Amaras? I wouldn't have been looking at a screen." He grinned sweetly.

"Me either. I was a total voyeur. And then I got a lap dance." I didn't say anything about seeing Melissa Burge. That was her story to tell. I didn't need to start rumors about that woman. She'd shred me with her manicure.

"Really?" Christopher put down his drink. His big blue eyes begged for an explanation. I let him wait. I took a big bite of taco and chewed slowly. "Did you pay for it?" he pressed.

"No, some banker from Dallas paid for it."

"And?"

"I sat on his lap and two girls danced ... uhm ... for me ... on me? It was over quick enough." I sipped my lemonade, an excuse to look away. "Honestly, it was really uncomfortable, but I just wanted to be cool."

"You mean, impress your boyfriend?" The edge in his voice was back.

"Yeah, maybe," I admitted. "But not just him. I wanted to show those businessmen that I was one of them, that I could hang."

"How did that work out for you?"

"It didn't. I was just part of the show. But whatever, I'm used to being that kind of entertainment."

"What do you mean?" he asked.

"Well, how is being a recruiter all that different from being a stripper? We both tease and dance and cajole to get men to do what we want. They get cash stuffed in their panties. I get offers signed so Kava will stuff a bonus in my panties." I slid the chips across the table.

Christopher picked at them. "Well, your clothes are on for starters. Right? Because if they aren't, I mean, call me." His silly expression made me laugh.

"Yes. They're on," I assured. "I entertain in a tight pair of jeans and a company t-shirt."

"Your boyfriend is messing with your head." Christopher's pale blue eyes looked placid, a little sad.

"It's even crazier now that I think about it, because instead of the boys paying me, I pay them—with bigger signing bonuses and exotic trips and luxury cars. I'm a stripper that pays her clientele. How messed up is that?"

Christopher placed both hands flat on the table and took a breath. I'd seen him do this when he was about to explain a complicated software thing to somebody who wasn't getting it. "You are not a stripper. You are a recruiter." His eyes weren't liquid, they were ice. "Sure, this company has a hiring strategy rooted in the basic tendencies of all guys—of all people. But you can't stereotype yourself like that and you can't stereotype me either. It's unfair. Have you ever considered how the other half of Kava Tech's recruiting model feels? You may be paid to lure, but we're paid to be lured. It's an insult to think I would make a career decision on behalf of my penis."

I looked away, but he kept talking. "Sure, I like to look sometimes, who doesn't? But I didn't come to Kava Tech to ogle ass. I came here to develop software with brilliant people. One stereotype—recruiter—cannot exist without the other—developer. And they both suck, but that's life. You're not a whore."

I didn't realize what I felt until he said it. Before the tear rolled off my cheek, his arms were around me.

"Chris, I'm making a mess of things," I said into his shoulder.

"Maybe, but you'll find your way."

A Proposal

The email from Rodrigues came from Henri. He wrote it in pieces between power outages and connectivity failures, answering many of the letters I'd sent. The line "Message Failed to Send" divided many of the paragraphs, but the long, disjointed note brought news of friends and their families and updates on the island.

We have power now, with electricity restored to most of the island. The café marron tree was found intact. We collected a cutting, and again, hope it takes. Conservation may have stalled, but our project continues. The cyclone killed many native species, but it also annihilated the exotics—the imports that were strangling the endemics to extinction. Olivia, it was hundreds of years of evolutionary justice exacted in a few hours. There are now substantial holes in the tree canopy and it's an opportune time to re-establish the Rodriguan landscape. We are ready for the aureum to come home.

I imagined the Rodriguan sun; its Capricorn rays blessing an understory of soft ferns and spiked palms; dusty yellow warblers flitting between the gnarly Pandanus branches; and Henri moving through the Grande Montagne forest searching for a place to root the *aureum*. What he wrote next yanked me from my ecological daydream. The words hit my chest like a cold, hard brick.

Rani asks for you all the time. She wants to know when you're coming home. She is doing okay, still living in a shelter with her parents. Their plot was leveled. You asked, and no, I don't think she'll be going back to school. It's the same for so many families here. After what they lost, there is no way to afford the extras, like supplies and uniforms and school fees. She got a job sweeping floors at the market.

I didn't want to think of Rani, a sparklingly bright 11-year-old, anywhere but skipping home from school, her knobby knees flying out from under her too short plaid skirt. But now I saw her; head down, moving sand over a cracked tile floor with a straw broom. Rani was cleaning floors. I was trashing hotel rooms. She couldn't afford primary school. I blew money for sport. I didn't know if I could ever help her, but I had to do better. I had to try.

As winter faded to spring and the blue bonnets blossomed down the Texas highways, I took on additional work as a floater, like Avery. Besides recruiting at my campuses in the northeast, I built our West Coast presence at Stanford, Cal Tech, and Berkeley. I banked on the extra work and the title promotion upping my bonus.

Weekly, I flew the "nerd bird," the direct flight between Silicon Hills, Austin, and Silicon Valley, San Jose. This connector boarded to capacity with frantic young men rearranging PowerPoint presentations, oblivious to announcements to stow electronic devices. Everyone had metallic frequent flyer cards colored gold, platinum, or silver. I held a green card, a biodegradable status that landed me in the last row between two dudes who'd rather code than shower. The attendants warmed the beef stroganoff just behind my seat, near the bathroom, wafting Worcestershire-fart funk down the aisle.

When I wasn't fighting for personal space on flights to Massachusetts or California, I worked with Jeremy to plan our final, and biggest sell event of the year—a weekend ski trip in Telluride, Colorado. Telluride was a winter playground for the rich, situated an hour's flight from Denver. Tom Cruise and Nicole Kidman built a cozy, $40 million log cabin there, and from what I understood, it was the best scenery and skiing the American West had to offer. We offered the trip to our most prized candidates, our alpha wolves who had not yet signed on the dotted line.

Months ago in the searing August heat, a ski trip sounded like a great idea. Now in the thick of it, it felt like we were planning a wedding for a dozen bridezillas, and our candidates grew more difficult the longer they held out. It was our own fault for enabling the brats with holiday presents, birthday presents, and presents "just because we're thinking of you!" Could the wolves smell our weakness, our growing desperation to get them to sign? Even our "easy" candidates demanded bigger cash signing bonuses and starting salaries. A $100,000 base and a $25,000 sign-on bonus weren't enough for some 22-year-old college graduates.

On top of this, we were again working closely with Avery Stone, the cranky Pegasus spy. Though I had spotted Avery smooching Mr. Pegasus at the Marriott, she still had the sole line of access to our top MIT alpha wolf, Conor Walsh. With us both angling for the same bonus, and having to work together toward it, our relationship teetered like a passive-aggressive seesaw. I'd threaten Price and she'd threaten Conor. Why Conor Walsh responded to her was a mystery Jeremy and I could not solve.

"Misery loves company," Jeremy guessed, and we would shrug and work with the hand we had been dealt. With the ski trip fast approaching, our bickering with Avery on the uptick, and so much still undone, the three of us agreed (probably the only time all year we agreed on anything) to divide the remaining to-do list credit card roulette-style—by pulling pieces of paper out of a hat.

I made sure we used Jeremy's baseball hat, which hadn't been washed since his freshman year of college. The inside rim, I presumed once white, had turned the color of earwax. To be fair, I let Avery hold the hat and pull the mini to-do lists from deep within. Jeremy towered over her, spitting into a full dip cup, which he placed on the desk next to her black coffee. In the end, Jeremy pulled the lists for flights and transport, Avery ended up with activities and ski reservations, and I got gift baskets and restaurant reservations. When we were done, Avery walked away abandoning her coffee mug on our desk. Jeremy spat in it.

Per my assignment, I shopped for the 20 invited guests and stocked the house. A high-end event coordinator, I learned everyone's sizes and their favorite colors, and I purchased them the best ski jackets and pants, long underwear, and wool socks Austin had to offer. I was on a first-name basis with the L.L. Bean salespeople. I also made gift baskets for each candidate to open upon their arrival. Recruits would find their favorite liquors, cigars, high-end ski equipment, and Godiva hot chocolate, among other Kava Tech must-haves such as our t-shirts and bouncy balls. Every basket also had a Tiffany pen to get them thinking about signing their offers.

Though I was outfitting candidates and the attending Kava Techies, Avery thought of me as her personal shopper. She walked by my desk to tell me she needed a pair of ski pants and a parka. I squelched the urge to throw my computer at her head. "What size?"

"Four petite," she called over her shoulder.

Later that day, I purchased her pants, a size-two in neon yellow. I bought her a rainbow-colored parka to go with them. I thought about making her a welcome basket full of tampons and condoms but decided there were better uses of my time. I had to plan an engagement.

The idea that popped into my head at that first career fair, when I watched James and Julia stop at the DeBeers booth, had turned into him popping the question. Over the last few months, I saw that the power couple looked for their first jobs together. Jeremy was adamant that James would never find another girl like Julia, who was brilliant, sweet, and a talented writer. He'd be a fool to lose her, Jeremy insisted, and we made sure James knew it.

I did what I had to do. I promoted their romance with dinners, gifts, and opportunities for them to be alone—courtesy of my corporate Amex card. In one of Jeremy's man-to-man talks with James, it had come out that he was considering proposing to her. My partner being a dude had paid dividends. James was a lot more comfortable opening up to a guy—not that I didn't three-way into these conversations to keep tabs on the couple's emotional pulse. In the end it was understood, that if we enabled James' proposal on top of the picturesque Rocky Mountains, that he would accept his offer at Kava Tech, and bring his fiancé with him. After all, Austin was a great place to start a family, wasn't it? I had no idea.

I went with James to pick out a $15,000 engagement ring in Boston. He chose a 1.5-carat diamond solitaire in a carved platinum band designed by Varna. My hand shook when I handed my Amex card to the jeweler. I thought of how Amara Young had gotten fired over a $1,500 bottle of tequila. But—I assured myself—this purchase was a calculated move. James and Julia would earn for the company way more than their recruitment costs, even with a diamond ring thrown in. Plus, I reasoned as I signed the receipt, it was the same as upping his signing bonus, which I totally had the authority to do.

When James gave me the ring to hold until the trip, I entertained selling it back to the store and running across international lines. I wasn't even sure I'd be able to smuggle a couple of seeds through customs, so I abandoned the fantasy of high-end theft. Back in Austin, I put the black box in its velvet embroidered bag on top of my mantel where it kept my tampon box company—or at least they stared one another down.

I envisioned James proposing on a Saturday afternoon atop the mountain, and that night, we would go to dinner to celebrate. That's where he and Julia would accept their offers in front of the other candidates, who would follow their alpha wolves to Kava.

For dinner, I chose the New Sheridan Chop House. It was a nineteenth-century, Wild West brick building nestled in the middle of Telluride's quaint town center, the dramatic backdrop of the Rockies visible all the way around. From our rented house on the slopes, the group would take a gondola over the mountains and walk down to the valley to reach the cozy restaurant. We'd have a beautiful dinner, after which we'd celebrate more in the hotel's Ballard Suite, a network of rooms with a view of Ballard Peak—all 13,000 feet of it. I had the suite stocked with champagne, chocolates, candles, and flower arrangements. I asked the florist to sprinkle the king-sized bed with rose petals, and I bought Julia and James silk pajamas. After celebrating at the hotel, I figured the group would leave the happy couple alone to enjoy their night and continue the party back at our rental house.

On the eve of the ski trip, Jeremy and I sat around the office fixing last-minute glitches.

"Liv, Avery's kid, the one that transferred to Carnegie Mellon, he missed his flight." Jeremy looked up from his email.

"Are you kidding me? It's snowing pretty hard in Denver, there aren't going to be a lot of flights out."

"I know. I'll call travel. You call him." Jeremy went to work.

"Can I tell him I'm rescinding his offer for being a lazy shithead?"

Jeremy answered me after hanging up with the travel department. "No, but you can tell him that we booked him a later connection and a private car from the airport, since he'll miss the van that is picking everyone else up."

I rolled my eyes and grabbed the phone. "Great life lesson. Be an irresponsible jerk and we'll get you a private car." When the candidate answered, I switched to my sweet, accommodating recruiter voice and explained his updated travel plan. "Maybe we can get him an extra signing bonus for making the private car?"

"Stop it," Jeremy warned. "You better check that attitude and get your butt to the airport."

"I will. Any idea if Conor is coming?" Naturally, Avery had been tight lipped on his whereabouts.

"Avery said yes. He's included in the headcount for all the reservations. You have the ring?"

I patted the zipper inside my purse. It was good practice for the tampon box. "I can't believe we're orchestrating an engagement. This is crazy. We're matchmakers."

"I know. But it'll work. They'll come and then everyone else will. And we'll have recruited the best programmers in the country."

"Except Conor."

"We don't know what's going to happen yet. At least he's going to ski. Or so Avery says. Even if she takes credit for that hire, everyone else who comes because he did … they'll be ours."

At the airport I grabbed a newspaper to entertain me on the flight to Denver. Stock market speculation had become my hobby, and I wasn't alone. The market continued to reach new highs with investors forecasting another month, another year, of record shattering gains. Any company with a dot-com on the end of its name was going through the roof. Of course there were the naysayers: the analysts who said that the bull horns around which we all hung would dip under our collective weight. Some wrote about Y2K jitters, theorizing that the turn of the century would cause a computer-driven apocalypse that would erase our bank accounts, crash planes, and launch nuclear weapons.

But I knew, based on the morale and pace at work, that this was all nonsense. The naysayers were wrong. Our company's valuation unfurled like a lotus leaf towards the sun. Optimism, and consequently the pressure to grow, were palpable. Faster, bigger, smarter, better. Kava Tech was not going to be left behind, and we recruiters pushed the pace. We glowed with avarice fed by unchecked ambition.

This was the celebratory, if not predatory, energy we brought to Telluride. Corks on the Dom Pérignon popped open with the frosty door locks. Even this group of candidates, which had grown so used to our recruitment excesses, looked wide-eyed around the insane "cabin" I'd rented.

It was built for entertaining, and thanks to me, it was stocked for the weekend. The Viking appliances were stuffed with champagne and beer. The granite counters sparkled under an array of giant-bowed gift bags. Oak bunk beds, draped in snuggly plaid comforters, were a showcase of new ski equipment and clothes, all laid out for the candidates to claim. I waited for Avery to find her miniature Life Savers-colored snowsuit before going to put my own stuff away.

She held up the jacket and looked at me. "You suck."

"That's what Price said."

She threw the coat on the floor and left the room. It was going to be a colorful weekend.

The one thing that wasn't available at the house, or anywhere in Telluride for that matter, was good connectivity. Once we had arrived, communications to the outer world were patchy at best. This cut me off from Jeremy and stopped me from reconfirming my reservations for the engagement. There was no way I would risk anyone, especially Julia, hearing me talk on the landline. Without an internet connection or cell reception, there was nothing left to do except hope that everything went according to plan.

After trying five times to reach Jeremy to let him know everyone had arrived, I gave up and joined the party that had already started around the blazing fireplace. Aside from greeting him at the airport, I had kept my distance from Conor. He chatted with one of the developers, and I let them talk shop. I poured myself a glass of wine and found a spot next to James and Julia. They, and a few other recruits, marveled at the views of our ski-in, ski-out residence.

"You all set to tackle those slopes?" I asked.

"We've never skied," James said.

"At all?" The heads shook. "None of you?"

"Well, I have once, in Pennsylvania," a recruit said.

Telluride was a place for serious skiers where the easy trails were hard and the hard trails were absurd. The house stood on a double blue that led to a lodge where, I hoped, Avery had booked lessons for everyone.

"It's easy," I assured them. "You'll have fun." I took a big swallow of my drink.

"I'm going to try snowboarding," somebody said.

Brutal, I thought. I could still feel the bruises on my butt from the time I had tried it years ago. "Well, there's lots of fresh powder. It'll be like falling on a pillow. Plus, there's nothing a little liquid warmth can't help." I smiled and held up my wine.

When he went to refill his glass, I followed James into the kitchen. "Are we all set?" I whispered.

"I guess so," he stammered.

"Top of the mountain, tomorrow afternoon, right? You take the lift together. Hop off, take a knee, and pull the ring. Easy. I'll be right behind you on a walkie talkie with the operator to give you a moment after. She'll be thrilled. And I have everything all set to celebrate."

"Yeah. Okay." He was trying to convince himself.

"James, it's the right thing to do. She is perfect. Irreplaceable." We looked over at Julia, still chatting by the window. "Is something wrong?"

"I'm not sure." James was clamming up. I needed Jeremy here, or at least reachable on the phone. Damn cell service.

"It's perfectly normal ..." I pep talked, but people came into the kitchen. Another recruit pulled James into their conversation, and I lost my chance. I left them when I saw Conor sitting by himself on the fireplace ledge. I swallowed my wine, left my glass in the kitchen, and approached him.

"Hey, Conor. The place is great, right?"

He gave me a shrug.

"Can I sit?"

"Sure," he said, looking at the fire.

I took a seat in a plush leather chair next to him. "I'm sorry I never got a chance to talk to you more that night you spent in Austin." Apologizing was the last thing I wanted to do, but I had to try.

"That was a great night," he said, perking up. "Especially the way it ended." He scanned my face for a reaction, but I was too prepared.

I mustered my best fake smile. "It was pretty

ridiculous getting thrown up on. Typical in my line of work, I guess."

"About that."

"About what?"

"We never finished our conversation from dinner," he said.

"Which one?"

"You know," he said tartly.

"I'm serious. I don't have a clue." I went for the dumb, flirtatious recruiter act. I widened my grin and softened my expression. And then, I took a chance. I put my fingertips on his knee. The way I touched him; it said I was engaged, sorry, and really interested. Usually, I used this gesture on people's shoulders, but his knee was all I could reach from the chair. When I went to take my hand back, he reached out and caught it. But this time I couldn't hide my surprise. I jerked my hand away, and Conor smirked at having disarmed my mask.

Avery, of all people, rescued me when she stole Conor away. I knew that she would do all she could to prevent me from recruiting him, but I never thought I'd be grateful for it. I sat by the fire alone until one of the Kava Techies announced it was time to hit the slopes.

Avery and I locked eyes in acrid agreement. This wasn't on the agenda. The first ski lessons were set for tomorrow morning. Tonight was supposed to be mingling at the house and dinner. True to form, our company leadership was drunk and taking us off-script. Like kids on Christmas morning, the recruits tore apart their gift baskets to open goggles, hats, gloves, lip balm, and anything else they might need to brave the elements. Forty-five minutes later the house was trashed.

The default house mom, I carried a garbage bag between rooms collecting cellophane, torn boxes, and wrapping paper. After that, I had "children" who needed help getting into their snowsuits, who couldn't zipper their coats because their gloves were already on, and who didn't know how to buckle ski boots or attach the boots to the skis. I ran between the mud room, the bedrooms, and the entrance to slope.

It was past 4 p.m. when everyone assembled outside the cabin, and a Kava Techie led the charge down the hill to the lift. He glided, despite being a few drinks in, soundlessly and effortlessly out of sight. The recruits, sensing a rite of passage moment in which they could impress their (hopefully) soon-to-be colleagues, all went at once. The three in front fell 20 feet from the door. This caused a chain reaction of accidents as the group behind them picked up speed but did not know how to turn. Like a cartoon, the bodies piled on top of one another, leaving behind a trail of hats, skis, and poles. Neither Avery nor I had dressed to ski, and we stood under the awning watching as candidates collided and rolled out of sight in the snow.

I couldn't help myself. I burst out laughing. Even Avery, who I had never heard laugh, cackled. I looked in disbelief at her smile. Granted it was at somebody else's expense, but still it counted as a smile. "If that's not a metaphor for working at this company, I don't know what is," I said.

"Seriously," she said and crossed her arms.

"I'm going to finish cleaning up the house."

"Fine. I'll ski down and help out below."

"You might beat them there." I joked, but the moment between us was gone. She turned away and said nothing.

Though my wool socks were already soggy, I tiptoed around the snow clumps and puddles on my way back to the great room. In the mayhem to get everyone outfitted and outside, I overlooked James and Julia. They hadn't left to ski. They were, instead, arguing in hushed voices in front of the fireplace.

"Julia, I'm telling you, it's the right place," I heard James say. He held her hand in his, but her arm was limp.

"These people are batshit crazy. We should go to ... —— ... it's more stable," she argued. I inched closer to hear better.

"But that's the exciting part. And they're great people. Austin is the place to start our life. I'm sure ..." James grew quiet when Avery entered the kitchen. I stayed hidden in the hall with my back pressed to the wall.

"You aren't skiing?" she asked. "You should come down with me."

I felt their heavy-hearted pause. "Yeah, we're going."

I didn't have the chance to get them alone, but at least I knew what the problem was. Julia was the holdout. Would a diamond ring be enough to change her mind? I stomped my feet and entered the room as though I had come in from outside.

"It's cold out there. About an hour or so left of light to ski. You love birds going with Avery?" I picked up ribbons and paper bits as I spoke and watched as they scampered to their bedroom.

The next day the recruits dressed themselves and went down for the lessons Avery had booked. James looked like a startled animal. I felt bad for pressuring him to make a marriage proposal, but he had agreed to it. I mean, we didn't force him, did we?

In the hall, I pulled him aside and handed him the velvet black box with the ring. "Zip it in your jacket. It's now or never." He swallowed audibly and did what he was told. "James, that's a $15,000 engagement ring. You're getting it for free. And with it, you are also getting the most incredible woman I have, you have, ever met. You got this." He wiped a bead of sweat from his forehead.

"What if she says no?"

"That's what you are worried about? Not a chance. She loves you and you're about to give her an incredible life." I took his shoulders in my hands, pinning him to the wall. I heard somebody coming down the hall, so I leaned into his ear and whispered. James bent to hear me.

"Everything here is an opportunity of a lifetime. This company. This moment. Her. Take. It."

Conor turned the corner and stopped to stare when he saw me holding James and murmuring in his ear. I jerked away when I saw him.

Conor laughed, a deep laugh. "Am I interrupting?"

"We're finished," I said, letting go of James who patted his zippered pocket and darted away.

Conor scoffed, "Excellent," and walked past.

That afternoon, according to plan, I cut the lift line and got behind James and Julia. I watched him tuck his pole under his arm and pat his coat pocket yet again when they caught the chair. He put his other arm around her and she leaned into his shoulder. Perfect, I thought, as they ascended over the aspens and into the snow globe wonderland. At the right moment I radioed the lift operator, who had agreed after I bribed him with a bottle of Dom and a restaurant gift certificate, to stall the chairs on my call.

The wonder couple approached the apex. As the ground met her skis, Julia slid off and stopped at the top. But not James. Checking the damn box for the thousandth time, he got his ski pole caught in the side of the chair. By the time he tugged it free, the chair had turned and begun its descent with him still on it. The lift operator, who did as he was bribed, stopped the chairs. But now James dangled some 15 feet off the ground facing down the steep slope. Julia stood alone – at the top looking confused.

Under normal circumstances, James would have been the idiot who missed the drop and rode the lift around again. But nope, swaying in the breeze, I watched with horror as he panicked. He looked left, right, behind him at Julia, and across to me. But before either of us could yell stop, he did the unthinkable—he jumped.

James dropped like a hunk of raw cookie dough, disappearing in the powdered sugar below. A moment later the lift resumed its function, and I stood next to Julia watching James crawl military-style on his belly up the slope. Without poles or skis, he pulled himself along with his elbows under the path of the returning, empty chairs. More people gathered, watching how the gap between the metal seats and his head narrowed the closer he got to the top. Why didn't he get up and walk around the chairs?

Showing timing and coordination I didn't think he had, James rolled to the left to dodge one last fast-moving guillotine. We heard him moan, the unmistakable, guttural expression of true pain. Julia ran to him, but before she could say a word, still on his stomach, James held out the velour box. Julia dropped to her knees.

Instead of popping the question, James wailed, "My leg, it's broken!"

Someone else yelled to call a medic, and I handed over the walkie talkie without looking at the people behind me.

James' head rested on Julia's lap. He looked up at her and then, he did it.

"Marry me?" he asked and opened the box.

Maybe it was his herculean effort to ask the question, or his broken leg that made Julia forget the reservations she had earlier, because she did not hesitate. "Yes. Yes, I'll marry you." Her hands held his face, and she smothered him with kisses.

"Keep him still," someone said, but before we could

intervene to perform group medical care, two brawny guys in gray ski jackets with red crosses on their backs arrived with a stretcher.

Julia gushed. "All this for me? You're crazy."

"Put it on," he said as his head was strapped to a red board.

She held up her glittering finger and called out, "I love you." But the mountain version of Baywatch had begun their descent with James moaning between them.

Julia followed and a crowd with a great story to tell made its way down the hill.

Alone on the mountain top, with the lift paused yet again, I screamed into the open air, "She said yes!" Two down and one big one to go. I made the sign of the holy trinity and skied down the mountain.

It was near dark when James and Julia returned from the emergency room. We had been drinking for a couple of hours already, which meant everyone was stupid before sunset. While Julia showed off her ring to a bunch of guys who feigned interest, James sat with his casted ankle on the ottoman and discussed their plan to start their lives together in Austin, at Kava Tech. This announcement, that James and Julia would come to Kava Tech, prompted another hour of toasts.

Though James was in no condition to take the gondola (the only way in and out of the town center from our cabin) to the Sheridan, I kept our dinner plans. It would be impossible to get another reservation in this two-block resort on a Saturday night, for this many people. And it was way too late to cancel the suite

I had booked. So after dark, we left James and Julia and trekked out in the cold, starry night for a celebratory dinner on their behalf. From what I caught of the recruits' side conversations, the Alpha Wolf Strategy was working. With James and Julia committed, talk of offer signing upwelled. I watched Avery all but shove Conor in a gondola with a star Kava developer.

At the restaurant, steak and potatoes did not dent our buzz. Drinking was one thing. Drinking at 10,000 feet after a day on the slopes was a different beast. I floated when I walked, my heartbeat heavy in my ears but my head light. I watched a candidate stumble to the restroom. Conor sat next to Avery. His eyes were droopy drunk, and her cheeks were wind-burned and red-wine pink. I had long stopped trying to sell the recruits around me. Conversation was a candle flame—lively, unsteady, and melting the very structure that held it together. At the end of dinner, somebody suggested we continue the party in the suite upstairs.

"What about the happy couple?" somebody asked.

"Give them time alone at the cabin," somebody else said.

"There's an awful lot of champagne upstairs," I told them, "and chocolate."

There was immediate agreement and movement. Everyone was so off-balance, I couldn't imagine they would have made it up the slippery, snow-covered steps to catch a gondola home. Instead, we braved the warm, steady elevator to the Ballard suite. The moon illuminated the snow on the peak towering over the hotel. We smudged the windows with our noses until somebody uncorked more booze.

"To building an empire," a star Kava Techie said, popping the Dom and spilling it on the rug. "You wanna be stupid rich?" He chugged from the bottle and handed out the others from the bar. The recruits opened their slit-drunk eyes as wide as they would go. "Do you know how much my stock is worth? Do you?" Pop! Pop! Pop! The corks flew around the room. "Chug!" he yelled. "And if you can't chug, we don't want you here anyway." Everyone gulped the Dom, and when they surfaced for air, he said, "Then you're in. All of you." They hooted and high-fived. "Again," he said. Avery grabbed more bottles out of the bar, and I knew the offers were all but signed.

With the initiation party in full swing, I realized Conor wasn't with the group. Was he in the bathroom? Oh, the bathroom. I needed to go. I disappeared down the hall and pushed the door to the master bedroom. The hotel did an amazing job. Rose petals covered the floor and bed linens. Heart-shaped chocolates topped origami folded silk pajamas. Housekeeping had lit the candles not long ago. I picked up the spaghetti straps of the camisole meant for Julia and inspected the top. I needed to remember to take it with me to give to her.

"You really did it up for them, with all this." Conor startled me, and I dropped the shirt. He closed the door behind him.

"Yeah, well, that's what we do at Kava Tech. We take care of people," I said folding the shirt. "Seems hard for you to understand."

Conor walked to me and sat on the bed. Rose petals

tumbled into the dent he made on the bedspread. "I want to be taken care of too, you know."

"What do you want, Conor? Who will give you more than us? We're a developer's paradise. Our billionaire CEO takes care of everyone. Where else does that happen?"

"Maybe I want to be the CEO."

"You wanna start your own thing? Why keep up the charade? Just to party? You don't seem to enjoy it."

"To party with you," he said, slurring.

"You're Avery's candidate. Want to tell me why?" I sat down next to him on the bed.

"Money. She and Price linked their offers."

He looked super drunk, and I suspected he was telling the truth. "What does that mean?"

"Avery and Price said that if I came to Kava Tech and didn't get big money or bonuses or whatever that my offer at Pegasus would still stand. They said they'd pay me for information on Kava's plans and products while I was there. They met with me together."

I sat speechless on the bed next to Conor. Avery was sleeping with Price and feeding Kava's human capacity and intellectual property to our biggest competitor. If our crazy start-up didn't pay out fast, Pegasus would siphon off our top talent and get company secrets in the process. I wondered how many of her recruits had this deal, or worse, how many of mine?

"Avery and Price already paid me to be quiet about it," Conor slurred.

But then, I thought, why should I care? If the candidates came, even for six months, I would still get credit for the hire, get my bonus, and get back to Rodrigues. Maybe Avery was doing me a favor.

My head was spinning—the altitude, the drinking, and now this. Conor reminded me he was sitting next to me. He put a hand on my knee. "I know how this works," he said. "Avery's the negotiator and you're the closer." He leaned towards me. "It's time to get me to sign my offer."

"Wait, what?" I tried to think. I needed to out Avery to Kava Tech. How could I do that? "Did you get this deal with Pegasus in writing?" I asked him, but it was too late. Conor's lips buried mine, and his tongue pressed between my teeth. He grabbed my shoulders and shoved me to the bed. Before my head hit the pillow, my fist caught his jaw, just below his ear. He crumpled into the rose petals and lay there dazed, his underwear tenting out of his open fly.

I ran from the bed and opened the door into Avery.

"You," I hissed. I grabbed her shirt and pulled her into the room. I slammed the door, and Conor groaned on the bed.

"Did you tell him I'd sleep with him before or after you paid him to betray Kava?" Avery surveyed the situation. She looked at the half-conscious candidate and then back into my fury. "Answer me!"

"Or what? You'll tell on me?" Avery taunted.

"I'm going to let everyone know what's going on," I said, pointing at Conor.

"Sure, you will. After I tell them I found you alone in the honeymoon suite with your star recruit."

"He attacked me. Right after he told me everything."

"That drunk, skinny kid attacked you?" she laughed.

"I knocked him out."

"You hit a recruit?" Avery snarled. I took a step towards her, but she didn't move. She raised her chin and stared me down. "You came-on to a recruit to get him to sign, and when he turned you down, you assaulted him? That's what I saw."

Like a scared, cornered animal, I bolted from the room. I ran past the Dom chugging candidates, so drunk they never registered me coming or going. I heard vomiting in the hall as I tore open the suite door. They would all be passed out soon anyway and not a single one, save James and Julia, would wake up in time to catch tomorrow's flight home.

I ran into the freezing air and didn't stop until I was on the gondola. I exhaled into the seal of its frosty doors. When I saw my reflection in the glass, sure I was alone, I cried. Tears of rage, of fear, of panic. Tears of having lost. I screamed and punched the plexiglass, bruising knuckles already sore from hitting Conor's face. "You stupid fucking girl." Drunk in a honeymoon suite with a star recruit. Hadn't I seen enough to know better? To see it coming? On the other side of the valley, I sat on an icy curb and sunk my throbbing hand in the snow. "Fuck." Who would believe my story over his? Over hers?

I searched for a way out, thought about every angle I could play, that Avery or Conor might take. A few hours later, I did what I did best—I ran. I flew out early in the morning with Julia and James, before anyone else returned to the cabin. I helped James with his broken leg, a perfect cover for leaving Avery and Conor behind.

On the flight home, I wondered if Conor would even remember what he did last night. Could I forget it too? Back in Austin, when asked about my wrapped hand, I said I slipped on my way to the gondola. Jeremy bought it, and my bruised knuckles healed. Everything else, that you couldn't see, I buried. The anger, the shame, the guilt, the fear, all of it. I never said anything about what Avery was doing with Pegasus, too afraid she'd come after me and accuse me of hitting or soliciting a recruit. Once again, our secrets kept one another in check.

Acceptance and Avoidance

The entrance to the department of Corporate Culture and Human Resources was a long uninterrupted stretch of corkboard. Though initially it was a place to pin sale notices, requests for roommates, and embarrassing happy hour photos, More transformed it when she hung an airplane-sized tow banner to remind us that "Size Matters!" Under the giant sign, she placed a whiteboard, a satchel of pushpins, and a massive brass gong and accompanying mallet. She said nothing about the change, but we knew what to do. From then on at the 'wall of acceptance,' recruiters pinned their signed offer letters, changed the tally on the whiteboard, and beat the celebratory gong.

At first the noise startled me out of my chair, but I made peace with the sound of money. And I got such pleasure out of striking it, as one after another, my candidates accepted their offers. Though I never received a single thank you for the $75,000 ski trip, every recruit except Conor signed with Kava. Still, Jeremy didn't understand why I had stopped fighting for one of our alpha wolves.

"I pushed too hard in Colorado. He's Avery's kid now," I said. "Besides, look at what's happening, he doesn't matter anyway. James and Julia were the ones we needed."

"Our numbers are fantastic. We might even win that trip to Paris," Jeremy said, giving me a cigarette-fumed bear hug.

"Would you believe I forgot about that?" With everything going on, and with how badly I needed cash, it wasn't the prize I cared about. I fixated on the numbers, the key to our individual and group bonuses. I watched the wall of acceptance tally rise by the week, then the day, and then the hour.

I was one of the few early birds in the office when we hit the triple. It was before 8 a.m. when two Penn State recruiters changed the count to 1,201, hitting and surpassing the target. They rang the gong twice, and I went over to see the board. I stood with the two of them staring at the number. We knew this moment was coming, but now that it was here, we didn't know what to do.

"Should we go tell More?" one of the recruiters asked.

"Is she here? It's so early."

"What's going on?" More asked, coming down the

hall from her office. Her eyes widened when she saw the number on the whiteboard. She observed it with reverence. "Can I have that?"

The recruiter handed her the mallet. We stepped back as More beat the gong until the mallet cracked. I uncovered my ears after she dropped it on the floor. "Congratulations. I'm so very proud," she said and gave us each a high five. Then she straightened her shirt and walked back to her office.

"Didn't see that coming," one of the recruiters said.

"No, not at all," her partner agreed.

And after a length of stunned silence, we decided to go out for breakfast.

Later we came back to find "Fuck Yeah" written on the whiteboard under the tally. More sent a lively email congratulating everyone and encouraged us to keep going. So we taped the mallet back together and began tacking acceptances on top of acceptances. The wall was a constant reminder that we had not only hit our goal, but exceeded it. I expected big things.

While I took my time walking by the wall, mulling what fortune it would bring me, I always hurried past Avery's desk. For weeks, I heard nothing, not a whisper, about the Conor incident, though I waited for the hammer to drop. Consequently, avoiding Avery at the office became a sport. I went to the bathroom with friends, stayed out of communal areas like the kitchen, and took the long way around places I thought she would be. She must have been playing too, because I hardly ever saw her. Maybe she was finally transitioning to the marketing department or a job with Pegasus. I didn't know, and I didn't ask.

Yet, part of me wanted the truth to be out, not only about what Avery's recruits would do to Kava, but what Conor did to me. The more sensible part of me said to keep quiet, that really nothing happened, and it wouldn't be worth the consequences of a he-said, she-said ordeal, especially because there was more than one she involved, and she hated me. Still, that night changed my perception of the things around me, like how I felt when my colleagues orgasmed their way through my name. What had been a harmless joke now meant something else. I curbed the dancing and the drinking, even skipping a few happy hours, including the one where we celebrated hitting the triple. The party went on without me.

When Marion didn't find me at my usual haunts, he asked me out to dinner.

"Up for Jeffery's?"

"Sounds amazing." I slumped, breathing in the new car smell that he somehow maintained. All the nights we had shared, and this was the first that felt like a date. Neither of us was drunk. There was no plan to drink. I should have been thrilled, but I felt tired, empty. Tupac rapped low on the stereo. He sang about shooting somebody. "That's one angry man," I said after a while.

"You'd be too if a gang tried to kill you."

"Are you angry? I mean, about anything?" I had

always meant to talk to him about the strip club and to ask him about Vegas, but I never did. It was never the right time.

"I'm not sure what you're asking."

"Me either," I said and reached out to touch the top of his hand resting on the gear shift.

Jeffery's was high-end, but it was still Austin. A place where you could wear jeans and cowboy boots but accidently sit next to a politician or a movie star. We cozied into a table, and away from the Kava kitchen, I ate. Thick steak, bleu cheese-doused bib salad, and dark chocolate mousse topped with sweet cream and raspberries. We didn't talk about the company. I didn't think about what waited for me there. Instead, Mars shared stories from his job, new businesses they were funding. Other places, other things.

I thought he was just as beautiful as when I first saw him at the information session at Dartmouth. The physical draw had never waned. Beyond that, the connection we had, the familiarity, revolved around drunk sex and Kava Tech. For almost a year now, we had met intermittently after company parties and late flights in from long work weeks. There was little in between to call a relationship, and I thought that Kava was worse than college that way. Work, travel, and the constant company of the company; it was all so emotionally crippling.

But maybe I was also the problem, I thought. I'd put my own wedge in the relationship, hadn't I? Kissing Christopher. Never telling Mars about my plans to cut and run after bonus payouts. He was so close to the leadership that I worried my secret would leak and I'd get less. Or maybe I worried he'd care more about losing me for the company than he would for himself. I wanted him to want me.

"Olivia? Did you hear me?"

"What? Sorry, I was thinking."

"Clearly. Want to go for a walk?" he asked.

"You mean together?" Was he offering to do another thing that didn't require a condom, liquor, or bedsheets? He gave me a look. "Yes, together." I hopped out of my chair.

We walked, my hand in his, to the dirt trail that ran around Town Lake. The sky was a patchwork of pale pinks, smoky oranges, and deep purples, and a swarm of Congress Bridge bats took to the sky. We found one of the shabby wooden docks connecting the trail to the lake and rented a rickety rowboat. Too lazy to paddle, we drifted out to the middle of the water. Marion sat down on the floor of the damp hull. He pulled me down to him, and I rested against his chest. We watched as, one at a time, the stars introduced themselves to the night.

Our fingers dangled in the tepid lake water, and the clouds moved slowly, morphing through the evening sky.

"An orange hair dryer," I said, pointing to one.

"No way. That's a dragon."

"What kind?" I asked, surprised he would even play this game.

"Pink-fire. Sweet looking, but very dangerous," he mused, twirling a ringlet of my hair around his finger.

He let it fall across my forehead.

"Like you," I teased, brushing it out of my eyes.

"Maybe, but it looks like a donut now."

After everything, I knew this was what I wanted from him now. No more clubs, drugs, or drinks. Maybe we had made our mistakes, had one too many wild Kava nights, but that didn't change the way I felt around him. No matter how long I was away, in Boston or San Jose, thinking of Marion made my heart leap and my insides twist. Maybe we could make it work when I went to Rodrigues after all, maybe he would visit. I pictured us, sun drenched, skinny dipping in one of the hidden volcanic coves.

I reached up and put my palm on his smooth cheek. "Mars?"

"Yeah baby?"

"Stay with me."

"Of course." I laid against his chest and he held me close. The black water chopped against the wooden bow, eventually drifting us back to the dock. Night fell around us like a soft blanket.

Out Loud

Among the many dip cups that adorned our cube, Jeremy and I kept a gift box. A red bow held its cheap plastic together around two crystal glasses and a bottle of some amber-colored liquor. It looked like a Christmas gift from TJ Max, and we had long since forgotten who had given it to us or why. Still, it was the nicest thing on our desk, and we joked that we'd open it together when we got our bonus checks.

I put the ridiculous box on top of my closed laptop and straightened the tacky ribbon. "Today's the day."

"You nervous?" Jeremy asked.

"You have no idea," I said.

"Big O, we exceeded our goal."

"Do you think we're contenders for Paris?" I asked.

"Hard to tell. Nobody's ever seen the weighted outcomes."

"They'll announce everything at the assembly this afternoon, who won the trip and the departmental bonus for hitting the triple."

"It's a big day," Jeremy said, his voice trailing off. He fidgeted in his chair.

We waited in our cube to be called for personal performance evaluations. I went first, when More asked me into her office. The sun scorched through the tilted blinds. Her cardigan hung on the back of her chair. "Please, sit."

I did as she asked and sat across from her desk in a folding chair. I put my hands on my lap. Ready.

She began. "Olivia, you did a great job this year, and we're very proud of your accomplishments. You and Jeremy were a solid team that brought in stellar talent."

"Thank you," I said, trying not to smile too much.

"This performance review is based on four indicators compiled by senior management. They include: one, whether you hit your hiring goals; two, how well you worked with your team; three, your ability to problem-solve; and four, your hallway reputation. Each recruiter is ranked on a scale of one to five, with five being the highest. Your individual bonus is based on your average score."

"Got it. Wait, what was that last indicator?"

"Hallway reputation. It's how you're perceived in the company, which is important if you're a recruiter. Human Resources needs to be a unifying force," she said.

"Okay."

She continued. "First, you exceeded your hiring goals. You received a five for this indicator because you hit 120 percent of your target number. Congratulations."

I smiled again. "Your ability to problem-solve was excellent as shown by your performance throughout the year, as various issues came about. You received good feedback from the managers and interviewers that traveled with you. You earned a four in problem-solving."

"Why not a five?" I asked.

"An incident on Harvard's campus? I'm not sure what happened that day, but I understand that candidate interviews were suddenly cancelled, which caused confusion. Recruits were calling the main line here to reschedule when they couldn't locate you."

Willy and Vi had kept their word. The Madam O incident was still under wraps. I should have never gotten into that mess. I'd live with a four. "Okay, I understand."

"On your ability to work with your team, you received a 2.5." More's expression was unforgiving. "I understand that you and Avery Stone had a troubled working relationship. She came to me repeatedly with ideas for improving your collaboration, and even brought me lists of career fair candidates she screened for you. Candidates she said you rejected, despite her advice. You should have accepted the help of your floater instead of competing with her."

Avery had outwitted me again. I never thought of making sure More was on my side. I hadn't thought ahead. I hired the best kids and exceeded my goals despite Avery Stone, who was a divisive Pegasus spy, but how could I explain that now? I crossed and uncrossed my legs and didn't say anything. More's expression told me it wasn't my turn to talk. "When I dug deeper into these issues, I learned that there were several occasions where you argued with Avery and made others uncomfortable in the company."

Still, a 2.5? That was unfair. It wasn't like I had a catfight in the office. I looked down at my hands and didn't argue. "Okay," I said. "I'm sorry."

More nodded that she heard me. "On hallway reputation, in this category, you received a two out of five."

"What?" I dug my nails into my palms.

"We received a phone call about you from a candidate." Shit. Conor. I closed my eyes and waited for what More would tell me. "He said you insulted his father because he drove a cab." She looked up from her notes and waited for my reaction.

I laughed, a cackle of involuntary relief. Colorado had been swept under the rug. Did Conor not remember? Did Avery think I had too much on her? At least Conor didn't call and say I punched his drunk ass in the mouth. I smiled, wide.

More's tone was sharp. "Not everybody comes from money, you know. We take diversity, in all its forms, very seriously at Kava Tech."

I stifled another laugh. What diversity? We hunted for culture fits, didn't we? Everyone we hired was the same person – a white guy, under 25, and from the most privileged of educations, I thought, but I said something else. "That candidate, Conor Walsh, was very disrespectful. He insulted Levi, he insulted Kava Tech, and he insulted me, more than once, and more than you know. I was standing up for myself and the company."

More raised her eyebrows unsympathetically. "Did you say something about his father's occupation?"

"It was after he——"

"It doesn't matter, Olivia. We have a zero-tolerance policy for——"

Fear tagged her sister anger, and she jumped in the ring. I cut More off. "A zero-tolerance policy for what? I wasn't aware this company had any policies for anything. Do you also have a zero-tolerance policy for sexual harassment? Because I'd really like to see it."

"I don't understand how that's relevant. Besides, isn't your nickname 'Big O?'"

Anger hulked through her shirt. "Is that what this is about? That name isn't my fault." And it became clear to me, obvious then, hearing myself say it out loud for the first time. So, I said it again and louder. I said it for me. "None of this. None of this is my fault." Not the obnoxious nickname, not all the ass grabs on the dance floor, not Dallas at the strip club, not being accused of running a prostitution ring, and certainly not Conor. All around me was a culture—an industry—thriving on sexism. I saw it clearly for the first time. "You're pegging my bonus to rumors. Do the developers and tech sales reps—do they get bonuses based on hallway reputation? Or are their bonuses based entirely on results?"

"Olivia, I don't see how that's relevant. You're a recruiter and your role here is very different from theirs. Would you like a bonus, or not?" I saw that it was over and swallowed the dry burn in my throat. I needed the money. "Based on the average of your indicators, management awarded you an individual bonus of $5,000. Thank you for your work."

"That's it?"

"Yes."

"5k?"

"Yes."

"For hitting 120 percent of my goals."

"Yes."

Three thousand dollars, maybe, after taxes. I'd lost way more playing roulette. I left without shaking her hand. More said to my back, "Department announcements will be this afternoon. Assembly attendance is mandatory." Jeremy wasn't at our desk, and I didn't want to see him anyway. I needed to get out of that nightmare of fluorescent lights and chatty cubicles. I grabbed the liquor gift box from our cube and sprinted to my car.

I wanted Marion. He'd be able to explain it and tell me how they'd make it right this afternoon. They'd announce something big at the assembly, they had to. I called his cell, but he never answered it during the day. I drove straight to his apartment, putting together a plan as I sped down the 360 Loop. I'd use the spare key under the mat, sip some gift box liquor, and message him to join me. Even if he didn't come, I'd have a quiet place away from everyone at the office.

I clicked open Marion's front door and dropped my bag on the floor. I kicked off my shoes and padded up the stairs. The large double doors to his room were open, and there he was, laying naked on top of his bed, legs spread wide, and his entire package in Amara Young's mouth. She was on her knees, her perfect head bobbing up and down.

At first, which was absurd, I wondered how the hell she fit all of that in her mouth. Is that what deep-throating looked like? How is she not gagging? I stood there unnoticed with my head cocked to the side, watching for what had to be seconds, but felt like an eternity. I trembled as anger welled from my core and radiated like white hot lightning to my hands. By the time it registered in my head, it was too late, I had already hurled the bottle and both glasses in rapid succession. They hit like crystal bombs, exploding on the headboard behind them.

Marion screamed. Not a moan of pleasure, but a high-pitched squeal of pain. Amara whirled around. I stared at her, naked and vulnerable, glass sprinkled over her back.

"You bit me!" Marion yelled and jerked his hands back from the broken glass on the mattress. He froze when he met my eyes and realized what had happened.

I had always known I wasn't the only one. The others. The scratch marks on his back. I looked at my hands. The pink t-shirt. I never wanted to deal with the truth. Now that it was right in front of me, I had no choice. "You were just a dick," I muttered. "Really, what else did you give me?"

Soft Pitch

For the next hour, windows down and stereo up, I drove the Texas freeways. I thought of nothing except how to pass the cars in front of me, mechanically shifting through the gears, the white lines blurring into the blacktop. By the time I went back to work, the assembly had started. I walked in the back door of the crowded room. More was well into her introductory remarks. I found a place next to Jeremy who always stood behind everyone so he wouldn't block their view.

"What'd I miss?" I whispered. More wasn't alone at the front. Next to her stood Bill Watts, the Congo Scripts founder I'd met at the HereBeer launch party. Next to him was Marion, well dressed and pressed, like he hadn't been busy a little while ago. "What's going on? Why are they here?"

Jeremy shrugged. "Where did you go?"

"Did you get your bonus?" I asked. He nodded. "What was it?"

"Later. I want to listen."

"What was it?" I pressed.

"35k," he said not looking at me.

"$35,000?" I said it so loud that people turned around. Jeremy's expression pleaded with me to be quiet.

Of course Kava paid him. He didn't fight with candidates or get into trouble on campus or bicker openly with Avery. He did his job without incident. His only misstep was an association with me. But, was I worth $30,000 less than him to the company? Wasn't I half our team?

Jeremy looked enthusiastic as More extolled the department. "... it was such a pleasure and an honor to work with you all. I look forward to doing it again next year, but instead of another triple, we'll aim for zero attrition. Recruiting will keep this company thriving and fulfilled," she said.

"I bet it will," I scoffed. People shushed me.

"And for the next few weeks," More continued, "you will focus on helping your candidates transition into their life at Kava, like so many of you did a year ago. Make them comfortable, show them the ropes. I don't need to tell this group to open their arms and invite people in. Now enough about the work you will have to do. Let's celebrate the work you've done. That's the reason we're all here now."

People clapped and fell quiet, waiting for what More would announce.

"First, let's call up the winners of the Paris trip. An all-expenses paid trip to the city of love. It's awarded to the team that brought in the highest number of recruits, weighted to the size of their universities. Get excited, people! This is it ... and the winner is ... drumroll please ..." She opened an envelope like someone was taking home an Oscar. "Jeremy and Olivia! The recruiters for MIT and Harvard! Come on up here!"

More waved two golden faux plane tickets in the air to a standing ovation. Jeremy high-fived our cheering colleagues as he moved through them towards the front. I followed in his wake, numb, until we walked past Avery. She rolled her eyes and mouthed the words, "You owe me." I stared at her until I tripped on the back of Jeremy's shoes.

I did what Jeremy did. I shook More's hand, smiled, took the ticket, and moved down the receiving line. Bill Watts congratulated me next, and then I stood in front of Marion, the gentle warmth and smell of a fresh shower coming from his skin. A wave of sadness, anger, and longing crested and crashed. I held my breath in its swirling tide. Marion followed protocol. He reached for my hand. I looked for a lifeline, something else to grab, but I saw nothing in the black depths of his eyes. Neither resentment nor passion nor regret.

"Why?" I asked.

"Congratulations, Olivia," he said and let go of my hand. The waters stilled. There was no current left to fight.

More moved the show along. "Okay people. Good work. Jeremy and Olivia, stay up front." I stood sandwiched between Marion and Jeremy, our elbows touching. More sounded like a depraved gameshow host. "The big announcement ... are you all ready? The departmental bonus for hitting the triple is ..." My colleagues cheered and hooted. "Nope. I'm not going to tell you." People laughed. They quieted when she didn't say anything. They looked around at one another until More pointed at Marion and Bill Watts and blurted, "Our esteemed colleagues will have the honor! And they have some very exciting news."

Marion bowed his head and raised his palms to the crowd, a simultaneous show of deference and control. "I know you all so well, having handpicked many of the recruiters in this room. I have an eye for talent." He smiled and my co-workers stared, starry-eyed. I took a deep breath and let it out slowly. "With intimate knowledge of your skills and your reputation for success—you didn't just get to third base; you crushed a home run—it was a no-brainer to turn human resources into a profit center for the company. It is with great pleasure that today, we announce SoftPitch, a new Kava product. We will develop this recruitment tool borrowing from your expertise. Some of you will even move from recruiting into consulting, billing your time to the companies that purchase and deploy SoftPitch. Congratulations, you will all be considered founders of this new product and given an additional 5,000 stock options in Kava Tech."

Marion built an army of recruiters to develop another Kava product? I tried to understand. That's why we had to hit the triple, to prove we could be a profit center? And now that Kava didn't need to grow, it would turn us into consultants to support SoftPitch?

What difference would it make if I had "product founder" or "consultant" on my resume? And additional stock options? How long would it be before I could do something with them? Our departmental bonus was like throwing a ball on a roulette wheel that could spin for years.

"I'd like to recognize Bill Watts," Marion said, "who has agreed, based on your track record alone, to pilot SoftPitch and use the product to meet Congo Script's human resource needs on the West Coast. Thank you Bill, for coming on board as our first client and for believing in our product from its inception." People clapped and Bill gave a gracious bow.

Then the conference room door swung open, and Marion waved. "You're just in time, my friends. Come. Join us," he said. "Everyone, let's welcome the principal investors for SoftPitch. They will support, advise, and help fund product development and deployment." I leaned to see who had come into our meeting. "Please give a warm welcome to Logan Mangold, head of the Dallas-based investment firm Skylight; and the renowned restaurateur, Chef David Cadena."

Dallas and Chef? The guiding investors for SoftPitch were Dallas and Chef? They made their way to Marion. Before I could shut my dry mouth, Chef was shaking my hand. Dallas clasped my shoulders and spoke in my ear. "Nice to see you again, Recruiter."

"And one more super exciting announcement," More hollered over the applause. "Marion has agreed to come on board as the new head of the SoftPitch Business Unit. We will all work closely together to guide the product to success. Let's give Marion, David, Logan, and Bill a huge and warm welcome to the Kava family."

Marion, the head of a business unit of recruiters? I wanted the gift box crystal back so I could throw it again, but instead, I turned to the men next to me, and I hissed, "You can keep your fucking escort service. The three of you can fucking keep it." I walked off stage and let the door slam behind me.

I filtered through the maze of grey cubicles, the cradle of Kava's culture. The flimsy corkboard anchored this nonsensical circus, a show that would never end. There would always be another product. Another gamble. Another goal tacked to the contemptable material. More recruits like Conor, guys like Marion, and colleagues like Avery. I walked through it and into the communal kitchen.

A ticket to Paris would get me halfway to Rodrigues, but what would it cost to break my lease and cover my debts to Kava and Sky and pay off my loans? If I left this company, what would I do for money? Could I hang on until my stock sale date? Would the market hold? I sat at one of the flimsy tables, not realizing Avery had followed me out of the meeting. In a light pink linen suit, she looked like a naked mole rat—puffy and wrinkled and pale.

"That outfit is becoming," I said. Avery opened her mouth and then closed it. "Did you know that naked mole rats fight each other to the death to become queen? Terrible bloody battles. The losers, if they live, eat the queen's shit. Literally, eat her shit."

"At least you know who your queen is," she said.

"You won the race, Avery. You're the top rat." Her back to the entrance, Avery didn't realize More had followed me too. I guess when you sneer at a beloved board member and his high-powered friends, and walk out of the biggest meeting of the year after winning an award, your Director might want to know why. "But I'm done with your shit." I raised my voice, for More. "How many of Kava's best candidates will be spies for Pegasus? How much inside information did you give them on our recruitment tactics? On our products? And for what? A piece of ass?"

"A great piece of ass. And a nice fat check. Something I'm sure you didn't get."

"Price paid you to steal candidates and Kava secrets for Pegasus?"

"Of course Price paid me. Why settle for a chintzy hotel in Paris when I could buy myself a villa?"

"You're a total fraud."

"You're also in violation of Kava's non-disclosure agreement," More said. Avery turned on her heel, her face as pallid as her blouse. "Give me your laptop." Avery didn't move. "The laptop. Now." More's voice was never more serene, and Avery's hand trembled as she handed her the computer bag. "In my office," More said and walked away, leaving Avery no choice but to follow. I didn't need to watch the queens battle to the death. I knew who would win.

With Marion, Chef, and Dallas still holding court in the conference room, and Avery behind closed doors with More, I turned off my phone and left the office, intent on taking a few days away. On my way out, I walked

by the wall of acceptance. Our departmental triumph
was a cluttered mess, and one of the acceptance letters
had slipped to the floor. Out of habit, I looked for a
place to tack it. I found a small space above where the
banner had drooped, revealing a photo collage from
our first few weeks of work. Someone had pinned up
several Polaroids from the day we went sky diving,
including one of me in my jumpsuit. My face was
flushed with thrill, and I pointed and smiled at a plane
in the distance. I didn't remember taking that picture,
but I'd never forget what it felt like to fly and then to
land. I thought, as I tucked the photo in my bag, that if
Kava Tech had taught me how to do anything, it was to
close my eyes and jump.

Paris

Paris was a victory lap for Jeremy and me, before the next cycle of recruiting began. He made me tell him the Avery story again and again, howling with laughter every time I compared her to a naked mole rat and described her face when she realized she had outed herself to More.

"I can't believe she left everything on ICQ," he said. "Brought down by her chat history. How ridiculous."

"I wonder what her music collection looked like," I mused, thinking of her laptop.

"Britney Spears MP3s."

I giggled. "Remember when Napster crashed the Kava network?"

"Now that was a crazy couple of days."

We reminisced some, but mostly Jeremy frequented the nightclubs and slept all day. I meandered through the city, joyously alone. I walked the cobblestone streets and canals, stopped to pet designer dogs, and browsed the beautiful shops. On our last morning, I met Jeremy for breakfast. I sipped a café au lait and listened to his plans for the year ahead. He chattered incessantly until I rendered him speechless.

"What do you mean you're not coming back? The flight leaves in a few hours." He checked his watch, his rollaway luggage under the table.

"There's something I need to do, and I'm halfway there already," I said. "I have to stop in Rome, but that's a quick side trip."

"So, you'll be back later then."

"No."

"What do you mean, no?"

"No, Jeremy. I'm not going back to Kava." I sipped my coffee.

He lit a cigarette and blew out the smoke. "Because of your bonus?"

I shook my head. "It's not about that. I delivered Avery's head, and More paid me like a bounty hunter." Jeremy raised his eyebrows.

Not only did I negotiate forgiveness of my debts to Kava from both rounds of roulette, but I talked More up to a $50,000 bonus. It was easy to find leverage once More learned the depth of Avery's misdeeds and most of what I dealt with. Above all else, I thought More rewarded my comparative loyalty, and I liked to imagine the bonus money moving from Avery's account to mine. Regardless, after taxes and various other expenses, I walked away from Kava with a bank account big enough to get to Rodrigues and stay awhile. "Let's get more croissants, okay? The chocolate ones."

Over what I thought was a proper French breakfast, I told Jeremy the thick of it, where I was going, and why. At the end of my story, he stubbed out another smoke.

"You've lost your mind."

"Probably."

"I'll miss you, Big O."

"Olivia," I corrected.

"Olivia," he smiled and stood to hug me goodbye.

"Your next partner, whoever she is, will be very lucky," I said into his armpit.

Later, in Rome, I greeted Sky with a $2,500 check and a present from Paris. She looked beautiful, maybe a little fuller from all the pasta and wine, but gorgeous, nonetheless. She opened the delicately wrapped box and unraveled a scarf imprinted with a teal jaguar, green and fuchsia quetzal feathers, and bright green palm fronds.

"It's wild. Only you would pick this."

"Hermès seemed like the thing to buy in Paris."

Sky thumbed the silk. "It's gorgeous. Thank you. You really didn't need to ..."

"It's not the *haute couture* dress I wanted to get you, but it did set me back almost $500. I wanted to thank you for the loan and all nice things you've given me. You've been so kind and I've never been able to give you anything in return."

"You're my friend. A very true friend. That's been more than enough."

"Sure, but now you have a really expensive, gaudy scarf, too." She laughed and draped it around her shoulders.

Sky and I drank a lot of wine that night, swapping tales about life after college and our plans for the future. With each story I told, I untangled myself a little more from the Kava web. We watched the sunrise from her balcony, the white light of morning flooding the city. After a long silence and before we fell asleep on her patio furniture, Sky asked me one more question. "What happened to Christopher?"

"I said goodbye the night before I left for Paris."

"That's it?"

"I kissed him the way I should have kissed him in Vegas. The way I should have kissed him at the swimming hole." Sky pulled her scarf around her shoulders and waited for me to say more. "He asked me to stay, but I told him I couldn't."

"And then?" she asked.

"And then he let me go."

Epilogue

After Rome, I landed in Mauritius. And then, finally, Rodrigues.

The sun sunk below the bluff overlooking Port Mathurin, a few clouds obscuring its hazy descent into the sea. I had to hike back before it got too dark to find my way, and before Rani needed light to study. Even with a flashlight, it was easy to lose the dirt path that ran through the forest to my home, a newly constructed cement slab with a tin roof. This time though, I had a small generator for electricity and a laptop. Sometimes the internet connection was fast enough to read a few emails and get some US news.

From this speck in the Indian Ocean, a place where time passed languidly, I reflected on my year at Kava Tech. I tried to forgive myself for so many missteps. I rationalized Marion. Doesn't every girl fall for the wrong guy at least once? Sometimes more than once? I knew it was going to end badly, had seen the signposts, but I did it anyway. He was like the roulette wheel. The odds were against me, but I plunked down my cash for the thrill of it, to entertain the hope that the ball might land on my number.

Half a world away and nine hours ahead of Eastern Standard Time, I watched the turn of the century in the Western Hemisphere. I braced for Y2K to end the world. Nothing bad happened, minus a few firework-related injuries and the globe's obsession with the song "Mambo No. 5." SoftPitch launched as planned, Marion at the helm and Amara on the brochure.

I also followed Kava's stock. With my eye on the prize, I never saw the real catastrophe coming. I wasn't the only one. A few short months after ringing in the new century, the stock market imploded and the dot-com bubble burst. Kava's stock price fell off a cliff, and overnight, I lost a bunch of money I never really had. This time I was one of the lemmings, one of the investors who believed the good times would never end. Refusing to see that the party was over, we held on until the bitter end, when valuation hit zero and everything collapsed.

Jeremy gave me updates on the apocalyptic end of HereBeer and SoftPitch. He told me how employees who still believed worked without paychecks until everything dissolved, like salt in a water glass. Eventually he took a job with a Europe-based start-up, where it was still socially acceptable to smoke. Maybe he met them on our trip to Paris. Around the same time, William and Viola jumped ship together and went to a tiny start-up called Google. Last I heard, they were trying to recruit Christopher, who had piled the passenger seat of his roadster with CDs and took a tour of Route 66. I thought about him often, and I wondered if I might see him again.

While Kava Tech disappeared, its people endured, and I kept in touch as best I could. The company culture may have been anchored in a bizarre, sexist social experiment, but Willy, Viola, Jeremy, Christopher, and many other quirky nerds that wove the company fabric became my forever friends. I learned that Kava Tech's real payout to me was not money, but an enduring network of brilliant and talented—albeit amusingly strange—people.

I watched the tech world implode, grateful to be thousands of miles away from the human resources department that had to fire all the kids I had hired. In the dry heat of Texas, the tech oasis I sold them turned out to be a mirage. I lost track of most of my candidates, but I did hear that Julia and James got married after they exchanged her ring for something less corporate. Who could blame them?

Later, on this new thing called Facebook (the online version) somebody by the name of Conor tried to friend me. I declined just to be safe. Maybe he didn't remember what happened in Colorado, but I'd never forget. That night crystalized my understanding of what was going on around me, how dangerous it could be, and that it needed to change. I realized that I was lucky—lucky he was small, lucky he didn't try harder, lucky I hit him when I did.

And my luck didn't run out. After I jumped out

of the Kava Tech plane, my chute opened. While I had plenty of school debt to resolve, I scored a job with a United Nations-funded project supporting the Rodriguan hurricane recovery. I watched over the *aureum* seeds sprouting in the nursery and I sent Rani back to school. When the post office reopened, I mailed pictures of my "children" to my parents who sent care packages in return. What choice did they have? I was too far away for them to be more disappointed than worried. Plus, I had a fancy bureaucratic title, United Nations International Civil Servant, and my salary sounded amazing, provided you didn't convert it from rupees to dollars.

Though it was without luxury, my life in Rodrigues was meaningful and peaceful. I spent my days working in the forest and my evenings swimming along the shoals. I picked the wild pineapples growing in my backyard and occasionally fished my dinner out of the cove. Often I read by candlelight until the wick burned low and the fruit bats—the noisiest of nocturnal company—munched their way through the woods. There was a natural and restorative rhythm to my time, and my future felt as unbound as the sea.

THE END

Acknowledgements

I'd like to thank:

Brian Anderson, familiarity has only bred fondness, and one day you just might laugh at my jokes;

Joy Kolin, founder of givingjoygoods.com, my life adviser, and my sister who listened to self-doubt expressed in every way possible and never stopped encouraging me to finish;

Reuben Swartz, thank you from the front end through to the back end, and all the compilers in between. The screenplay is all yours;

Ellen Meister, my developmental editor and writing advisor. I was lost before I met you. Thank you for everything you taught me; and

Kevin Jablonowski, thank you for your thoughtful and thorough copyedit.

I also owe a very special thank you to Jean Alfred Begue, Emmanuella Biram, Jennifer Butler, Frank Bruno, Brandon Cohen, Linda Esposito, Will Esposito, Roben Farzad, Mijha Butcher Godfrey, Runako Godfrey, Eve Hesselroth, Graham Hesselroth, Sarah

Beth Johnson, Noelani (Misty) Lee, Susan Leiser, Faye Leone, Tracy Vargas, Catherine Whalén, and Ellen Wong—friends and family and colleagues who shared their stories, gave advice, read drafts, and offered me endless encouragement and ideas.

I'd like to also give a nod to the "Couch Club" of Natalie Scola Scaffidi, Stacie Brookbank, Stacy Shifren, and Gloria Shifren at Flyers Gymnastics in Hammonton, NJ, where this book took shape; to the township of Medford, NJ, for keeping so many of the trees and giving me such a bucolic setting in which to write; and to the Princeton Writers Network and the many Princetonians who offered their sage advice.

Finally, thank you to Margi Prideaux and Donna Mulvenna of Stormbird Press for taking a chance on me as an author.

About the Author

Following her graduation from Princeton University, where she studied ecology and evolutionary biology, Lauren Anderson worked as a high-tech college recruiter on and off for five years to finance her further education and adventures at the nexus of conservation and development. She has studied and worked in Costa Rica, Mauritius, and Rodrigues. Lauren earned her master's degree in international relations from the Johns Hopkins University School of Advanced International Studies (SAIS) and launched into a career with the United Nations. Under the United Nations family of organizations, she has supported the sustainable development of island countries and global efforts to fight Ebola and COVID-19. Lauren also serves as an eco-writer and editorial consultant for the International Institute of Sustainable Development (IISD) and an adjunct professor in the Africana Studies Program of Rowan University. Lauren currently resides with her family in South Jersey. *Recruited* is her first novel.

Legal Note

An Invitation from Stormbird Press

Stories about our world, and our relationship with nature, have been told by people for thousands of years. It is how we share our moral tales, empower ourselves with knowledge, and pass wisdom to the future.

Our titles all passionately communicate people's reverence, wisdom, and inspiration about the places, plants and animals, habitats and ecosystems, of our shared home— Earth. They whisper where we've been and foretell where we are going.

Around campfires and hearths, beside streams, across tundras, under the shadow of mountains or the wide branches of mighty trees, and in the pages of Stormbird's books, people's stories and wisdom carry like feathers in the wind.

Become part of our community.

We will keep you up to date with our latest catalogue, give you access to new releases before they arrive in bookstores, give you chances to win signed editions, and much more.

Stormbird Press

www.StormbirdPress.com

CPSIA information can be obtained
at www.ICGtesting.com
Printed in the USA
LVHW030353300421
686058LV00006B/561